A DIRE WARNING

"Mister Newspaperman, this here message is from the good folks at the S and RG . . . be a mite respectful next time you write about the railroad.

"Right now, you feel like a plow horse walked on you. Isn't that right? Thought so. If we have to come back to teach you another lesson in manners, you'll feel like a locomotive ran you down.

"Remember your poor old ma's advice. If you can't think of something nice to say, don't say nothing. You clear on that, Mister Newspaperman?"

STEPHEN OVERHOLSER

FIRE IN THE RAINBOW

LEISURE BOOKS NEW YORK CITY

A LEISURE BOOK®

December 2003

Published by special arrangement with Golden West Literary
Agency.

Dorchester Publishing Co., Inc.
200 Madison Avenue
New York, NY 10016

ISBN 0-8439-5294-6

The name "Leisure Books" and the stylized "L" with design are
trademarks of Dorchester Publishing Co., Inc.

Printed in the United States of America.

Visit us on the web at www.dorchesterpub.com.

FIRE IN THE RAINBOW

Chapter One

"Edna! Edna, you be careful. Hear?"

Eddie Pauls heard her mother's parting words and turned in the saddle to wave at her as she left the home ranch. Marietta Pauls would watch her daughter from her wheelchair on the sunny verandah, staring after her until she splashed through Ute Creek and rode out of sight.

Eddie knew that without looking back. She knew her mother worried about her safety. Marietta stewed and fretted about real and imagined dangers, terrors ranging from her daughter being bucked off the horse to a rattlesnake bite, from capture by renegade Indians to rape by roaming bandits, from lightning bolts to flash floods. She worried herself sick even though her worst fears had never come to pass on the Rainbow Ranch.

Eddie let the horse have his head. Her destination was Rainbow Arch at the mouth of the valley, and, if this retired cutting horse had any memory left between those ears, he knew her destination and would plod along in the right direction.

Eddie pushed her guilt aside, or tried to. She did not intend to torment her mother. Far from it. She loved her dearly. But Eddie simply could not stand to be cooped up in that house, day and night, without some freedom and a change of scenery now and then. Marietta Pauls had been bound to the wheelchair for six years. In all that time, from the age of eleven to this day, Eddie was her caretaker, her only solace. The mere thought of another horrible event such as the accident that had crippled her was more than Marietta could bear.

Eddie's father and two brothers understood the underlying causes of this incessant brooding—fearfulness and helplessness. They also knew it was unreasonable to expect Eddie to be housebound from now until forever. When she needed breathing space and a change of scenery, she had permission to saddle up and ride out, alone. Her sole restrictions were to leave word of her destination and a promise to be home by sundown. Then, if something untoward did happen, the men would know where to begin their search.

Now at an hour past noon under a hot Colorado sky, Eddie took the deep breath of fresh air she had craved. The warmth of the sun seeped pleasantly through her jacket and the heavy cotton material of her divided skirt. She exhaled, scanning the terrain around her. The land, stretching out in all directions, seemed barren, as though baked by the sun since dinosaurs had roamed, a region now devoid of all creatures and most vegetation.

She knew better. A variety of animals and plants were capable of surviving weather extremes from summer heat to winter chills, from bone dry to sopping wet, with most bearing colors that faded into desert terrain. Lizards and rattlesnakes blended in with the predominant browns and ruddy reds, as did the plumage of prairie chickens and the coats of scrawny coyotes—all of them crouched low to the ground, poised to move fast. In this region, quickness and camouflage meant survival.

Ute Creek was marked by tall grasses growing along the muddy bank on its course through a land of sage, cacti, and scattered piñons. The stream flowed out of the distant mountains year around. Eddie had seen the headwaters herself.

In the saddle since childhood, she had often ridden with her brothers from the home ranch into the mountains, helping them and seasonally hired hands drive Rainbow-branded cattle to summer range. At those higher altitudes Ute Creek gurgled out of fissures in the floor of a mountain valley. Building speed, the water charged downslope, slowed on the flat plain, and eventually flowed past the home ranch into the Paulses' reservoir behind the earthen dam. From the spillway, the creek meandered twenty-five miles to its confluence with the Río River in the town of Red Rock. Beyond the town, it flowed southward into New Mexico Territory, and water that was not diverted by countless ditches there eventually joined the Río Grande.

From a keen interest in local history inspired by her father's reminiscences and by books in his library, Eddie knew the origin of that repetitious name, "Río River". An American Army officer's misinterpretation of Spanish, the name fell into common use after the conquest of Mexico in 1848. In that year General Micah Lewis Moresby announced to the populace that the laws of the United States were to be obeyed from this day forward. Those laws would be enforced by troopers from "Río River" in southern Colorado all the way to the "Río Grandee" in Moresby's mispronunciation. The Río Grande now defined the southern border of the United States. North of it lay the spoils of war.

"Orders from my blue coat troopers shall be obeyed by all United States citizens!" Moresby was reported to have shouted in every town, village, adobe pueblo, and *ranchería* he could find. The general neither spoke nor understood a word of Spanish, and he squinted at words in an *Inglés-Español* dictionary. When his index finger ran down the page to "river", he spied *"río"*.

That was enough for Moresby. "Río River" it was. He so proclaimed it while his horse forded that very creek, and like a stubborn nickname, wrong-headed or not, "Río River" stuck. Later, a translator was said to have been slightly more successful when he repeated the general's bellowed commands: Spanish land grants were hereby null and void; promises and treaties between Spain and the government of Mexico were rescinded; boundaries drawn by agreement between Mexican officials and tribes native to the region were not recorded on American maps.

"Man, woman, child, or dog! If you aim to live under the yoke of Mexican authority, pack up! Pack up and head south until you cross that Río Grandee!"

Now Eddie rode beside Ute Creek, her gaze moving from the brown and dry terrain to clear, cool water sliding over its rocky bed. The horse remembered, and, after a drink through the bit, he veered away from the creek. Eddie rode past sandstone spires standing like sentinels, and reached Rainbow Arch two hours later.

The formation was a magnificent sight, a seemingly impossible band of reddish sandstone arching between two cliffs. At one hundred and fifty feet in length and some forty feet overhead at the highest reach, the landmark was well named. Against the blue sky on this day, the shape of the arch eroded in stone resembled a petrified rainbow.

As she liked to do, Eddie rode under it. She looked back, gazing under the arch toward the ranch. The barns and outbuildings were long out of sight from here, but sometimes she could see a haze of smoke if green wood was in the stove.

Clear blue sky today. She kicked out of a stirrup. Saddle leather creaked when she dismounted.

Tying the reins to a sagebrush, she followed her own

boot prints in the powdered red dirt to a sandstone cliff. Her tracks from previous visits were all around her. She gazed down at rounded heel and triangular sole impressions among fine chips of cream-colored flint. Among them, she saw a few broken spear points and shards from clay vessels.

At the base of the cliff she came to simple markings at eye level, dozens of petroglyphs showing rams and deer and rabbits, as well as several human hand prints. Off to one side, she studied spiraling designs and webs of intersecting lines in crosshatch patterns. In the center of this gallery, she reached out and placed her own hand over a reddish handprint from long ago, as though reaching across the ages.

No volume of history helped her make sense of these graceful drawings. Perhaps that was part of the allure. Her imagination conjured up images of ancient peoples who had passed this way long before she passed this way—who?, when?, how?, or why? she did not know. She supposed they ranged from north to south with the seasons to follow migrating herds of animals. She supposed summertime had brought them here every year on their way to cool mountains and freshets. She supposed generations of mothers and fathers, of sons and daughters had walked this very ground scuffed by her riding boots.

Whether she heard a sound or caught a scent, she did not immediately know, but the sudden awareness that she was not alone brought her out of deep imaginings. A shiver ran up her back as though she had awakened from a vivid dream. For as she looked down at the ground, she saw other tracks in the powdery red dust, footprints overlapping hers—moccasins.

Lifting her gaze slowly, she looked left and right, drawing a sharp breath when she saw an Indian. He was a young man. He stood perfectly still a few paces beyond the arch, dark eyes on her. The old cutting horse did not object to his presence, and, as Eddie met the youth's gaze, her instincts told her to show no fear.

The lone Indian stood naked but for a breechcloth and moccasins. He held a bow. A quiver of feathered arrows slanted across his back. The leather carrying strap of the fringed quiver was decorated with lines of red and blue beads. Standing there in full sunlight beyond the arch, his braided hair shone as black as a crow's wing, his skin a rich, earthen color.

Prolonged staring signaled hostility to Indians of the region, or so Eddie had heard, and now she lowered her gaze. She did not know how long they faced one another, but in those moments her mother's warning came to mind, reverberating through her thoughts like echoes in a cañon.

She glanced at his face. His dark-eyed expression gave no hint of his intentions. Suddenly he turned. He strode away and broke into a run. Eddie watched him disappear in the afternoon shadows of the steep-walled cañon curving away from Rainbow Arch.

Lips moving under a graying walrus mustache, Ben Pittock muttered to himself as he drew type from his composing stick and positioned each letter with stubby, ink-stained fingers. He read the whole page upside down and backwards, made two corrections, and locked the form by tightening the type in place with a pair of toggle levers. After applying ink with a roller, he brought a sheet of paper to the press, and ran his first proof. The banner across the top featured an incongruous masthead of his own design—a lighthouse in the desert.

The Red Rock
SIGNAL

Truth Shines Bright
In Our Beacon of Light

Benjamin Pittock, Editor-in-Chief &
Floor Sweeper

Our Motto and Guiding Light: The Truth shall make you free, dear reader, but this four-pager will cost you ten cents. Job Printing & Advertising Rates by Request.

Dept of Bear VVith Us. A new shipment of type arrived via rail car. Unfortunately our order vvent avvry, misdirected all the vvay to Santa Fé, Nevv Mexico Territory. VVhat happened? VVell, vve received a Spanish font by mistake. VVe say "unfortunately" because the Spanish language does not employ the letter VV. So as you alert readers have spied, vve are forced to use tvvo Vees paired together until the manufacturer can ship good old American VVs.

Still muttering, Ben half smiled at his little joke. His account was a flight of fancy. The wrong font had not been sent to him. New type had not been ordered or shipped. He would use Ws in the next issue. Rather than confess that hoax, he would perpetrate another by announcing to readers that he had merely turned upper and lower case Ms upside down, thus solving a printer's problem. He could hear his readers' mock outrage now:

"A joke all along!"

"You tricked us!"

"You lying you-know-what!"

"Hang the editor!"

In Ben's thinking, deceiving readers was a practical art, the key to success in his profession. Readers were amused by hoaxes. Curiosity must run high in the copy he churned out, or the newspaper withered. He had seen failure in other town papers, humorless rags listing marriages, births and deaths, lodge meetings, church service hours, various comings and goings, all of them tedious and largely unnoticed unless (horrors!) an error crept in. Pittock had learned to string readers along. A whopper here and there made them yearn for the next issue.

RED ROCK, COLORADO
POPULATION 999
EVERYONE PRAYING FOR A BABY

The eye-grabbing headline marked a brief story claiming: **Your faithful editor has counted everyone at least once. Come on, folks, can we make it an even thousand?**

Pittock heard the door open. By habit, he wiped ink-stained hands on his ink-stained printer's apron as he turned to face a customer. This one was Joe Gilmore.

" 'Afternoon, Sheriff."

"Howdy, Ben. Am I interrupting you?"

"Sure, but talk anyway. What can I do for you . . . Reward dodgers?"

Gilmore shook his head. "I'd like to get a story in the paper."

"Story. What about?"

"Theft."

"What kind?"

"Cattle."

Pittock eyed the lawman that sported a full, dark beard, neatly trimmed. "Stockmen have been stealing mavericks from each other for years, Joe. I believe they call it 'replenishing the herd'."

"This is different."

"How so?"

Gilmore shoved his wide-brimmed hat up on his forehead. He wore a wool vest over a white shirt even in summer, gray wool trousers, and box-toed boots. The brass five-pointed star pinned to his vest and the Colt Peacemaker holstered on his right hip were well-worn tools of his profession.

"I got a report of cattle with doctored brands sold down in Caliente," he replied, adding: "Thirty, maybe forty head belonging to local ranchers."

Pittock knew "Caliente" to be a common name in the Southwest. "You mean, that dusty, adobe burg across the Colorado line in New Mexico Territory?"

The lawman nodded. "The stolen livestock are probably long gone in old Mexico by now. Most ranchers won't miss them until autumn roundup."

"So you're telling me somebody used a running iron," Pittock said, "to alter legal brands of thirty to forty head culled from several different ranches?"

"That's what I'm telling you," Gilmore said. He handed him a list diagraming half a dozen brands. "The rustlers must have been in a hurry because they made a poor job of it. Most of the original brands were still readable. A drover trailing the herd produced a bill of sale, collected his money

15

from a buyer, and then he and the other riders got scarce. Stanley Harrison, the Southern and Río Grande agent, was suspicious. He sent a report to me by the next mail car."

Pittock ran an inky hand through his mustache as he looked at the list. He lifted his gaze to Gilmore. "That bill of sale was a fake?"

The sheriff nodded.

"So you want me to run a report of the theft?"

"I want folks to be on the look-out for strangers," Gilmore said. "A bunch of horsebackers. Probably leading pack animals."

"How do you figure that?"

"Nobody I've talked to in these parts spotted a group of riders," Gilmore said. "The rustlers are probably living out of panniers on pack animals, filling canteens in the crick at night while watering livestock, careful-like." He added: "With easy pickings in Red Rock County, they may come back for more."

"So you want the story in the *Signal* to advise folks to report to you or a deputy if they see a wad of horsebackers passing through our fair county."

"That's about the size of it."

Pittock looked into the distance as though he could see inked type locked in the form. " 'Sheriff Joseph Gilmore warns of cattle thieves'. That's the headline, Joe. You'll read it in the next issue. Page one."

"Obliged, Ben," Gilmore said. Turning, he tugged his hat down on his head and left the print shop.

The day was hot, but Eddie felt a cold sense of dread when she spotted a familiar saddle horse in the corral. After her encounter with an Indian, she had returned early from Rainbow Arch, only to find the brown and white mount be-

16

longing to Buster Baldwin here. He had come for supper, and she would have to feed him. Worse, she would have to pretend he was a welcome guest.

Baldwin was one of two lawmen patrolling a county the size of Delaware, but he was the only one who managed to show up—without fail—at suppertime every two weeks. Eddie had learned to set an extra plate when she saw his horse in the corral, and to add just the right amount of fresh cream to his coffee, as well as avoid his lingering gaze. At first she had been embarrassed when she felt his relentless stare, but now she was annoyed by his attention. He was a braggart, his clothing tattered, not clean of face or hands. She wanted nothing to do with him, and gave him no encouragement. Still he stared.

She knew better than to mention this to her father. Tom Pauls would not hesitate to run him off the property, officer of the law or not. Worse, her brothers, Alex and Roger, would take care of it in their own way: *"No problema, pronto,"* as they liked to say when faced by a dilemma. Knowing her brothers, Baldwin just might fall down and hurt himself as he was leaving the house under their escort.

Wanting no trouble, she kept quiet. Besides, Alex and Roger were gone for several days, staying in outlying line shacks on the eastern sector of the ranch. Tom Pauls did not allow his sons to ride alone out there.

Eddie looked at her mother. Her face was creased in deep lines plowed by pain. Eddie had noticed she was quiet while a guest sat at their table. When they were alone as a family, Marietta routinely complained of ailments in a dull monotone. On these occasions Eddie saw her father looking on, brow furrowed, clearly distressed by his helplessness to relieve her pain and troubled by her mental state. Once good-humored and light of spirit, Marietta had lost not only

17

vitality after the accident, but her smile, too.

Tom Pauls sat at the head of the table. Broad-shouldered with keen blue eyes, his thick hair had turned snow white in the last few years. He still possessed a quick and charming smile, and now he frequently acknowledged Baldwin's comments with an agreeable nod or two. He was a polite host, but Eddie knew her father privately ridiculed the deputy's crude boastfulness. Tom Pauls had once said: "A stall mucker would need a gold-plated shovel to move Baldwin's load."

Eddie had fried steaks and potatoes, boiled vegetables, and now she served supper to her mother and father, and Buster Baldwin. She added cream to his coffee, and was just as glad when he did not thank her for it. Instead of grinning and leering at her, he was busy puffing up a yarn about his career as a lawman, claiming to have once served as marshal in Dodge City back in the days when it was a wild town.

Over supper Eddie idly listened to a dull conversation dominated by the deputy. She did not mention seeing the Indian at Rainbow Arch. For one thing, she knew her mother would fret if she knew. For another, Baldwin would undoubtedly pester Sheriff Gilmore into making an official report to Fort Crawford. Blown out of all proportion, the whole thing would make Baldwin look heroic.

Over one hundred miles away, Fort Crawford was the nearest Army post in Colorado. Based on the fate of past crime reports forwarded from Red Rock, the Pauls knew there was slim chance infantry would be dispatched to this southernmost county. Far away from the population center of Denver, nothing short of an incursion by Mexican revolutionaries or an attack by Indians would bring the Army down here.

Besides, Eddie well knew her father's attitude toward the prospect of a column of two hundred troopers tramping through his rangeland. Like most pioneer ranchers who had built their private empires in remote reaches of the West, he figured he could handle things himself. He always had before the law came out here. Bluecoats were not needed then, or welcomed now.

Eddie thought about the Indian she had seen today. A sentry, he was probably traveling with family members. She wondered who he was—his name, where he was from, what his day-to-day life was like. Before her birth, all the tribes had been banished to distant reservations, and she did not know one clan from another. The young man she had encountered at Rainbow Arch could have been a Ute, a Kiowa, a member of the Navajo tribe, or a Pueblo.

That last one was not a united tribe so much as a region populated by clans, large and small. Eddie had learned that from a Chautauqua speaker visiting Red Rock last year. Two hundred and fifty years ago, according to the lecturing anthropologist, Spanish conquerors had lumped together all the tribes living in the upper Río Grande Valley. Friars labeled them "pueblos" due to a perceived similarity of their adobe and stone structures.

These dwellings with thick, solid walls were accessible by ladders. Taken up at night, or in the presence of enemies, the ladders had served as an effective defense from attack for centuries. Then came the *conquistadores*, "men from the south", as they were called by native peoples. These invaders brought swords of razor-sharp Toledo steel, pikes, and firearms.

With no means of escape, the inhabitants found themselves trapped in their homes. Warriors attempting to resist with weapons of stone and wood were mutilated by fusillades of cannon fire or slain by Spanish musketry. Women and children, huddled together, were slashed with swords wielded by soldiers charging under the flag of Spain. In a bloody conquest, powerful tribes were conquered in a matter of days, entire clans annihilated.

Survivors were bound in servitude by Spaniards. Slaves were chained, penned at night, and worked by day, just as Africans had lived under the whip for centuries throughout Mediterranean Europe. In the New World once proud men and women with long heritages in this land spent their lives in servitude—farmers, ditch diggers, household servants, miners, or laborers building great missions with bell towers. The irony was not lost on the workers. Bells summoned them to an all-knowing deity, a fearsome god promising violence against heathens.

During two centuries of rule by Spain across the Sea of Darkness, as the Atlantic Ocean was first known to Europeans, tribal identities were lost. This destruction of centuries-old cultures continued when the Spaniards were driven out by Mexicans, and the Mexicans defeated by Americans. Native clans merely noted different flags and unknown uniforms of the "new men".

Invaders repeated the error committed by Columbus in the spring of 1492. Even after two more voyages across the Sea of Darkness, Christopher Columbus failed to recognize his mistake. He went to his grave in 1506 believing he had opened a route for the lucrative spice trade, that he had made contact with the people of India—*los Indios*.

Eddie knew clans of various "Indian" tribes routinely jumped reservation boundaries. Such illegal travel was not born of hostility toward conquerors so much as a disregard for arbitrary lines inscribed on maps. Some clans traveled northward in a pilgrimage to the sandstone arch opening into a twisting cañon. Passing under the arch brought good fortune and protection from evil, the clans believed, and the deep cañon itself promised safety. Each stone spire embodied unique spiritual powers, too.

Those were sketchy beliefs Eddie had heard whites ascribe to Indians over the years. The accuracy of those accounts was unknown to her. She had never actually tried to communicate with an Indian. Until today she had never stood within a quarter mile of any of them. With their air of quiet mystery, they were strangers to her—distant, unknown, vaguely feared. And she knew, as her father often pointed out, from antiquity this land had been theirs.

The difficulty of a long and arduous trek in moccasins of leather or sandals fashioned from yucca fibers was testament to the importance clans attached to their beliefs. Entire families eased past white settlements and ranches at night. Footprints in the muddy banks of Ute Creek over the years had helped Eddie determine their route. They followed the creek, skirting the ranch house and outbuildings, and angled toward the arch—the same route she had followed today.

Clearly the clans bound for the sacred cañon did not want a fight, or even to be detected by whites. They answered the call of their ancestors. Small groups came and went without confrontation from Tom Pauls, even when discovery of a horned skull and sun-bleached bones proved they had butchered a beef from the Rainbow Ranch herd.

"A small price to pay," Eddie had often heard her father comment, "to folks who called this place home a whale of a long time before we landed here."

Chapter Two

Deputy Cale Parker reined up. Half turning in the saddle, he looked down at the churned earth. He was no tracker, but he had worked in livery stables long enough to know what he was seeing here.

Cattle had passed this way, a small herd in the last week or ten days. His estimate of the elapsed time was based on the color of droppings as observed from the saddle rather than the time-honored technique of dismounting to plunge an index finger into the brown mound. An experienced tracker tested for moisture content with that finger, and then sniffed it to estimate the freshness of a wafting bouquet.

Cale lifted his gaze and looked uptrail. Half a dozen other imprints were stamped into dry soil by horseshoes. Scattered among them were burro tracks.

Cale scanned the empty horizon. As far as the eye could see, this was a bleak terrain studded by gray sage, clumps of green pear cactus, and tufts of thin, almost colorless grass. Not a tree in sight.

His gaze returned to the tracks. By his reading, five horsebackers had herded thirty-some head of cattle and a handful of donkeys. They were moving south, probably headed to the Colorado border with New Mexico Territory. His first instinct was to follow.

Cale thought about that. Pushing a herd this size in the heat of summer was unusual, and that was what had caught his attention. Nothing to be gained now, he figured, by following a cold trail to the state line. That was where his jurisdiction ended.

This trail led toward the Río River. Following it downstream would take the herd across the line into Caliente. Cale remembered seeing the village from the underside of the freight car that had brought him here. He recalled a cavernous sale barn and complex of corrals and chutes along a Southern & Río Grande siding. Maybe a rancher somewhere in Red Rock County, one of the smaller operations, was cashing out and selling his herd at auction in Caliente during the off season.

Due back in Red Rock in three days, he decided his best course of action was to report this to Sheriff Gilmore. Then, after a trim and a hot soak in the back room of Dave's Tonsorial Parlor, he would feast in a sit-down café on Broad Street—a slab of sirloin steak, mashed potatoes dammed up to contain a sea of beef gravy, green beans, corn, and a soda biscuit twice the size of his fist. Buttered. Plenty of butter. Then came apple pie. He envisioned a triangle of fresh-baked pie capped by a peak of whipped cream like snow on a mountaintop, all of it served by a girl with a pretty smile. . . .

Cale made vivid promises to himself about food and women as a way to cope with this bleak region. Not only could a man get himself hopelessly lost in a land with few landmarks, but the longer Cale roamed these parts with no company other than his horse, the more he felt his identity slipping away, too, his inner sense of self-awareness swallowed in the vastness of this place.

Thinking about the feast placed before him by a beautiful woman with a smile just for him, he lifted his canteen to cracked lips and gulped water. Then he watered his horse from his hat. He could almost see the imagined menu in a Red Rock café, and he could almost taste a fine cut of steak steaming on a white porcelain plate. Almost.

Ten months ago he had not thought much beyond his next meal when he had taken the job advertised on page two of a newspaper from a distant town, the *Signal* of Red Rock, Colorado. Orphaned at fourteen in North Platte, Nebraska, Cale had camped alone by the Platte River at night and mucked out horse stalls and corrals by day. Then he went to work for the railroad. His job was to clean passenger coaches and freight cars on the Union Pacific line. He left his camp on the riverbank and took up residence in a rooming house. He had moved up a step from shovel work in a livery, but only a step.

As time wore on, he gave up his dream of ever becoming a locomotive engineer. Or a brakeman or fireman, either. Every able-bodied youngster within earshot of a steam whistle wanted a job on the railroad, and none of the cussed graybeards on the UP payroll would quit to make room. *You gotta shoot some old-timer iffen you want to get a job on the UP went the standing joke in North Platte, but chances are the body won't even be cold when some danged shirt-tail relative of the dead man slides into that job ahead of you.*

The day Cale found that crumpled-up copy of the *Signal* on the floor of a passenger coach, a job opportunity in Colorado was all he needed to shove him into a decision. He hopped a midnight freight on the UP line, and traveled west to Rawlins, Wyoming. Dropping south, he rode the rods under a S&RG coach all the way to Caliente, New Mexico Territory. From that Spanish-style village he took the spur to Red Rock, Colorado—all of this illegal travel risked on the off chance the job was still open at "premium pay".

It was, and Cale's days of swamping train cars were over.

Claiming twenty, he had lied about his age by adding three years. The other answers to Gilmore's questions were more or less accurate. He did not mention three days of train travel without the nicety of a ticket.

The lawman seemed particularly interested in the fact that Cale had been orphaned, that he was alone in the world with no family depending on him, that he had the gumption to hunt for opportunities. As an added benefit, should something happen to this pup while performing his lawful duties, the line of mourners would not be long.

Gilmore had leaned back in his swivel armchair, eyed Cale Parker, and then slammed forward, boots resounding on plank flooring. Meeting the lawman's flinty gaze, Cale figured he had smelled a fib. He braced himself. Instead of demanding the lying applicant leave the premises immediately, though, Gilmore turned from his desk and opened the safe.

With his signature on a Red Rock County voucher, the sheriff advanced enough money to pay for a month's bed and board at Bess Loukin's rooming house. He outfitted his new deputy with a horse, saddle, bridle, and saddlebags, and handed him an old Whitney Navy .36-caliber revolver, holster, and cartridge belt—this gear accepted long ago from a drunk in lieu of a fine.

Ears ringing after target practice that afternoon, Cale was on duty. Gilmore used the county map on the wall for reference, and instructed him to patrol the south sector of the county. The bald truth, it turned out, was that this was a new law enforcement position created by the county commissioners as a way to extend protection to outlying ranches. No one else had offered to pin on the badge. Volunteers eager to patrol remote outreaches of Red Rock County numbered exactly one.

Now Cale clapped his hat on his head and swung up. He turned the mare, and spurred her. On the way to Red Rock he would stop off at three ranching operations—Henry Taylor's T-Bar-H, Aaron Miller's Circle M, and Sam Aikens's spread, the Diamond Bar—and inquire about matters of the law.

Sam Aikens's Diamond Bar was a one-man deal, a hard-scrabble ranching operation. With fifty head of cattle under his brand, Sam survived for one reason and one reason only—a reliable spring. Located "halfway beyond the middle of nowhere", as the old-timer described this stretch of high desert, barren terrain yielded to grassland near a cabin, slab barn, and pole corral.

An underground spring seeped to the surface, and a shallow well provided water year around to the rancher and the Ute woman who lived with him. Named Chipeta, no one knew where she came from or why she had thrown in with a "hairy mouth". The best guess, according to tales Cale had heard, speculated Chipeta was shunned from her clan for violating some tribal rule or taboo, giving her no choice but to leave. She took up with a white man, un-doubtedly leaving loved ones behind in her clan.

When Utes were forced onto reservations, Chipeta could have joined them. A translator came to the Diamond Bar and told her that. But she elected to stay on the ranch with her garden and endless chores in the company of an old man who did not share her language. In truth, after all these years, the small spread, branded cattle, and three breeding bulls were as much hers as Sam's.

Cale hailed the cabin when he approached from the chimney side, a windowless plank wall. He rode around the corner past a stack of uprooted sagebrush used as firewood. Drawing rein, he swung down as the door opened. A mangy dog trotted out, tail slowly wagging, with the old rancher a step behind him.

"Howdy, young 'un."

"Sam," Cale greeted the rancher. "How are you?"

"Still breathing."

Cale grinned.

Sam Aikens rubbed his eyes, and grimaced as he flexed his fingers. He was thin, a raw-boned man with white beard stubble on his jaw, bowlegged, gnarled fingers pained by arthritis. Barefoot and hatless now, Cale saw thin white hair standing on end, and figured his shout had awakened Sam from an afternoon nap.

Cale bent down and petted Cyclone. The brown and black dog, sniffing his boots, had earned his name from the habit of chasing his tail at high speed. "Gol-danged dog gonna corkscrew hisself straight into the ground someday," Sam often predicted. "Just hope I live long enough to see it happen."

Cale opened a saddlebag. He drew out a sky-blue tin of Mail Pouch, the rancher's favorite brand of tobacco, and handed it to him.

"Much obliged," Sam said, his face brightening to show missing teeth. "Come in, come in. Come in, afore the mosquitoes knock you down, and horseflies carry you off to hell-and-gone."

Cale often used this ranch as a way station when passing through, staying overnight in the shed. He left small items in return—thread, needles, thimbles, and sewing scissors for Chipeta, chaw or smoking tobacco for Sam. He always thanked Chipeta for her hospitality even though she had never spoken to him. Whether the stout woman understood his words or not, Cale did not know. But he saw the wrinkles in her face deepen, a warm expression in brown eyes that went beyond spoken language.

Night or day, she wore long, shapeless dresses pieced together from White Star flour sacks. She decorated the cotton fabric with fine stitches of colored thread in the shape of flowers and stick-figure animals. From his previous visits, Cale knew she had fashioned baggy underwear for Sam, and pullover shirts with bone buttons halfway down a fabric yoke in the old style favored by frontiersmen. To Cale, both Sam and Chipeta seemed ageless, somehow eternal, like the land itself.

Sam had an untamed fondness for flapjacks made from hand-ground graham flour, served with honey and freshly churned butter. Cale watched Chipeta scoop the coarse powder out of a mouse-proof barrel and stir heavy cream into a crockery bowl to make batter. When sausage sizzled in the frying pan, she dropped dollops of thick batter into the popping grease. She boiled water for coffee while turning the pancakes and adding them to a stack in the warmer of the stove.

After eating and swapping tales, Cale spent the night in the oversize shed that served as a barn. He knew Sam slept on a cot in the cabin with Cyclone by his side and eight or ten laying hens at his feet. The floor was covered with back issues of the *Signal*, supposedly for the purpose of catching the alkali-white droppings of chickens.

Cale had noticed most of their leavings and stray feathers ended up smeared into the wool blanket thrown across the cot where the hens preferred to roost. Sam seemed oblivious to the stench and the filth. With a note of pride in his voice, he had once explained this unusual sleeping arrangement to Cale: "With me and Cyclone on guard, this here's the bestest way to perteck my chickens from coyotes and hawks."

Chipeta apparently disliked it. She bedded on a buffalo hide on the floor near the fireplace, often sewing by the light of flames late into the night.

At dawn Cale said his good byes, and mentioned the tracks he had seen. "Missing any livestock, Sam?"

The old rancher squinted. "Dunno. Reckon I'd better take a count."

"If I had time, I'd lend a hand. . . ."

"Don't worry about me, young 'un," he interrupted. "Ain't much of a trick to count steers wearing my Diamond Bar brand. In this danged desert they don't wander far from water and grass."

Farther north, Aaron Miller's Circle M encompassed eighty thousand acres with a mile of it along the Río River. Rich soil was irrigated there, much of it planted in oats and wheat. Not large, nevertheless, this was a fine ranch in the desert country. Miller himself had profited mightily and become an absentee owner. In recent years he and his family of six children had lived in a house in the Capitol Hill section of Denver. Miller depended on his ramrod, Griff Monroe, to mind the place.

Cale spoke to Rollie, the ranch cook, and learned the Circle M foreman was out on the range. Like most ranch cooks, Rollie was a man who had given his best years to the saddle. Crippled up now with bad knees and one lame arm that had healed improperly after a fall from his horse, he was able to stay on the home place by keeping the chow coming when hungry men wanted it.

Riders were expected at noon. Cale waited in the shade of the verandah. He was eating roast beef and boiled potatoes on a much-dented steel plate brought by the cook when a dust plume caught his eye. Cale finished eating and stood, his gaze on a lone rider coming off open range from the east. He was mounted on a white horse.

"That's Griff," Rollie said as he headed for the cook shack in his gimpy stride. "The others, they won't be far behind."

Cale stepped down from the porch. Every man sat a horse in his own manner, and Monroe's style was easily recognizable from a distance. He had a way of arching his back and holding the reins high in one gloved hand, his stockman's hat pulled low. Coming into the yard at a canter now with an unlit *cigarillo* clenched in his teeth, he made a beeline to the verandah. He sawed back on the reins hard enough for his mount's hoofs to raise dust. The maneuver was not a friendly one.

"Parker," he said, speaking around the *cigarillo*.

"Howdy, Griff," Cale said, and stepped back from the dust cloud.

Eyes shaded by the brim of his hat, Monroe's gaze lingered on the steel dinner plate with a fork and knife on a step of the verandah. "What brings you out here?"

"Making my rounds."

"Looks like you lassoed a free meal while you're at it," Griff said.

They regarded one another in a long, unblinking challenge. Griff Monroe was heavily muscled, with short-cropped hair, blunt facial features, and a thick mustache. He was armed with a holstered revolver and a lever-action repeater in his saddle scabbard.

Both of them knew the practice of offering food to a traveler was a time-honored tradition in the American West. By loading a plate, Rollie had simply done what was expected of him. Monroe's attitude seemed to be that Cale had somehow used his position to take advantage of the custom.

Cale broke the silence. He came straight to the point and

described the trail he had cut. "Are you missing any critters, Griff?"

"Besides the one you just ate?" the foreman asked.
"Look, kid, I can't answer that until fall roundup when we
take the tally."

He spoke as though stating a fact known to all but Cale.
One way or another, Monroe was always quick to label him
a newcomer, a green kid with no ranching experience or
horse sense, either.

Ignoring the implications of his remark, Cale asked:
"Have you seen any suspicious riders around here?"

"Nope. Just you."

"I'll pass that along to the sheriff," Cale said dryly.

"Deputy," Griff Monroe said with rising anger, "if cattle
thieves are robbing us, do your damned duty. You and that
lazy town lawman track them down. That's what you're
paid to do. Earn your money. That's what I say. Tell that to
your almighty sheriff." Monroe drew a breath and added:
"Or send for the Army. It's probably those Utes that are
picking us clean. Starting with that old she-bitch down on
the Diamond Bar pointing the way for the rest of her tribe."

"I saw tracks left by shod horses," Cale said.

"The Indians could 'a' stole saddle mounts."

"They were trailing a few donkeys," Cale said. "From
what I hear, Utes won't touch donkeys." He eyed the big
man. "You already knew that, didn't you, Griff?"

"Smart, huh?" Monroe said, glowering. "I'm just the
man to knock the smart outta you."

Hoof beats signaled other riders drifting in. Cale looked
past Monroe. He counted four men, and saw the ramrod
glance back at them as they headed to the corral adjoining
the barn. Smoke plumed from the cook house stovepipe
now.

Monroe had not dismounted or invited his visitor to stay overnight. On previous patrols, Cale never had, and he had not planned to tonight, but the message was clear enough—Lawman, you are not welcome here.

Cale went to his mare, tightened the cinch, and swung up. As far as he was concerned, Mr. Aaron Miller had given his foreman too much authority. The power to rule the Circle M had gone to his head.

Without a parting word to Monroe, Cale rode out. In the ten months since he had taken this job, they had not seen eye-to-eye on much of anything. The Circle M foreman had disliked him from the first, determined to take him down a notch at every opportunity. Why? Cale did not know. That night, stretched out under the stars with his saddle for a pillow, he wondered about it.

Cale searched his mind. He still did not know what he had done to earn such rancor. At least he did not know the reason from Monroe's own words. After pinning a deputy's badge on his vest, though, he had learned a thing or two about human nature. For one, some folks walking this earth disliked law officers on general principles. Maybe Griff Monroe belonged to that breed.

There was another possible explanation, one Sheriff Gilmore had cautioned him about when he had taken this job. In remote cattle country, a good many cowhands were men on the dodge. Some had undoubtedly escaped the hangman's noose by a thread. Having left notoriety in their dust, such men fled to a region where no one knew them, where they would not be found.

Recalling the hard stare in Griff Monroe's gaze, Cale wondered if there had been a blow-up in his past. Maybe a deadly encounter had taken place, one that he did not want local folks to know about, and he was reminded of it every time a lawman hove into view.

The opposite side of the hospitality coin was exemplified by the friendly manner of Henry Taylor. From the moment Cale drew in sight of the home ranch on the T-Bar-H, Taylor himself welcomed him as a guest. He insisted Cale take his meal with him in the main house. He apologized for not having an extra bunk in the bunkhouse, but offered the haymow in the horse barn to him for the night.

Tall, with an unruly shock of black hair almost hiding his large ears, Taylor struck a Lincolnesque figure. He customarily dressed for supper, and ate alone by the light of a single oil lamp. Taylor was said to be a widower. In Cale's experience, the rancher rarely spoke of his past. As a matter of common courtesy, Cale had honored the unspoken rule of etiquette in the West—never ask a man about his back trail. Now Taylor stated his pleasure of welcoming company for supper, and ordered the ranch cook to bring an extra serving.

From previous visits, Cale knew Taylor was a hands-on owner. No meerschaum pipe and rocking chair on the verandah for him. Ranch life kept him busy from sunup to nightfall. With some eight hundred head of cattle and a fine string of horses, he was a successful rancher, as successful as any in southern Colorado with the exception of Tom Pauls, owner of the famed Rainbow Ranch.

Well-to-do by local standards, Taylor was, yet Cale had noted the man seemed lonely, eager for company. He found out why. It was imperative, the rancher explained to him, to maintain a certain distance from the hired hands.

"It pains me to say so," he confided to Cale, "but a boss cannot be a pard."

Well-designed with a barn and outbuildings perched on high ground, this ranch overlooking a stretch of the Río

River stood a few miles south of Red Rock.

Cale knew Sheriff Gilmore counted Taylor as a friend. Not only a rancher, Taylor was a county commissioner, and an influential one. It was a friendship, Cale judged, that Gilmore cultivated as a political necessity. The two were about the same age, the front-side of fifty, and they had hunted game and fished for native trout together in week-long treks on horseback to the mountain valleys far north of Red Rock.

Over coffee that evening after supper, Taylor listened intently to Cale's account of the tracks left by an unknown group of riders herding livestock.

"I'll have men fan out tomorrow," Taylor said. "If we pick up that trail as you described it, we'll know thieves have hit us."

Eddie was gathering eggs in the chicken coop when the sounds of pounding hoofs reached her like a distant drumbeat. Basket in hand, she backed out of the low-roofed coop. She looked around, expecting to see her brothers coming on horseback at full gallop with the horses' nostrils flaring and tails flying.

She was right. The two of them raced across open pasture on lathered geldings, Roger in the lead as usual with Alex bringing up the rear.

"Beat you!" Roger shouted to Alex when he passed the coop and approached the corral by the barn. "Beat you!"

Next came a shout from the house. "Somebody's going to get beat, all right!"

Eddie turned. She saw her father step out on the porch, hands on his hips. He had bellowed like a bull, and even though he demanded strict obedience, neither of her brothers was deceived by his stern demeanor.

They halted at the corral, leaping from their horses. Roger yanked his hat off his head, tried to hit his brother with it, and missed when Alex dodged away. The horses shied, but were quickly brought under control by the two boys.

"I beat you!" Roger said again.

"Wind-break two good horses," Tom Pauls shouted from the house, "and you'll need six months to work off the debt! Tell me who wins then."

"Yeah!" Alex said as he shoved his brother. "You lose, numb nuts!"

Roger pushed him back, mimicking him as though taking their father's side. "Yeah, hatchet face!"

"Tend those horses!" Tom Pauls shouted. "Wash up and get in here! Both of you!"

Eddie grinned at the shouted exchange between them. Lifting her free hand to greet Roger and Alex, she headed for the kitchen door to the house.

At suppertime, with their heads still wet from washing at the pump, Roger and Alex reported to their father. Eddie listened and watched, smiling at her brothers. The level of excitement was always elevated when they were on the home place, and now she welcomed a surge of energy to her daily routines of cooking, cleaning, care-taking.

Stood side-by-side, Alex and Roger would never have been picked out of a crowd as brothers. At eighteen, Alex was Ichabod Crane—rail-skinny, beak-nosed with high, pointed cheek bones, thin lips, and owlish eyes. According to his father, Alex had to stand up twice to cast a shadow.

The oldest by eleven months, Roger took after his father's side of the family. He looked older than he was, somehow wiser. Roger was broad-shouldered, square-jawed, strong and handsome, quick to flash the grin that made him look like a young Tom Pauls.

Eddie shifted her gaze to the other end of the dinner table. Marietta sat in silence in her split cane wheelchair, a mother's loving gaze embracing her sons as though all pain was alleviated in these moments.

Ben Pittock set type for the back page of Volume 12, Issue 7 of the *Red Rock Signal*. He had just finished his column, "Methinx", and now he proofread the piece. His editorial subject concerned the second greatest pet peeve among women in this town—unpublished changes in the schedules of S&RG trains.

Just about the time the arrival of a thundering locomotive can be predicted in our fair city, the powers that be in the S&RG bust their own schedules and send an engine our way. With no more warning than two toots and three blasts of the whistle, coal smoke darkens the sky. Pity the poor lady who has hung freshly laundered clothing and bed sheets on her line that day. A cloud of smoke obscures the sun, and cinders drift down from the sky like black snow, quickly ruining a morning's work. Oh, yes, and pity the poor S&RG man, methinx, who foolishly confesses responsibility for this unwarranted abuse. As women wronged, the ladies of Red Rock shall band together. They shall go after said gent, seeking justice—and just revenge.

The S&RG spur from the main line at Caliente had pumped life into Red Rock. The rail line brought steel closer to coal mines, logging operations, and a few hard-rock mines in the mountains.

Pittock knew folks disliked the roughshod exertion of power by railroad barons, and nearly everyone resented their wealth. Freight rates were sky-high. So were passenger tickets. Men routinely hopped freights at night rather than pay the fare to the main line.

One local man, apprehended while burglarizing a boxcar last year, had stated to Sheriff Gilmore: "Them see-gar chompin' railroaders waddle through town like fattened hogs. Me, I ne'er would 'a' turned to robbin' iffen my family had enough to et."

Pittock ran that quote on page one. He had little to lose. The S&RG had never purchased an inch of advertising in the *Signal*. He figured readers would sympathize with the point of view of a family man rummaging for food. Now a strong word of advice on the subject of scheduling would show readers where their editor stood on the railroad issue—and his "Methinx" column just might spark newspaper sales.

His eye caught movement outside. Through the plate glass window of his front office, he saw a lone horseman making his way down Broad Street.

Pittock recognized the young deputy, Cale Parker. Armed with an old revolver holstered on his cartridge belt, and outfitted with spare canteens, a rolled blanket, and saddlebags, the youngster rode easily in the saddle. Something in his manner, though, his squared shoulders and the set of his jaw, hinted of purpose, if not urgency.

Pittock moved closer to the window and peered out. The deputy was headed toward the sheriff's office down the block. Pittock recalled Gilmore's request for an article about cattle theft in the paper last week.

Might be a follow-up story here, he thought as he untied his ink-stained apron.

Chapter Three

Cale entered the sheriff's office on Broad Street, finding Gilmore in conference with two men seated in chairs on either side of his desk. Both of them wore suits and polished street shoes, and both held narrow-brimmed hats of black felt on their laps. One carried a black briefcase.

City dudes, Cale thought immediately. The one who had been speaking stopped in midsentence. Cale drew up, sensing the gravity of this meeting without knowing the subject under discussion.

Joe Gilmore lifted his hand in greeting. "If you don't mind, Deputy, we'll get together later, and I'll take your report."

Cale nodded, and backtracked to the door.

"Reckon you've had your fill of campfire fare by now," Gilmore added with a grin.

"Yes, sir."

"Go ahead and get yourself a decent meal," Gilmore went on. "Steak and beer on me. I'll meet you in the Pair O' Dice."

Stepping outside, Cale closed the door. He turned and came face to face with the editor of the *Signal*. Their gazes met briefly before Cale stepped past the man.

"Good afternoon, Deputy Parker," Ben Pittock said.

Cale nodded at him, and moved to his mare at the tie rail. He knew Pittock by sight only. The newspaperman had never spoken to him before. He had always talked to the sheriff, interviewing Gilmore for news items "fit to print", as he liked to say.

Cale took loose the reins, and jerked his head toward the sheriff's office. "Sheriff's busy with a couple gents right now."

"You're the one I want to talk to, Deputy," Pittock said.

"Me? What about?"

"Cattle rustling, altering brands, that sort of shenanigan."

"Sir?"

"You just now got back to town, didn't you?"

"Yeah."

"Sheriff Gilmore has everybody and his dog on the lookout for stock thieves," Pittock replied. "Did you find any rustlers in your travels through the far-flung hinterlands?"

Cale blinked. Whatever "hinterlands" meant, he figured this man ought to be speaking to the lawman in charge, but did not know how to sidestep the question.

"No."

Pittock eyed him. "You found something, though, didn't you?"

Cale met his stare. "You'll have to talk to Sheriff Gilmore about that."

"Deputy, I'm talking to you."

Cale thrust a boot into the stirrup. He swung up, and turned the horse.

Pittock moved to the edge of the boardwalk. "I want an answer, Deputy."

Touching spurs to the horse, Cale repeated: "Like I said, Mister Pittock, you'll have to get that from Sheriff Gilmore."

He heard a muttered curse. Aware Pittock stared after him, he rode away from the lawman's office and crossed Broad. He headed down Fifth Street toward a weathered plank sign on a barn:

Red Rock Livery Barn & Stables
Wade Powell, Blacksmith

Cale boarded the mare. Since his arrival in Red Rock with a grip in hand and the clothes on his back, he had not spent enough time here to become well acquainted with townsmen. But Wade was a friendly soul. He had welcomed him from the start, even offering the haymow for a place to sleep after learning Cale had worked in livery stables in Nebraska.

Cale was surprised to learn this easy-going man had once been a pugilist, that he had fought professionally in New York and New Jersey. Short and bull-like with rounded shoulders, he was powerfully built. A crooked nose and thick ears marked his former profession. As to his fight record, Wade had shrugged in reply to Cale's question.

"Lost count," he said. "You win some, you lose some. I can tell you one thing for sure."

"What's that?"

"The younger the challengers get," he said, "the more bouts you lose."

Now Cale left the barn with saddlebags slung over his shoulder. He walked the five blocks to Bess Loukin's rooming house, and climbed the outside staircase to his rented room. He gathered up clean clothes, and hiked to Dave's Tonsorial Parlor on Broad. The barbershop was located midway between the sheriff's office and Pittock's print shop. With no sign of the editor on the boardwalk, he figured Gilmore was being interviewed by now.

An hour later, shaved and bathed, Cale donned his clean clothes. He hiked to a café adjoining the Pair O' Dice Club and bought the supper he had promised himself.

More or less. The steak was boot-tough, an oily gravy

floated islands of congealed grease, and the corn-on-the-cob should have been left in the field. The meal was served by a fat cook with a ratty beard, not the smiling young woman Cale had dreamed up in idle fantasies. The cook wore a much-stained shirt with buttons missing where the fabric yielded to a bulging stomach, the aperture exposing his dirty bellybutton at eye level. Cale turned away from fish-belly white skin forested with dark, curling hairs.

He ate hurriedly, paid the bill, and immediately went next door through an arched entryway. Not a gambling man, Cale moved to the Pair O' Dice bar. From there he watched faro, roulette, blackjack, and five-card draw poker games. He drank a nickel-mug of dark beer, not for the purpose of washing down his supper, but to purge his mouth of an aftertaste of rancid grease. He was still trying to get the image of that hairy stomach out of his mind when Joe Gilmore caught up with him.

"You did the right thing, Cale."

While the sheriff waved to the barkeep for a mug of beer, Cale cast a questioning look at him.

"Pittock's steamed at you," Gilmore said with half a smile, "but he'll get over it." He paused. "Ben figures you know more than you told him. Do you?"

Cale nodded. "Yeah."

"Well, you did the right thing," he said again, "when you sent him to me."

"Did he barge into your meeting with those two gents?" Cale asked.

"Nothing in this town counts for more than Ben Pittock's next deadline," Gilmore replied. "Earthquake, cyclone, plague, you name it." He shook his head. "Those two gents came all the way from Denver. They had a train to catch, but that didn't stop Ben from horning in."

The mustachioed barkeep slid a beer across the bar to Gilmore, refusing payment. The lawman admired the dark brew. He raised the mug to his mouth. Taking a long gulp, he set the mug down and wiped foam from his beard.

Gilmore turned to Cale. "Now you can tell me, son."

Cale described the tracks he had seen. Gilmore nodded slowly as he listened. When Cale finished, the lawman re-counted Stanley Harrison's report from Caliente, noting brands registered in Red Rock County had been crudely altered by a running iron. Among the brands in question were the T-Bar-H and Circle M. Sam Aikens's Diamond Bar was not on the list.

"Stock thieves," Gilmore said. "No question about that. But we don't have enough to go on to warrant raising a posse, either."

Cale watched Gilmore heft the glass mug again, take another swallow, and wipe his beard as he set the mug on the bar.

"One of two things, I figure."

Cale looked at him questioningly.

"Either those thieves will take their money from the sale of steers and head south to Santa Fé or maybe old Mexico," Gilmore said, "or they'll spend that money in Caliente, and ride back here for more cash on the hoof."

Cale was aware Gilmore eyed him after he drained the mug and waved off a refill from the barkeep.

"What I'd like you to do," the sheriff said at last, "is ride back to the spot where you picked up the trail. Can you find it?"

Cale nodded.

"Ride back there," Gilmore went on, "backtrack 'em, and take up a position where you can see far and wide. I'll give you my telescope to take along. In my experience, thieves sometimes return to places where they have been successful. If this bunch is still in the region, they just might visit again."

"What if they do?"

"Come back to Red Rock on the double," the lawman said. "I'll get up a posse, pass out the rifles, and we'll ride the bastards down."

Eddie left the house after her father stretched out on the settee in the library for his midday nap. Her mother worked on a knitted scarf for next winter, long needles clicking in a familiar rhythm.

Crossing the verandah, Eddie went to the barn in search of her brothers. She knew they were mucking stalls and forking fresh hay down from the mow—tedious, horsefly-bitten chores assigned as punishment for running saddle mounts too hard. Over breakfast their father had handed down a verdict, as stern as any judge from the bench: "You boys can sweat off that extra energy in the horse barn today."

Roger had groaned.

"For how long?" Alex had asked.

"When I tell you you're done," their father had replied. "If you're still full of beans after that, I'll throw a saddle on you and spur you both into the ground."

Eddie had ducked her head to hide a smile.

Now she entered the barn and searched for Roger and Alex amid deep, fragrant shadows. Near silence in cavernous near darkness was disturbed only by the *swish* of tails whipping flies and the movements of confined horses. Several lifted their heads to nicker as she passed by in the runway.

"Sis," Roger said.

"Where are you?"

"Back here."

She moved toward the voice. "What are you doing?"

"Feeding my blood to skeeters and horseflies," he replied.

She found him in the next to last stall. Overhead, muffled sounds came from the mow. Alex was up there, wielding a pitchfork as he tossed clean hay down to his brother.

"Did you see any Indians on our range?" Eddie asked.

"No," Roger replied. He stopped shoveling. "Did you?"

"One," she said.

"When? Where?"

She told him about her ride to Rainbow Arch and her encounter there.

Roger asked: "Was he hostile?"

"No," she replied. "He was so close to me . . . well, if he had been hostile, I would not be standing here talking to you."

Alex had overheard and called down to her. "Don't tell Mother."

"I won't," she said.

"Eddie," Roger cautioned, "you'd better start carrying a gun when you ride out by yourself. . . ."

A strange sound reached them. Eddie heard shrill, bleating cries. The cries came from the house. Eddie saw Roger drop the shovel. Exchanging a quick glance, they both turned and sprinted toward the bright sunlight. Alex shouted down to them, demanding to know what had happened. Eddie was a step behind Roger when they reached the big door of the barn.

"What happened?" Alex repeated. "What's going on down there?"

On the heels of her brother, Eddie lunged outside. She saw her mother on the verandah. A ball of knitting yarn and a pair of long needles lay at her feet. She waved frantically from her wheelchair, her cries sounding like a wounded animal. Eddie saw Roger surge ahead. He jumped the verandah steps in a single leap, and sprinted past their mother as he rushed into the house.

Eddie took the steps two at a time. Seeing her mother distraught but unhurt, she hurried past. Inside the house she turned in the hallway, slowed, and came up behind Roger in the library. She drew up, hands flying to her mouth like birds.

Eddie saw their father lying on the settee, perfectly still. His white hair was neatly brushed straight back from his forehead, eyes closed.

Roger dropped to his knees as though felled. He sobbed suddenly. Eddie stared. Then she moved closer. She put her hands on her brother's quaking shoulders. A moment later she heard Alex's heavy footfalls on the porch, his anguished voice again demanding to know what had happened, what was going on?

Cale led a pack mule this time, a big, sturdy animal bearing panniers packed with an extra box of .36-caliber ammunition, dried beef, tins, a sack of grain, and corked demijohns of water. The mule and gear were rented from Wade Powell on a county voucher signed by Sheriff Gilmore. The liveryman sent Cale off with a hearty—"So long!"—and a wave good bye.

Prepared for a long ride without alerting ranchers to his presence, Cale skirted the Río River drainage. He was watchful as he rode, using the borrowed telescope to glass distant terrain. In this way he avoided herds of grazing cattle, along with the cowhands tending them.

Angling eastward, he well remembered the lay of the land where he had cut the tracks of steers and horses and a few donkeys. At that time he'd had a fair notion where the party was headed. Now the question was—where had they come from?

Cale recalled his first view of this land from the under-carriage of an S&RG freight car. Sliding by at twenty miles an hour, the terrain seemed flat and dry, devoid of life. This was a forbidding place, empty but for hot breezes launching dust devils into the sky.

Later as a deputy on horseback, he had discovered undu-lations and significant land features—swells and gullies and rock outcroppings. This arid region was home to creatures ranging from bounding jack rabbits to skittering lizards and silent, slithering snakes. He found more vegetation than he could have guessed before he rode out here, alone, with a polished deputy's badge pinned to his jacket.

Springs were small and far-flung, many hardly more than seeps. But water was here, life-saving water for man and beast who knew where to find it. And while nothing but sage and pear cactus grew in profusion, feather grass and balsamroot had supported animal life for centuries. Boiled balsamroot would keep a two-legged critter alive, too, as native tribes had discovered long ago.

Cale crossed T-Bar-H range, as well as the Circle M and the Diamond Bar without being observed. This was Sheriff Gilmore's suggestion when he had pointed out the fact that they did not know who they were up against—a band of quick-hit thieves from a distant place, or rogue riders from a local ranch.

Find the high ground, Gilmore had advised Cale, and keep your eyes peeled. Whether he meant it so or not, his advice was the preëminent lesson of survival in the high desert. Motionless creatures were unseen, gaining a distinct advantage over the active ones busily attracting predators.

With no rain for weeks, the tracks Cale had spotted were still visible in soil barely disturbed by gusting breezes. He turned his mare and led the pack mule along the trail churned by steers. Backtracking, the trek was long. At noon of the third day he spooked a flock of small birds. Two hours later he came to a granite uplift and a hidden spring.

He looked down from the saddle. Tracks in the damp soil told the story. Cattle had been gathered, watered, and driven south toward the Río River. In a brief search Cale found opened tins, blackened fire rings, and *cigarillo* butts and chaw littering the ground.

He rode in a widening circle around the muddy bank. The thieves had met here, each of them herding a hatful of steers to a common site. Judging by the ashen remains of sagebrush, brands had been altered here, too.

He turned the mare. With a tug on the lead rope, he led the mule to the back side of the stone outcropping. A dry wash there was just deep enough to conceal his animals. He dismounted and hobbled them, putting on nosebags to discourage wandering.

Following Gilmore's suggestion, Cale took up a position behind the outcropping. Hot from the sun, the flat-topped stone concealed him and at once allowed a view of the spring and surrounding terrain. From here, the sheriff's telescope brought the whole area closer to his eye.

As a pioneer rancher known far and wide in Colorado, Tom Pauls was a man who had spoken eloquently of his life experiences, but he had never mentioned death, particularly his own. Now, with his body wrapped in a bed sheet and covered by a favorite quilt, he lay in state in a spare room of the ranch house, door closed.

In a hushed family gathering during those hours after his passing, Roger expressed his conviction that his father would want to be buried on the home place. He suggested the crest of a sage-dotted hill overlooking the ranch house and distant reservoir Thomas Pauls had dug out himself as a young man. His long-time *segundo,* Spud Jenks, was buried up there. The site seemed fitting.

Alex shook his head in disagreement. "The funeral should be in Red Rock, the burial in the town cemetery. We have to order the coffin and a grave marker. I don't know how. Maybe Mister Pittock can tell us. When he writes the obituary, we can ask him. . . ."

Roger glowered at him. Then he glanced at his sister, clearly seeking her support in the first salvo of a family dispute.

Eddie said nothing. She made her point by turning to their mother.

Marietta had been silent throughout this anguished discussion, listening to the low, halting voices without speaking herself. Grief lay over them all like a blanket of cold iron, and words came hard.

Eddie gazed at her mother's lined face. The skin was puffed now, her eyes reddened from tears. Marietta was quiet for several moments. Then she drew a deep breath and squared her bony shoulders. She spoke with surprising force and certainty. None of her three children was prepared for her words.

"The town of Red Rock," she said, "was nothing but a few shacks on a dusty cattle trail when your father first saw it. You've heard him tell about camping by the confluence of the Río River and Ute Creek forty-odd years ago. And now we all know if the S and RG rail spur fails, Red Rock will fall into decline. It will be reduced to nothing more than a camp, as it was in those early days. I do not want my Thomas buried in a windswept boothill outside a shabby little town in the desert."

Marietta paused, taking a moment to look into the eyes of each of her three children. "I shall live in Denver. That is where Tom's final resting place will be." She added: "Mine, too."

Eddie shouted—"No!"—and clapped a hand over her mouth.

Her brothers were struck silent. Having been born and raised here, none of them could imagine living anywhere else. Roger recovered his wits first. He tried to talk their mother out of this notion. When that failed, Alex suggested she give it more thought. Both were silenced when Marietta repeated her determination to leave the Rainbow Ranch, to put Red Rock County behind her. Forever.

Marietta reminded them of her correspondence with a long-time friend, Mrs. Aaron Miller. The Miller family had left their Circle M Ranch in Red Rock County to live in Denver. In letters Sharon Miller often remarked how much easier life was in the city than on the ranch where endless chores had filled their days, where summer's heat and winter's cold had confined them to the ranch house. She cited other advantages, too, such as the ladies' reading and discussion group she had joined. Sprinkled through her letters were comments on the lyceum. In search of cultural enlightenment, she enjoyed visiting orchestras, lecturers, humorists, ballet troupes, the circus arriving in train cars, and colorful Fourth of July parades replete with black powder cannon fire and Civil War veterans marching in their uniforms.

After a glance at her daughter, Marietta spoke to her sons. She addressed them with a tone of finality: "You boys make up your minds about what you want to do with this ranch. Keep it, sell it, divide it, that's up to you two. Edna and I shall live in Denver."

Eddie bowed her head. Her tears came not only from grief still raw, but the shock of her mother's pronouncement. This plan had never even been hinted at before this moment.

Now Marietta turned to her, reaching out from the wheelchair to rest a hand on her shoulder. "You will have more opportunities in Denver, Edna."

Eddie knew what she meant—marriage. She shook her head. Marriage was the last thing on her mind.

"Don't think I haven't seen the way that grubby deputy, Buster Baldwin, looks at you," Marietta said, withdrawing her hand. "He's not the right man for you, but if you stay out here on this high desert . . . well, I think you know what I mean."

Red-hot emotions surged through Eddie. She blurted her reply: "Mother . . ."—she cleared her throat—"Mother, I do not want to leave our ranch."

"Now, now, dear, after you've had time to think. . . ."

"Mother, I do not want to leave here!"

They stared at one another, neither blinking.

"I will not leave," Eddie said in a voice barely above a whisper.

Marietta winced as though slapped. She bowed her head for a full minute. Then she turned her wheelchair, and left the room.

Cale did not own a pocket watch. If he had a timepiece, he figured he could just about set it by the red-tailed hawk that swooped overhead daily. Every morning, after sunrise, the winged predator appeared in the western sky, circled the spring in a wide arc, and flew away, fast. Cale figured the hawk normally drank here before starting the day's hunt for field mice, but the presence of strange critters had spooked him, sending him winging through the blue sky to a safer spring in this desert.

Long, hot hours dragged into one full day, and then two. By sunset of the third day, the summer heat had taken a toll on the mare and the mule. On Cale, too. His resolve weakened as his body lost strength in the scorching heat. Gilmore's plan to wait in hiding with the hope of catching sight of cattle thieves seemed far-fetched now.

He strapped panniers on the mule. Saddling the mare, he swung up and rode away with no specific destination in mind. All he knew for certain was that he could not stay there any longer. He rode in a wide circle, and soon picked up the tracks of half a dozen steers and shod hoofs. He backtracked them, aware the trail took him in the general direction of Circle M range.

At noon he spotted a cluster of piñon trees growing up the side of a low, sloping ridge. He rode to the grove, tied the horse and mule in a patch of shade, and hiked to the crest. The elevated position gave him a long view of the terrain. The sweep of the telescope took in several miles in all directions.

No water was here. Cale knew his time in this location was limited. He would have to move on soon and search for a spring. His plan changed, though, when he spotted a dust plume. He brought the telescope to bear on a pair of riders and focused the lenses. He observed the cowhands until they halted. The riders abruptly turned back. Heading away from the ridge, they disappeared in the shimmering distance.

Pounded by the heat of the sun, Cale forced himself to be alert and watchful through the course of that day. He rationed water, and protected his animals by moving them from one patch of shade to another as the day wore on. In the evening he made a cold camp, knowing even a small flame could be seen for miles. He was careful. So he believed. Too late, he discovered his own overconfidence when he was awakened in the night by the *click* of a revolver's hammer, a cocked gun.

"What the hell you doing out here on Circle M range?"

Startled, Cale recognized the voice of Griff Monroe. He threw off his blanket and sat up. In night shadows cast by starlight he saw the ranch foreman standing over him, handgun drawn. Cale got to his feet and faced the man.

"Parker, I asked you a damned question."

"Making my rounds," Cale replied.

"The hell," Monroe said. "That lazy town marshal sent you, didn't he? What's his game?"

"Catching stock thieves," Cale replied. "You favor that game, don't you?"

The ramrod swore. "Told you once. I'm just the man to knock the smart outta you. Ever' last bit of it."

Cale's cartridge belt lay across his saddle. Monroe bent down and grabbed it, yanking the old revolver out of the holster. He cocked his arm and heaved it.

Cale heard the gun clatter as it bounced off rocks below. "I don't know what you're trying to prove, but this isn't Circle M range."

"If I say you're standing on my land," Monroe countered, "you are."

"Your land," Cale repeated.

"That's what I said," he replied. He added: "A couple of my riders saw a flash of sunlight off glass. Dead giveaway of trespassers. Hell, for all I know, you're stealing my live-stock."

"You know better than that," Cale said.

"Do I?" Monroe said.

When he waved his gun, Cale saw a dull gleam of blued steel by starlight.

"You wouldn't be the first lawdog to turn bad," Monroe said. "I'm asking again. What the hell are you doing here?"

"Making my rounds. . . ."

Before Cale could finish, he glimpsed a blur of move-ment. His ears roared. Knees buckling, he went down as though the earth had fallen out from under him. His mouth filled with dust before he realized he had been pistol-whipped to the ground. Warm moisture trickled down the side of his jaw.

Struggling to stand, Cale got to his hands and knees. He felt a sharp pain in his ribs after a boot scuffed dirt, and knew he had been kicked. He dropped down and lay flat. Kicked again, he tried to escape the pointed toe of Mon-roe's riding boot and rolled into a clump of pear cactus. The spines pierced his clothing. His howl of pain was an-swered by rough laughter.

"You don't amount to much, do you, kid?" Monroe said. "No, you sure as hell don't. Now, be a good little boy and go home. Go home, so I don't have to hurt you no more. Hear?"

Cale made no reply.

Monroe kicked him again, harder. "I said . . . hear?"

"I hear. . . ." Cale spoke in a pained voice he scarcely recognized as his own. Kicked once again, he drifted away like a feather on the wind.

The hot sun of midday brought him around. He managed to sit up. His mouth was cotton dry. Vaguely remembering more blows, he was not sure if he had been punched or kicked, but he knew he had been hit several more times, struck until he slipped into a state of unconsciousness. Now with a brassy sun directly overheard, the heat revived him. He had never felt such thirst.

Cale drew a deep, ragged breath. Pain shot through his ribs. His jaw ached. Raising a hand to his face, his fingertips touched caked blood. He felt a gash in the skin where the gunsight had raked him.

He stood. Hunched over, he gingerly made his way downslope and retrieved his gun. Then he checked his mare and the mule. He found the animals in the piñons where he had left them last evening. Lifting demijohns out of the panniers brought more pain to his ribs, but he managed to water both critters, and then gulp some himself. He doused his head and washed his face, trying to clean the wound. Cooling water brought a measure of relief, but he was aware of more bleeding.

After both animals were grained, he rested in the shade of a piñon, eyes closed. Waves of pain coursing through his chest and ribcage had sapped his strength. He slept for a time. Then he got to his feet.

He managed to saddle and bridle the mare. Loading the mule, he involuntarily cried out as he hefted the panniers over the mule's back. He leaned against the animal and took a slow, deep breath. Then he strapped the packs snugly, and picked up the lead rope.

Cale thrust a boot in the stirrup. He swung up, grimacing again with the effort. He looped the rope around his saddle horn. Touching spurs to the mare, he rode out of the trees with the mule in tow. Head bowed, he veered north from the base of the ridge and headed for Red Rock.

Chapter Four

Eddie consoled her mother, or tried to. Wracked by sobs and crazed by grief, Marietta cried with a child's abandon, mouth open, her lined face shiny with tears.

"My loving husband is gone," she said through her sobs, "and now you have forsaken me."

Eddie knelt at her side, and took her hand. She thought of a runaway locomotive. Her mother's emotional state was a hurtling force on a single set of tracks, steaming at full power into a black tunnel, unable to slow or change course.

Eddie helped her to bed, hoping she would sleep. Afterward she thought more about her mother's wish to leave this place. She wondered if overwhelming grief from the unexpected death of her husband had somehow tangled with her dream of living an idealized life in the city, a dream and a nightmare in overlay.

Perhaps. Eddie did not know. She knew her mother was a prisoner of grief. And she would not be consoled.

The awful day passed with Eddie alternately weeping from her own sorrow and worrying about her mother. Late in that dark and silent night after their father's death, Eddie, Roger, and Alex spoke privately to one another in the library, door closed.

No one had bothered to light a lamp. The three of them sat in near darkness, their shadowed faces without discernible expressions, their subdued voices seemingly detached from their bodies. This, against a backdrop of long silences. Disbelief and shock still filled their minds. Each of them expected, somehow, to hear heavy footfalls from the hallway, to see the looming figure of their father open the door, to hear him demand an explanation for idly sitting in this darkened room when there was work to be done.

In this strange setting Roger began the discussion by wondering aloud if their mother's desire to leave Rainbow Ranch would diminish as she came to terms with her loss.

Alex stated the problem bluntly. "If she ever comes to her senses, you mean. She hasn't been well for years. Maybe her mind snapped."

"I don't know what's happened to her," Roger said. "All I know is . . . we can't let her go off by herself."

Eddie was aware that he spoke to her.

"Sis?"

"Mother told me that she plans to hire helpers in Denver," Eddie said. "She's determined to leave. She wants to live in the city, and that's all she'll say about it."

"But we can't let her. . . ." Roger's voice trailed off. When he spoke again, he changed the subject. He still believed their father should be buried on the home place. Just as strongly, Alex still disagreed with him.

Eddie heard a tone of determination in their voices. This was new to her ear. No longer two overgrown boys chasing one another for sport, she realized they were young men, brothers at head-butting odds with one another. To her surprise, Roger acceded after she agreed with Alex and suggested a plan to protect their mother's welfare.

"If we can locate a rental house in Red Rock," Eddie said, "I'll stay with her after the funeral. We can visit the grave. Women will come calling, and Mother will talk to them. Little by little, she'll think about the future."

"I get your drift," Roger said. "Loosen the rein, and she'll come to her senses."

"I hope so," Eddie said.

"Hope," Alex repeated doubtfully.

"Whether she does or not," Eddie went on, "she needs time. I told her again I won't leave the ranch. I don't think she believes me."

"We can't run this ranch without you, Eddie," Roger said.

"We'll tell her that . . . ," Alex began.

Eddie broke in: "Arguing won't solve anything."

"All the more reason," Roger pointed out, "for the three of us to speak as one."

Alex was quiet while he battled his own grief.

"First thing in the morning we'll talk to her," Roger said.

"First thing," Alex repeated.

Eddie's eyes were tearing again when she answered the unspoken question looming in the darkened room. "Yes," she murmured.

With sunrise filling the east-facing windowpanes, Marietta swallowed chicken broth spoon-fed by Eddie. She would take no solid food. When Eddie had dressed her, Marietta co-operated in silence, avoiding her daughter's gaze as though pouting. She seemed surprised when her sons came to her.

"I heard one of you boys crying in the night," she said from her wheelchair. "Or both of you?"

"We have all shed tears, Mother," Roger said. His voice faltered when he added: "I still can't believe Father is . . . gone. I don't think any of us do."

Marietta cast a blank look at him.

Under his mother's gaze, Roger paused for a long moment. Not quite a man yet, Eddie saw him face a man's task. Alex stood by, his hat clutched in both hands before him. He had just come in from morning chores, and now he looked at his older brother.

"Mother," Roger said, "if you still want to leave the ranch. . . ."

She broke in: "How many times do I have to tell you? Have you have forsaken me, too?"

"Mother, we will help you," Roger said. He drew a breath. "The first step is to find a rental house for you in Red Rock."

"Red Rock," she repeated.

"Eddie will stay with you there," Roger explained, "while we make arrangements for your move to Denver. We have a lot to do . . . packing, taking bids from freight outfits, finding a suitable house for you, hiring caretakers."

"And we have a ranch to run," Alex reminded her.

"With Eddie's help," Roger said pointedly.

"Edna has forsaken me," Marietta said.

"Mother . . . ," Eddie said, her voice trailing off.

Alex advanced a pace. "Mother, the burial will be in Red Rock. We'll move the coffin later to the cemetery in Denver."

"In the meantime," Roger said, "while you are living in town, you can visit the grave."

Eddie saw her mother stare into space.

Alex added: "In Red Rock you can receive visitors."

Marietta did not answer.

"Mother?" Roger said, as though awakening her.

She held her gaze away from them, lips pursed.

In a strange way, Eddie thought, during the last several hours the children had become adults, the adult a child. Eddie thought about that, trying to comprehend this new set of relationships among her loved ones. She looked at her brothers. After some hesitancy, Roger had spoken with authority reminiscent of their father's tone of voice. Alex had done his best to copy his brother. Their words had been re-hearsed, and seemed to have the desired effect when at last Marietta answered with a barely perceptible nod.

Eddie had thought her mother might break down, but she did not. On the contrary, by noon of that day she seemed content, as though simply knowing what to expect in the immediate future was a relief, one certainty amid inner turmoil.

Red Rock Signal

THOMAS PAULS, PIONEER RANCHER, DIES

Sad news from the upper reaches of Ute Creek. Funeral Service in Red Rock Burial in Local Cemetery

THOMAS PAULS, aged 64, founder of the Rainbow Ranch, passed away in his home on Ute Creek last Tuesday. Well known and widely re-spected, Pauls's death marks the passing of a generation of pioneers. Those who knew him may recall his accounts of this region in the early days of settlement, an era when men lived by their wits and survived by sheer physical strength, durability, and a full measure of good fortune. Mr. Pauls embodied the stalwart quali-ties of his generation. Strong, hard-working, loyal and God-fearing, he possessed a clear-eyed view of life in the West. He was a man of good humor according to all who knew him, your faithful editor included. Thomas Pauls leaves his wife, Marietta, and their three children, a

daughter, Edna, and sons Roger and Alexander. The family will carry on a Red Rock ranching tradition with sons and daughter, thus honoring their father's memory and stellar achievements in our great American West. A man of common sense and uncommon valor, Thomas Pauls soared close to the ground. The pioneer rancher, husband, father, friend will be missed. He shall be laid to rest in the Red Rock cemetery.

Cale was mystified by the strange sight before him. A crowd filled Broad Street. Drawing closer, he saw a black-lacquered hearse drawn by matched black geldings. Driven by Wade Powell, the hearse was drawn slowly down the middle of Red Rock's main drag. Cale turned the mare and led the pack mule into a side street. He halted, and turned. Now he saw the hearse was followed by a low-slung landau, an open vehicle carrying four passengers. The driver was Buster Baldwin.

Silent mourners walked slowly behind them, women veiled, men in black suits, most of them hatless. Among them came a minister in a long black robe tied at the waist with a tasseled gold cord. Cale spotted Sheriff Joe Gilmore, Ben Pittock, Henry Taylor, and a few townsmen he knew by sight. Others crowded the boardwalks, standing still as they watched the procession heading for the town cemetery.

Weak from his injuries and dizzy from thirst, in one delusional moment Cale thought he was a witness to his own funeral. In the next instant a wind gust sent a dust devil spiraling into the air. His eyes fell on an auburn-haired young woman. She was seated in the landau behind the hearse. An older woman sat beside her, and two young men were in the facing seat.

The wind gust lifted the young woman's mourning veil as the vehicle rolled past. When she reached up to pull it into place, Cale saw her face in profile. She cast a glance at him, her eyes widening in a shocked expression of surprise or alarm—or both.

Cale saw her turn away. A strange sensation passed through him as she covered her face with the veil. In that moment he recognized the woman of his desert fantasies. The procession passed him by, leaving him with thoughts about her as though fantasy had somehow collided with reality. He did not know her, yet she looked familiar to him. Perhaps he had passed her on a boardwalk, and had forgotten the occasion but well remembered her lovely face and the auburn sheen of her hair under the brim of her hat. The curve of her chin and the shape of her mouth struck a familiar chord in him, and the memory came to life like an image from a dream. He sensed this one would not go away.

Cale had planned to report to Sheriff Gilmore. He had not taken into account the pain in his chest or this funeral. Instead of waiting for the graveside service to end, he touched spurs to the mare and rode down the side street three blocks to Powell's livery stable. Stripping the mare and the mule in the corral, he fought pain as he performed the chores of a liveryman. He left and headed for his room, perspiring from the effort.

He staggered past Bess Loukin tending her hollyhocks and snapdragons by the gate of her picket fence. Aware that she had straightened up and was watching him, he climbed the stairs to his rented room. Inside, he pulled off his shirt and undershirt. His clothing still bore cactus spines and bloodstains. After filling the basin, he started to wash his face, but winced when his hand touched the wound slanting across his jaw.

Looking at himself in the beveled mirror, Cale shook his head. He understood why the young woman in the landau had averted her gaze and why Bess had stared. He was a sight and a fright. Dried blood was caked on his face around the raw wound gouged in his flesh. His left eye was blackened, nearly swollen shut. An abrasion on his chin was scabbed over. And now he saw dark bruises purpling one side of his chest, injuries from the pointed toe of Monroe's riding boot.

"What the hell happened to you? What happened?"

Awakened by the insistent voice of Sheriff Joe Gilmore, Cale opened his eyes. For the moment he was uncertain where he was. He had no idea of the hour. Gilmore loomed over him, scowling, enraged.

Cale raised up on an elbow. He winced as pain stabbed through his ribs. He lay on a pallet's thin padding without remembering how he got here. He gradually recognized the bare furnishings of his room. Looking past Gilmore, he saw Deputy Baldwin standing near the open doorway. Ben Pittock was there, too, with Bess outside on the landing, key ring clutched in her hand. She gazed past Pittock and Baldwin, eyeing Cale with worry in her eyes. As if she could bear no more, she turned away and descended the staircase.

"After the funeral Bess chased me down," Gilmore explained to Cale. "Said you looked half killed. Said you must have been throwed and stomped by shod hoofs. Said we'd have another funeral if something wasn't done. Now, I'm asking you. What the hell happened?"

"I got on the wrong side of Griff Monroe."

Gilmore stared at him. "He handed you a whipping?"

"A kicking," Cale said, "after he pistol-whipped me."

Cursing, Gilmore yanked off his hat and slapped it against his leg. He demanded a full accounting, and listened intently as Cale described events since leaving Red Rock.

"Monroe won't get away with this," Gilmore said. "Not if I have anything to say about it." He turned to Baldwin. "Be ready to ride at dawn, Buster, with a rifle, extra ammunition, spare canteens."

"Yes, sir."

Cale sat up, wincing again. "I'll ride with you."

"The hell you will," Gilmore said. "Stay here and heal up. That's an order."

Cale sank back into the bed, eyes closing after the door shut. He drifted in and out of sleep. Darkness came and went. Bess came into his room several times, gently washed his wounds, and tiptoed out.

How much time had passed, Cale did not know. But every time he left the bed to go to the outhouse, descending and mounting the stairs made him realize his injuries were more severe than he had guessed. His ribcage hurt with every move he made. Worse, the open wound in his jaw swelled and ran with yellowish-white pus.

Wade Powell visited. He swore after taking one look at Cale's face, and departed. In a few minutes he returned. He carried a rag soaked in kerosene.

"You aim to set me on fire?" Cale asked.

"Kid, I'm a-gonna swab that tar-bull wound on your face," he replied. "The treatment works on horses and mules. Pugs, too. Reckon it'll work on you. Lay back. Take your punishment."

Cale winced. The kerosene stung. Horses deserved better, he thought. Even mules deserved better treatment. But the remedy turned out to be as effective as it was painful. Within a day he was aware of diminished pain. The next morning, when he eyed his bruised image in the mirror, no fresh pus was visible. The abrasion on his chin was healing, too.

Cale sat outdoors on the shaded porch of the rooming house when Sheriff Joe Gilmore and Buster Baldwin returned to Red Rock without a prisoner. Gilmore sent the deputy on to the sheriff's office, and came alone to the white picket fence of the boarding house. He opened the gate and strode to the porch steps.

"How are you feeling, son?"

"Better," Cale said.

"You don't look quite as uglied-up as you did the last time I saw you," Gilmore conceded. "You're not spitting up blood, so I reckon you'll live." He paused. "Wish I could tell you we did the right thing out there on the Circle M. All I can say is, we tried our damnedest, me and Buster."

"Monroe lit out?" Cale asked.

"That's about the size of it," the sheriff said. "I talked to Rollie. You know the ranch cook out at the Circle M, don't you?"

"Yeah."

"Rollie claims he doesn't know why the foreman packed his war bag," Gilmore said. "One night he was gone, simple as that. Where, nobody knows. That's the cook's story, anyhow. Buster and me, we camped half a mile away and belly-crawled close enough to the ranch house to watch. If Monroe had come sneaking in, we'd have spotted him. Last thing I said to Rollie was to tell Monroe to turn himself in. Give up, or get the hell out of the state. That was the message I left for him."

Cale said: "I've been thinking about it."

"Thinking about what?"

"Griff could have killed me if he'd taken a notion to do it," Cale replied.

"Huh?"

"He left me with water, supplies, and a saddle horse."

"Don't give the man credit for mercy," Gilmore said. "None a-tall. If he'd killed you, a hangman's loop would be waiting for him. As it stands, he's facing charges of assaulting an officer of the law. If he lays low for a spell, it'll blow over."

"You figure he's the one stealing cattle?" Cale asked.

Gilmore nodded. "Ramrodding a big spread for an absentee owner puts temptation directly under a man's nose. Some gents can't resist the scent of easy money. Griff Monroe probably got some trusted riders to do the job, and split the take with them. Likely they'll hit again before autumn roundup, and drift down into the territory." He added: "I figure that's why he didn't want you snooping around with that spyglass."

"I'm ready to saddle up and ride."

Gilmore shook his head. "Take a look in the mirror, son. You're not ready, not even close."

Cale cast a glance toward the staircase. "Staying in that little room is giving me a dose of cabin fever."

"Nobody ever died from it," Gilmore said with a grin.

"I don't want to be the first," Cale said.

"You got used to the wide open spaces of the desert, didn't you?" Gilmore said. "Now you feel penned up."

"Yeah," Cale said.

Gilmore paused in thought. "Tell you what, son. Drift over to my office. Make rounds with me until you're healed up proper."

The only rental properties in Red Rock were abandoned

homestead shacks on the outskirts of town, most with sod roofs either caved in or awaiting a shove from the next high wind. The best of them were well suited for snakes and mice.

At home after the funeral, Eddie and her brothers were busy with ranch work, all of them uncertain about their mother's emotional state, as well as her future. She was morose, often weeping, clearly troubled.

The matter was unexpectedly resolved when two men arrived at the home ranch in a high-wheeled carriage. Eddie heard a vehicle coming, and stepped out on the porch. From a distance she recognized Ben Pittock holding the lines. The rancher, Henry Taylor, occupied the tufted leather seat beside him.

"Hello, the ranch!" Pittock called out needlessly.

"Howdy, gents!" Eddie shouted back at him. She waited until they drew closer. "Get down and come in. You're just in time for coffee and lemon-iced cookies, the specialty of the house."

Pittock laughed heartily as he halted the carriage. "I was just telling Henry here that you're a sight prettier, but you've taken up where Tom left off, a man of fine hospitality that he was."

"My brothers and I are trying to do what he'd have wanted done," she replied.

"Honoring Tom's memory," Pittock said, climbing out of the vehicle, "just as I figured." He pulled off his hat and mounted the steps with Taylor a pace behind him.

After taking them into the library, Eddie wheeled her mother in. She left to stoke the fire in the cook stove and grind beans for coffee. She overheard pleasantries, and for the first time in a long while she heard a lilt in her mother's voice. When she returned to the library with a plate of cookies, napkins, cups and saucers on a silver tray, she understood the reason for happiness.

"We have a house in Red Rock," Marietta said immediately. "We can go there without delay."

Eddie passed the plate of cookies. "House?"

Ben Pittock said: "After the service, your brothers asked me to keep an eye peeled for a house in town to rent. Well, one came up, sudden-like."

"Which one?"

"The sheriff's house," Pittock replied.

"Sheriff," Eddie repeated.

Pittock nodded. "The news hasn't hit town yet, so keep it quiet. Joe Gilmore is taking a job with the federal marshal's office in Denver. He's leaving Red Rock in a few days . . . for good, looks like."

Eddie stared at him.

"Believe me, I was shocked when he told me," Pittock said, delicately holding a cookie between an ink-stained forefinger and thumb, his inky pinkie cocked. "Henry was, too."

"It's the reason I tagged along with Ben," Taylor said. His gaze moved to Marietta. "With all due respect, ma'am, if you aim to sell the ranch and move to town, I'd be honored to place the first bid on the finest horse and cattle spread in Red Rock County."

"The ranch is not for sale," Eddie said before her mother could reply. She drew a studied look from Taylor.

"Are you certain?" he asked, smiling as though he tolerated a child's attempt at adult conversation. "Time brings changes."

Eddie met the rancher's gaze. "I am certain."

Pittock chuckled again with an I-told-you-so look in his eye.

"My children will run this ranch for as long as they wish," Marietta said. "I'm the one who's leaving."

Now Pittock registered surprise. "Ma'am?"

"I shall rent the sheriff's house in Red Rock," Marietta said, "only until further arrangements can be made."

"Further arrangements," Pittock repeated.

"Arrangements for me to take up residence in Denver," she said, "where I shall live out my days."

Now Taylor stared.

"The Rainbow Ranch was Tom's dream, not mine," she explained. "He lived his dream from the age of sixteen to the day he died."

Eddie gazed at her mother while she paused in silent reflection. The eyes of both men were on her, too.

"A long time ago I married a handsome cowboy," Marietta reflected. "I told him I'd go wherever he needed me for as long as he wanted me, and I did. Now that our children are raised and he's gone . . . well, I have no interest in living out my days on this place, stove-up like I am."

Her words were met with silence. Eddie blinked away tears. At last Taylor spoke.

"Ladies," he said with a meaningful glance at Eddie, "just between us, if you should ever change your minds about selling, send word to me . . . if I may be so bold to ask such a favor."

"We will not change our minds, Mister Taylor," Eddie said, her sorrow replaced by annoyance.

Ben Pittock's walrus mustache lifted when he grinned. "Told you," he said to Taylor, and took a bite out of a cookie.

Chapter Five

Cale walked slowly along Fifth Street from Bess Loukin's boarding house. Turning, he followed Jefferson Street for three blocks, and then made his way back with a few dogs venturing into the heat of midday to bark at him before skulking back to their patches of shade. He looked around. Modest frame residences lined the streets in this part of town. Many sported whitewashed picket fences, some with flower boxes at the base of curtained front windows. Well-kept yards had been planted in cottonwood trees. Hand-watered, the scrawny saplings had grown into scrawny trees.

Ahead, half a dozen children played in the street, some chasing barrel hoops, all of them shouting in excitement when they heard the shrill blast of a train whistle. They ran in a herd toward the depot where black coal smoke plumed into the air.

Cale had not admitted weakness to Sheriff Gilmore, but privately he had to admit the lawman was right. Hunched over as he walked, Cale knew he was in no shape to saddle up and ride into the desert for patrol duty. He could manage rounds with the sheriff. That, and walking the residential streets of Red Rock, bent over like an old man, was the best he could do for now. He was on the mend, though, and regaining strength. Cale felt encouraged by his progress, slow as it was. Every morning he awakened with slightly less pain in his chest and ribcage. The wound gouged into his jaw was closing, with no more infection. Wade Powell had seen to that. He had returned to Cale's room and pronounced him fit. Cale expressed his gratitude. He offered to pay, but Powell declined. No physician was closer than Denver or Santa Fé. Cale figured one was not needed when a single treatment from a self-trained horse doctor and ringside fight doctor had done the trick.

He extended his walking distance by day, and kept pace with Gilmore by night. His posture straightened as the pain abated. Advancing from a few residential blocks to a dozen in a widening circuit, his route included the S&RG depot and business section of town.

He was walking on Seventh Street through Red Rock's finest residential section of town on a sunny morning when he heard his name called. He drew up, turning to see Gilmore step out of a single story red brick house. Hatless, the sheriff crossed the porch and beckoned. Cale stopped, realizing for the first time that Gilmore lived here on the corner of Adams Avenue and Seventh. The lawman hailed him again. Descending the steps, he hurried down the walk.

"Word's getting around," Gilmore said, approaching Cale, "and I wanted you to hear it from me before the rumors reached you."

"Hear what?"

He halted. "I've taken another job, son."

Cale stared at his bearded face.

"Up in Denver," Gilmore went on. "Federal marshal's office. More pay, they tell me, and less work than sheriffin' this big, dusty county. Couldn't turn that down, now could I?"

Cale shook his head in silent agreement while this information sank in. It was completely unexpected and would take some getting used to.

"I would have told you sooner," Gilmore said, "but I wasn't sure about it until yesterday when the telegrapher posted a message on the board with my name on it. I know this comes outta the blue. Everybody tells me that." He chuckled. "Reckon folks figured I'd be here forever. Anyhow, I wanted you to hear it from me, son. Ever since you pinned on the badge, you've held up your end of the deal and then some. I'm grateful to you. My only regret about leaving is that I didn't pull in Griff Monroe and make him pay for what he did to you."

Still in a state of shock, Cale had the presence of mind to shake the lawman's hand and wish him well in his new job.

"An interim sheriff will take over when I leave," Gilmore said. "You've met him."

"Who is he?" Cale asked.

"Buster Baldwin," Gilmore replied. "You don't know him well, do you?"

Cale shook his head.

"Didn't think so," Gilmore said, "what with you two covering opposite ends of Red Rock County. Buster's worn the badge long enough to know the ropes. He's a little rough around the edges, but he'll do. Hell, he may land the sheriff's job by the time all's said and done." Gilmore went on: "By the way, Cale, I'm throwing a little wingding at the Pair O' Dice this evening. Stop by after nine. Drink until the barkeep throws you out. On me."

That night the Pair O' Dice was packed with townsmen and a few ranchers, all of them standing shoulder to shoulder, downing free liquor as though flood gates had opened. Cale made his way to the bar. Across the room Gilmore shouted a greeting to him. Grinning, the sheriff raised his mug of dark brew in a mock toast.

Beer in hand, Cale saw Ben Pittock in the room, along with Henry Taylor and Wade Powell. Pittock came to him and spoke over the din of drunken voices. At close range,

Cale noted even his go-to-meeting suit and white dress shirt bore ink stains.

Pittock apologized for his behavior when he had aggressively sought information from Cale that day in front of the sheriff's office. Now Pittock knew Cale had not lied to him, and the city men parked in the office were offering Gilmore a federal marshal's badge for duty in Denver. Pittock admitted missing the news story of the year because he had been steamed at Cale. Instead of asking a few well-placed questions like a journalist should, he had vented his frustration and read the Riot Act to the sheriff.

Alcohol-lubricated voices ranged from loud to louder by the time Buster Baldwin punched through the batwing doors. The man swaggered into the Pair O' Dice. He drew up and looked left and right, eyes searching the room. His gray-eyed gaze landed on Cale. Baldwin bulled his way through the crowd and practically pushed Cale against the far wall.

"Have you been told?" he shouted over the din. In answer to his own question, he went on: "You're working for me now."

Cale nodded, seeing the sheriff's badge on his vest. "I've been told."

"You took a hell of a whippin' from Griff Monroe," Baldwin said, eyeing the scabbed wound. "Next time some bastard raises his hand or weapon to you, shoot him. You're the law, Parker. Remember that."

Cale did not reply.

"If you aim to ride for me," Baldwin went on, "you'll have to toughen up. And you'd damn well better be healthy."

"I'm healing."

"When can you hit the saddle?"

"A few days."

"Make it two."

Cale met his gaze, but said nothing.

"Make it two days," Baldwin repeated, "or step aside for a deputy who can get the job done."

Cale did not ask where he aimed to find a candidate, but agreed to be ready to ride.

"All right, then," Baldwin said, as though an important matter had been settled to his satisfaction. "Pack your saddlebags. Fill your canteens. You'll patrol the north sector of the county . . . same trails I used to ride. Follow Ute Creek to Rainbow Ranch. Cut due east to Colly Collins's Circle C spread. . . ."

Across the room men laughed uproariously at a remark or a joke. One man brayed loudly. Drowned out by the raucous laughter, Baldwin cast an annoyed look over his shoulder as though seeking some law-breaker to arrest. He turned his attention back to Cale.

"Parker, come to my office in the morning. I'll tell you where you're going."

Cale nodded.

"All right, then," Baldwin said. "Be ready to ride that mare and do your duty under the law." Over another burst of laughter, he said: "You will do your duty, Parker."

It was not a question. Cale met his gaze. He disliked this man. He had not missed the proprietary tone in Buster Baldwin's voice when he had said "my office".

Red Rock Signal

Methinx every man, woman, and child in Red Rock County will sorely miss Mr. Joseph Gilmore. Mister? Dear reader, that does not

sound right, does it? For a decade this gentleman has been "sheriff" to all of us. Sheriff Joe Gilmore. That sounds right, does it not? Henceforth, he will be known as "marshal" to the good folks of Denver and environs. Denver's bad apples, methinx, will come to know him and wish he had stayed in Red Rock.

Yes, we shall miss the lawman who worked so diligently on our behalf, who daily risked his neck to keep the peace in our fair county. Denver's gain is Red Rock's loss. A moment of silence, please, one and all, in honor of a sad occasion in the history of our town.

That done, we now throw our unbridled support behind interim Sheriff Homer Baldwin. For those of you who do not already know him, set your sail and stop by the sheriff's office posthaste. A finer man you shall never meet, we are told, a gent known locally by his nickname, "Buster".

Three cheers for Sheriff Buster Baldwin! Welcome to your new job, sir, and Godspeed!

From the seat of the ranch wagon Eddie spotted a lone rider in the shimmering distance ahead. Her mother, seated beside her with a ribbon-trimmed parasol sheltering her from the hot sun, saw him, too.

"Who could that be?" Marietta asked.

Carrying nothing of great value from the home ranch, Eddie was not particularly worried about road agents. In the wagon box were household goods, bedding, clothing, and personal items, along with the cane-and-wicker wheelchair. Even so, it was wise to be prepared.

Eddie heard her mother draw a sharp breath when she pulled a revolver from a folded blanket under the seat. The weapon was small, a .32 Smith & Wesson six-shooter given to her by Roger, but it was enough gun to provide defense at close range.

"Edna. . . ."

Eddie concealed the short-barreled gun in the folds of her dress and peered ahead. "Probably just a cowhand looking for work."

"Where . . . where on earth did he go?" Marietta asked.

On the earth or in the earth, Eddie thought, feeling uneasy now, too. The rider had simply faded from view as though swallowed by barren terrain. Two hundred yards farther Eddie glimpsed movement. A saddle horse was partially concealed in a dry wash off to her right. Hauling back on the reins, she pulled out the gun and cocked the hammer. A voice came from behind her.

"If you aim to shoot me, miss, you'll need to point that popgun back this way."

Eddie heard her mother gasp in alarm. Too late, she knew the saddle mount was a decoy. The riderless horse held her attention just long enough for this man to move through the dry wash, unseen, and come up on the road behind the wagon.

Eddie eased the hammer down and lowered the gun. She turned to look back. So did her mother. They saw a young man of medium height and build, dressed in the garb of a ranch hand, his face shaded by a dusty hat brim. He was armed with a large-bore revolver holstered on his cartridge belt. Eddie was relieved to see a badge pinned to his vest.

"Name's Cale Parker," he said, and pulled off his hat, "deputy to the Red Rock County sheriff."

Eddie winced at the sight of his face. It was rugged. One

eye was horribly blackened and a deep, scabbed wound angled across his jaw. As their gazes met and held in that moment, a vague memory crept into her mind. She had seen him somewhere, probably in town at one time or another. When, she did not know. While she wondered what an officer of the law had done to earn such brutality, her mother barked reprimands at him.

"You startled us, young man!" Marietta exclaimed. "You had no call for such outrageous behavior! Where's Buster Baldwin? He would never sneak up on two innocent women to terrify them. . . ."

Eddie put her hand on her mother's arm.

"Didn't aim to spook you ladies," Cale said. "I don't know this end of the county, and from a distance I wasn't sure who was on the road ahead of me." He added: "I've learned to be careful."

"What . . . what happened to you?" Eddie asked, and saw him grimace, embarrassed.

With a hand involuntarily seeking the scabbed wound, he answered: "I ran up against a gent who doesn't take kindly to lawmen."

Eddie studied him. "Have we met?"

Cale shook his head. "No, but in town I saw you ladies in the carriage behind the funeral hearse. . . ."

Now Eddie remembered. She had seen him in the intersection of a side street off Broad that day, slumped over and bleeding while he grasped the saddle horn. At the time she had guessed he was a cowhand who had been mauled. By what or by whom, she had no idea.

"Yes . . . yes, I saw you. . . ." Her voice faltered.

Cale cast a nod to Marietta. "My condolences to both of you ladies. I never had the pleasure of meeting Mister Thomas Pauls, but I've heard the name. Most folks have, I reckon. He was a fine man by all accounts."

"Thank you . . . ," Eddie began.

Marietta nudged her daughter. "We must be on our way, Edna."

Eddie lifted the lines, paused, and turned to Cale. "What brings you out here, Deputy?"

"I'm taking over for Baldwin while he's interim sheriff," he replied. "He's looking to hire another deputy. Until he does, I'll introduce myself to ranchers in the north sector of the county. Everyone down south toward the state line knows me, more or less, and I aim to get acquainted with folks up here, too."

Marietta peered down at him from her perch on the wagon seat, a severe gaze over her aquiline nose. "You go on about your business, young man. You shall find my two sons on the home place. In their father's stead, Roger and Alex operate the Rainbow Ranch now. You may be certain they are upstanding, law-abiding citizens."

"Yes, ma'am."

Marietta turned her back on him and raised a gloved hand. "Come now, Edna. We must go."

After a parting glance at Cale, Eddie fed slack into the lines, just enough to touch the backs of the horses. When she spoke to the team, the ranch wagon pulled away.

The mare caught the scent of water and broke into a jarring trot before Cale came in sight of the earthen dam. Founded single-handedly by Thomas Pauls some forty years ago, the Rainbow Ranch with its own water supply was legendary in local lore, and Cale had looked forward to seeing the place. Now he heard water churning through the spillway as he topped a low, stone-crested ridge. He reined up, pausing to take in this sight. Tossing her head, the mare objected.

He held a tight rein. A body of water stretched out before him like an oasis in the desert. In a sense, Cale thought, this was an oasis. Instead of the storied Arabian date palms towering over oases of the Middle East, fields of wheat and oats were irrigated by a network of canals, all of the hand-dug waterways reflecting the bright sky like a web of metallic ribbons.

Cale loosened the reins. He let the mare descend the bank and walk through boot-high grass to water's edge. After she drank her fill, he rode on to the home ranch, a cluster of outbuildings well beyond the upper reaches of the man-made lake. From the saddle, Cale saw an impressive complex of barns, corrals, and sheds, all of them backing up to a bunkhouse and cook house. One hundred yards farther, on a hill above the banks of Ute Creek, stood the main house, steep-roofed and wrapped by a verandah.

Manure dust filled the air over one of the corrals. Cale rode in that direction. He saw two men leaning against the top pole of the corral. A horse was confined in there, rearing to paw the air in his private madness. Cale watched the handsome roan with a black tail and mane run in a circle almost at full gallop. Distraught, the lathered horse bucked again, hoofs flashing as though pursued by grinning devils from a glue factory.

Cale was aware of the two men taking their attention off the roan. They watched him approach them. One lifted his hand in greeting. He stepped away from the corral. He came toward Cale, followed by a young man who was slender with hawk-like features. The one in the lead was broad-shouldered, heavier, older maybe.

Cale remembered the Pauls brothers. He had seen them both in the carriage during the funeral procession. Now he took a guess as he drew rein and halted near the larger man. "You must be Roger Pauls."

"I am," he replied, eyeing the wounds to Cale's face, and then the badge on his vest. He jerked a thumb at the slender man behind him. "This is my brother, Alex."

Cale introduced himself, and offered condolences. He described meeting their mother and sister on the road to Red Rock.

When invited, Cale swung down. He shook hands with both men. Behind them, the muscular roan horse—a gelding, Cale saw now—slammed into peeled poles of the corral. The animal fell back, struggled to regain his footing, and shook himself. Bleeding from the head, he trotted anxiously across the corral, circled back, and reared again, snorting and squealing.

"That horse was a favorite of our father's," Roger explained. "Went loco on us, running himself crazy ever since the funeral."

"Trying to kill himself," Alex added, nodding slowly. "That's how I figure it."

"That's about the only thing my brother and I agree on," Roger said to Cale.

"We're having us a debate about what to do with him," Alex said.

"Debate, hell," Roger said.

"Truth is, we're fixing to fight over it," Alex said. "Winner take all."

Roger cast a tolerant smile at Cale. "Don't mind him. He won't fight me because he knows he'll get his skinny ass whipped."

"Speaking of fighting," Alex said, moving a pace closer as he eyed Cale, "what the hell happened to you?"

Cale was starting to believe his middle name had become

What-The-Hell-Happened-To-You. As far as names went, he had not meant to drop any, but when he briefly recounted the nighttime attack, the names "Circle M" and "Griff Monroe" came out of his mouth. The brothers knew of the ranch and its ramrod.

"Tough *hombre*," Roger said. "Monroe's cleaned out a few saloons in his time."

Alex added: "He respects property lines, though, and we have not had any trouble with him ourselves."

"Trouble comes with that badge," Roger observed.

Cale nodded agreement.

"Deputy, to keep me and my ugly brother from fighting to the death," Roger said, "how do you vote on the question of the day?"

"Vote?" Cale asked.

Roger jerked a thumb over his shoulder. "On what to do with that locoed horse."

"What do you have in mind?" Cale asked.

"Chain a log to his neck," Roger said, "and make him wear the damn' thing until we bust his spirit and get a good saddle horse out of him."

Alex shook his head vigorously. "Turn him loose. That's what I say. Turn him loose and let him run free, free as the wind." He added in a voice suddenly thick with emotion: "Free as the spirit of our father."

"Turn that horse out," Roger predicted in a tone of dark inevitability, "and he'll be wolf bait."

"The wolf hasn't been born to catch him," Alex countered. "Besides, horses were meant to run free. Mankind enslaved them."

Roger turned to face Cale. "See what you're up against? My common sense and his flight of fancy." He shook his head. "Well, how do you vote, Deputy?"

Cale looked past the brothers to the corral. The big gelding was still rearing and kicking, eyes rolling wildly. Blood trickled from the gash in his head, reminding Cale of his own injury.

"Turn him loose," Cale said, "before he hurts himself so bad you'll have to put him down."

"Hah!" Alex said in triumph.

Roger said grimly: "You two yokels just sentenced that big roan to a painful death. Wolves go for the soft underbelly to bring a horse down, and they gnaw on the poor beast until the squealing stops. . . ."

"Hold on, gents," Cale interrupted. "I've got no call to vote one way or the other."

Roger dismissed his objection. "We asked your opinion, Deputy. You voted. You can't un-vote. Now it's up to Alex and me."

Alex turned to Cale and asked cheerfully: "Staying overnight, aren't you, Cale?"

"Well, I. . . ."

"Might as well," Roger interrupted. "The bunkhouse is empty, and Sis left some chow for us. Pull up a chair and put your feet under our table this evening."

Cale retired to the bunkhouse after supper, blew out the lamp, and fell asleep immediately. He did not awaken until after sunrise. He shaved and washed, examining the faded bruises to his chest. Stabbing pains had lost intensity. After a late breakfast of buttered bread with fried ham and eggs scrambled by Alex, he took a porcelain mug of steaming coffee out to the verandah.

From here he saw the corral adjoining the horse barn standing empty. Cale assumed the brothers had managed to calm the roan long enough to lead him into a stall in the barn. He soon learned he was mistaken. Without fanfare or a fight, Roger and Alex had opened the corral and turned the horse loose.

"Last we saw of that big gelding," Roger said, joining Cale on the verandah, "he was grazing in tall grass over there on the bank of Ute Creek. Then he was gone. Sudden and quiet."

Behind his brother, Alex spoke from the doorway. "Just like our father."

Chapter Six

After the carpenter had installed plank ramps and hand rails, Eddie relaxed a bit. Inclined planes slanted to walkways from the front and back porches of the red brick house. Marietta was able to maneuver under her own power, no longer dependent on her daughter to assist with her every move in and out of the place.

By Eddie's reckoning, a house had to be clean from top to bottom to be livable. Whether it was Joe Gilmore who had left a trail of stove soot and boot mud, or a previous tenant, Eddie did not know. She knew she could not bear it. So she cleaned. And cleaned some more.

From scrubbing soot-darkened hand prints off doors and even the walls in some places, to mopping floors and cleaning windows with wadded back issues of the *Signal*, Eddie concluded the bachelor's standards for cleanliness were several notches below hers.

With bucket and brush, she scrubbed from the washerwoman position on her hands and knees or stood on a chair in order to reach cobwebs overhead. In every room she cleaned floor to ceiling, wall to wall, corner to corner. Some of the smudged hand prints reminded her of pictographs left by the people of an ancient civilization at Rainbow Arch. In a dirty house, though, she could not bring herself to admire them as a cultural art form.

Having lived on the ranch all of her life, Eddie was surprised to discover new and modest pleasures in town. She found a certain novelty in strolling through the neighborhoods of Red Rock, waving to neighbor ladies and chatting

with them on her way to the business section of town.
Whether she walked alone with a marketing basket in the
crook of her arm, or wheeled her mother to the boardwalks
of Broad Street, she was entertained by the sights and
sounds of town life, more than she would have guessed before coming here.

Eddie had to admit her mother was right when she had
claimed living in town would be less strenuous than the
endless cycle of chores necessary for survival on the ranch.
Here, with clean water hauled to residences in a tanker,
there was no need for treks to a well and its long-handled
pump. Coal and firewood were delivered out back, too, per
order. Even in midsummer, blocks of ice could be ordered
from the ice house near the confluence of the Río River and
Ute Creek. And with the mercantile and shops close at
hand, she needed to stock her pantry a few days in advance,
not weeks or even months as required on the ranch.

As Eddie had expected, visitors arrived. Prominent
women of the town came calling—Mrs. Rose Waldron,
Mrs. Hazel Everts, Mrs. Ruth Mansfield, Mrs. Rebeccah
Olson, among others known casually to them but not so-
cially. Now these women were eager to get to know the ma-
tron of a legendary family, and, in the courteous fashion of
the day, visitors left calling cards bearing names and ad-
dresses penned in elaborate script. Several invited Marietta
Pauls and Eddie to share a pot of tea and *petits fours* or a
plate of shortbread cookies. Mother and daughter were invited to a china painting class. They were included in club
meetings where they were greeted with polite applause.

Eddie saw Marietta beaming, rosy-cheeked for the first
time in a long while as she enjoyed the stimulation and
comfort of feminine company. For Eddie, after the initial
awkwardness and self-consciousness about her grasp of

manners and the proper do's-and-don'ts, when-and-where, she had to admit she basked in newfound pleasures, too. She discovered elements of a social life previously unknown to her. Her mother accepted every invitation, and dressing for those occasions brought new pleasures. Now the challenge they faced was to purchase fabric and cut and sew at breakneck speed in order to have new dresses ready for the next *soirée*.

The company Eddie did not seek or welcome came from Buster Baldwin. Calling himself "sheriff" now, he claimed the appointment was permanent even though no announcement had yet come from the county commissioners. His authority was the editorial in the *Signal*, a now-tattered paper he thrust into the face of anyone he could buttonhole and insist the words be read aloud.

The fact that he had known the Pauls family before Marietta moved to town somehow, in his mind, gave him *entrée* into their private lives. Such reasoning was applied to the rented house, too. Having visited Joe Gilmore over the years, Baldwin was well acquainted with the lay-out of the place. He invited himself in, moving through the "sheriff's house" with a familiarity that alarmed both Eddie and her mother.

Baldwin frequently came calling, unannounced, sometimes more than once a day. He asked after the health and well-being of Mrs. Pauls and offered to perform heavy chores "fer you ladies." Eddie understood all too well why Baldwin rapped on the door, sweat-rimmed stockman's hat in hand, reeking of cologne. Her mother knew, too, and the day came when she blocked entry with her wheelchair. Baldwin drew up, a look of surprise lining his brow.

"I'm as well as can be expected, thank you, Sheriff Baldwin," Marietta replied to his usual question. "You do not need to traipse over here every day to get the same answer."

"Oh, it's no trouble, ma'am."

Marietta said: "We know where to find you."

"But it's no trouble, ma'am, no trouble at all for me to stop by. . . ."

Marietta cast a withering look, the meaning of it lost on him.

Eddie stepped forward. "Come here only if you are summoned."

Baldwin flinched as though he had suffered a blow.

Eddie repeated—"Please."—and pulled the wheelchair back just far enough to make room to close the door.

Baldwin withdrew a pace. Head bowed, he muttered something unintelligible as Eddie shut the door. She heard his footfalls resounding on pine planks.

Late the next morning Eddie left the house to walk to Pedersen's Dry Goods & Notions on Broad. On her way she heard the scuff of a boot behind her. She looked back. Baldwin followed at a distance of half a block.

Eddie halted, suddenly hot with anger. She faced him. Baldwin drew up, then edged closer. He ventured a yellow-toothed grin.

"Deputy Baldwin. . . ."

"Sheriff," he corrected her.

She demanded: "What are you doing?"

His grin faded. "Patrolling."

"Then tell me which way you will patrol from here," Eddie said, "so that I may chose another route."

Anger flashed in his eyes. "You figure you're too good for me." He searched her face for some hint of denial of the accusation. Finding none, he went on: "That's it, ain't it, Missy Prissy? You figure you're too good for me. Huh?"

Eddie made no reply. The man had spoken in a low, menacing voice, and in that moment she felt like prey fixed in the gaze of a predator. She knew he could commit no violence against her in full daylight here in this residential section of town, yet fear surged through her. A wild thought flew into her mind—she wished she was carrying the pistol Roger had given to her.

"Don't say nothin' you'll ree-gret, Missy Prissy," Baldwin went on in that growling voice.

Eddie demanded: "What do you mean?"

His answer was a baleful stare.

Eddie's anger overcame her fear. "I said, what do you mean by that?"

Baldwin turned and strode away. In his lumbering gait, he crossed the residential street and headed for Broad.

Cale rode away from the Rainbow Ranch, waving good bye to the Pauls brothers on the verandah as the mare splashed across Ute Creek. On the other side, Cale found dim ruts of a wagon road Roger had described, and followed them. With this late start, the brothers had advised him, he could expect to reach Michael "Colly" Collins's Circle C Ranch by sundown tomorrow.

Cale had alerted Roger and Alex to the threat of cattle thieves. A band of rustlers had managed to stay out of sight while working the southern sector of Red Rock County, he had told them, and repeated Gilmore's thoughts on the subject—thieves that had driven stolen livestock across the state line to the town of Caliente might drift back this way in an attempt to repeat their success. It was the message Cale would carry to Collins and other neighboring ranchers.

With time to himself now, Cale was lulled by a familiar

clinking of bridle chains and creaking saddle leather with the steady *clip-clop* of shod hoofs. His thoughts wandered, landing on memories of Eddie. He wished she had been on the ranch where they could talk and get to know one another. Most of all, he wished he had not spooked her and her mother on their way to town. He wondered what those two women thought of him, a man alone on the wagon road like that, bloodied, bruised, ghastly. He well remembered the sharp anger in the voice of Eddie's mother—anger masking fear, he figured.

Whatever they thought of him now, it was not the impression he had wanted to leave with either of them. Somehow he had to figure out a way to speak to Eddie in more favorable circumstances. Riding across barren lands under a hot sky, he schemed and daydreamed, rehearsing imaginary conversations.

In the past, when he had entertained such longings, women were either conjured up in his imagination or they were hard-eyed saloon girls barely known to him. Now the mental images were specific. He pictured Eddie vividly—the sweep of her rich auburn hair, her quick smile, the upturn of her small nose, and fine lips not quite full but captivating in a very pretty face.

Cale's daydreams of engaging Eddie Pauls in romantic conversations ended when he approached the top of a low rise. The mare shied, and halted. Cale looked around. Seeing no sign of danger or predators, he urged her forward with one kick, and then a harder one to show her who was boss. The mare obeyed. At the crest of the rise he abruptly yanked back on the reins. The mare tossed her head in an I-told-you-so gesture, and bucked once. Cale held on and regained control. He turned in the saddle. To his amazement he looked down upon a cluster of Indians in the bottom of a dry wash.

No more amazed by this unexpected encounter were the Indians. A group of eight, they stood as still as deer. All of them looked up at him in alarm. All but one.

Cale saw a corpse down there. The Indians—a young man and a boy, three girls, and a grown man and woman— were gathered around the body. The deceased was an old man, Cale saw, naked as the day he was born. He was gaunt, cheeks sunken from high, pointed cheek bones, and iron gray hair set free from braids. This group was his family, Cale figured, and they had gathered around, grieving as the old man breathed his last. A pair of spotted ponies stood nearby. One carried packs, the other pulled a travois, empty.

Cale stared, and the Indians stared back at him. He sensed they meant him no harm, and felt certain of it when his gaze moved to the young man. Armed with a bow and beaded quiver of arrows, and a sheathed knife, he made no move toward his weapons.

Cale figured the elderly man who had died was the father and grandfather, that family members had clustered around him in his last moments. Perhaps they had been headed toward the storied Rainbow Arch, Cale thought, one last trek to sacred lands by an elder who remembered the old times when his people roamed freely.

Cale turned the mare. He descended the sloping rise and backtracked for half a mile. Leaving the road then, he circled back. He gave the Indians a wide berth, at once watchful for other clans. Picking up the wagon wheel ruts again, he rode on without cutting sign.

As the day wore on, Cale thought about what he had seen in that dry wash. Aware of Indians "trespassing" in Red Rock County, he had been advised by Joe Gilmore to steer clear of them. "Most of 'em don't want trouble," Gilmore had informed him, "and we sure as hell don't wanna start something."

Sunset of the next day brought him in sight of the Collinses' ranch. In a grassy basin, dampened soil around a muddy pit looked like a pigsty, but obviously served as a well. Unlike the Rainbow Ranch or even the Diamond Bar, this place was run-down. More than run-down, Cale thought now as he looked at gnawed bones, rusting tins, broken glass, and dog droppings littering the yard. The cabin, small barn, chicken coop, and outbuildings were made of sawmill cast-offs—warped boards and scraps of lumber cut to odd dimensions, held together with rusty nails. *A hard wind,* he thought, *could bring the whole shebang down like a house of cards.*

Greeted by three skinny dogs with their tails buried between their legs, Cale called out to the windowless dwelling. No one answered. One of the dogs circled and came in too close behind the mare, snarling. A hoof lashed out, sending the cur rolling in the dirt with a howl of pain. Whining as he scrambled to his feet, the dog skulked away, head down as though he had been whipped. The other two followed, all of them seeking shade beside the ramshackle cabin.

The corral was empty, Cale noted as he rode closer, and the door to the oversize shed that served as a barn stood open. He reined up, took off his hat, and wiped a sleeve across his brow. Clapping the hat back on his head, he shoved it up higher on his forehead. He had just about decided no one was on the place when a shrill voice from the cabin startled him. A plank door hinged on leather straps slowly opened.

"I said, what the hell happened to you?"

Cale watched a thin woman emerge from the shadows of her home. Barefooted and wearing a tattered dress with a wide collar that might once have been white, she carried a long-barreled shotgun. She paused while eyeing this stranger. Then she leaned the weapon against the doorjamb, and stepped outside.

"I was a-watching you through a knothole," she said. "Didn't know what to make of you, what with your face all chewed up. Then I done spotted your badge. What in the name of hell happened to you?"

Cale introduced himself, at once thinking this woman was as thin and fragile as everything else on the ranch. He watched as she turned her head and expertly spit a brown stream.

"Where's Buster?" she demanded as she turned to face him.

Cale brought her up to date on the careers of Sheriff Joe Gilmore and his long-time deputy, Buster Baldwin. He wanted to avoid a discussion of the injury to his face, but quickly discovered Alma Juliette Collins was not a woman to take no for answer. She did not know any man named Griff Monroe, but felt inspired to announce to the world that if he had pistol-whipped her or her husband, the no-good some-bitch would be hunted down and dispatched like a mad dog. The same fate awaited thieving bastards, she said, when Cale told her about rustlers operating in the southern end of Red Rock County.

"My Colly's out on the range somewhere," Alma replied to Cale's question. "He ain't on the home place too often."

Armed with a Civil War–era sniper's rifle with a tele-scopic sight, Collins battled calf-killing wolves and coyotes. It was an endless war out there, his wife added, what with a sole rider protecting their livestock from predators and thieves.

"Don't know when my Colly's coming in," she repeated, her gaze moving to the door. "Maybe a week, maybe longer. Lotta ground fer a man to cover on horseback. My Colly, he always says . . . 'We ain't got much, but there sure is a lot of it.' Ride this-here desert for a spell, young 'un, and you'll know what he means."

Cale nodded in a silent reply.

Alma Collins added: "Stay over the night, Deputy, if you like. Buster always did when he came this way. Did he ever tell you?"

"No," Cale replied.

She frowned. "Reckon I won't be seeing him ever again, huh?"

Unsure if she meant that as a question or a statement, Cale did not offer an opinion.

After a meager supper amid swirling flies, Alma burned a tallow candle, spoke in a flat monotone about her lonely life in this-here desert, and quickly blew out the flame. In pitch darkness Cale realized she could ill afford an oil lamp or wax candles, and even burning a smoky tallow candle for more than a few minutes was beyond her means. In the darkness he heard a rustle of fabric as she slipped out of her clothes and lay on a creaking bunk against the far wall.

Remembering all of the trash and dog droppings outside, Cale had accepted her invitation and brought his blankets indoors. Bedded on the dirt floor of the cabin, he lay awake for a time, staring into darkness as he thought again about the Indians he had come upon today. Whether a few minutes passed or half the night, he did not know, but he believed he was dreaming of mangy dogs crawling under his blankets when he awakened.

"Asleep, Scarface?"

Cale heard Alma's voice in the darkness, her lips so close

to his ear that her foul breath gusted against him. She was under his blankets, and now she pressed her thin body to him, and repeated her question. As she spoke, her hands moved across his chest and then downward, slipping under his waistband.

"Buster, he likes it rough. Is that how you like it, too? Rough and tumble?"

Cale tried to speak. She might as well have grasped his windpipe and squeezed it shut. He could neither breathe nor talk. Her questions became more insistent, her grasp even tighter.

"Uh . . . uh . . . Missus Collins. . . ."

"Come on, Deputy Scarface," she said. "I'm a-gonna miss Buster, I am, but that don't mean you and me, we cain't do it. Ain't that right? Ain't it?"

Light as a bird, Cale thought, when he half turned and pushed her away. He sat up. He heard her curse as she pulled back.

"So that's the way it is. . . ." Her voice trailed off as she left the blankets. She returned to her bunk, boards creaking again under her weight, slight as it was. Cale was left to lie on his back on a dirt floor reeking of damp, soured chaw, breathing hard, his eyes open.

Red Rock Signal

Historians inform us Dodge City, Kansas in its heyday was the wild town to beat all wild towns in the Frontier Era recently passed. So wild, in fact, was Dodge City that two cemeteries were needed, one for men who died with their boots off, another for those who crossed the divide with boots on, spurs jingling in the heavenly

spheres. Six morticians had all the grim work
they could handle just to keep up with business.

The above is factual, commonly known to
Westerners, methinx. What is not so commonly
known is revealed herein: While outlaws settled
arguments by shooting and stabbing each other
and keeping the gravediggers busy, even more
men succumbed to skunks. Yes, dear readers,
skunks.

In those days Dodge City was a series of tent
camps beyond the outskirts of the business section, and honest, hard-working men slept in the
great outdoors under blankets thrown upon the
ground. Polecats were drawn to the warmth of
these temporary beds, and, when a sleeping gent
stirred, the skunks felt attacked and heartily bit
into bare flesh. Far and wide throughout the tent
camps, men awoke howling. And that was not
the worst of it, dear reader, for those poor souls
were condemned to an agony of long and painful
deaths.

At one time scientists believed a particular
variety of skunk attacked the bare lower extrem-
ities of sleeping men, Skunkus Hydrophobia
being the proper Latin name for the creature.
However, after a scientific investigation, it was
determined that no such animal existed, that the
underlying cause of so many painfully pro-
tracted deaths was the result of simple blood
poisoning from the fouled teeth of foul creatures.

One must ask, methinx, what possible posi-
tive purpose is served on this old Earth by mean,

disease-riddled, high-smelling skunks? Alas, the answer is well beyond the ken of mortal man. However, we can conclude after all evidence has been congregated, tabulated, and evaluated, that many more men died from skunk bites than saloon fights, and therefore Dodge City, Kansas was perhaps not so wild after all.

Ben Pittock heard the street-side door to his print shop open and close while he proofread his latest "Methinx" column. Reading the type upside down and backwards before tightening the page on the form, he nodded and muttered as though completing a conversation with himself. With minor editing, the skunk episode was lifted word-for-word from a back issue of the Kansas City *Star*. He figured *Signal* readers had not seen it, and would find the piece instructive and entertaining.

Finished, he wiped his hands on his apron, turned, and entered the front office. He shoved his wheeled swivel chair out of the way, and passed his cluttered roll-top desk. He was surprised to find his visitor to be Edna Pauls. He had not seen her since the day he had traveled to the Rainbow Ranch with Henry Taylor. Now he welcomed her.

She smiled and greeted him. "Mister Pittock, I have been remiss."

"In what way?"

"By failing to thank you properly," she said, "for the lovely passage about my father published in the newspaper. The obituary was a great comfort to us. On behalf of the Pauls family, I wish to offer my sincere gratitude."

"And I thank you, Miss Pauls," Pittock said, clearly pleased. He reflected for a moment. "Every obituary is well-intended, but not all are true. That one was. Every word. I knew your father, and I knew him to be a fine man. More than a pioneer, he was a gentleman in the truest sense of the word."

Eddie thanked him again, her eyes tearing as she reached into her handbag for a handkerchief.

Pittock averted his gaze while she regained her composure. When she cleared her throat and coughed softly into a white-gloved hand, he looked at her. She seemed to be searching for words.

"Mister Pittock," Eddie said at last, "I have been wondering. . . ."

"Wondering what?"

"If you know for a fact," she replied, "that Mister Homer Baldwin will be our next sheriff."

"Not for a fact," Pittock replied, choosing his words, "but a foregone conclusion, I'd say. Why?"

Instead of answering, Eddie asked: "No other candidates have applied for the job?"

"Not that I know of," he replied. "Do you have someone in mind?"

"No," she said. She added: "Well, I have wondered if that deputy, Mister Parker, will apply for the position."

Pittock shook his head. "Aside from being a newcomer, Miss Pauls, he's too young. We need a seasoned hand on the tiller of this ship, a man who knows folks. It would seem Buster Baldwin is the man for the job."

"Yes," she murmured, "it would seem so. But do you know anything about Deputy Parker? Where he hails from, that sort of thing."

"Well, let me think," Pittock said. "Joe told me the youngster was orphaned when cholera hit North Platte, Nebraska. He worked in livery stables until the Union Pacific hired him. He came here in response to a notice in the *Signal*."

The newspaperman paused in thought. "Joe liked him right off. I know that much. I've never seen him so riled as he was after the kid took a beating from Griff Monroe." Pittock ran out of steam, and posed a question of his own. "Miss Pauls, is there something I should know about Baldwin? Or Parker?"

Eddie shook her head. Lowering her gaze, she thanked him again, and cast a brief smile in his direction before turning away.

Benjamin Pittock reached out and opened the door. He bid her good day as she stepped onto the boardwalk. Closing the door, he moved to the plate-glass window. He observed Edna Pauls as she waited for the town's water tanker and then a mule-drawn freight outfit to pass by. After the dust settled, she stepped off the boardwalk and started across Broad.

Pittock looked past the backwards, frontier-style letters of **THE RED ROCK SIGNAL** sign painted on the inside of his window. Few people were out in the heat of day. He watched Edna head for Seventh, the street leading to the red brick residence that had been known locally for over a decade as "the sheriff's house".

Across Broad Street and down three doors, Pittock glimpsed movement in the narrow passage between two store buildings, Red Rock Mercantile & Supplies and Mrs. Catherine Reynolds Millinery. Buster Baldwin eased out of the shadows down there.

Chapter Seven

Cale completed his sweep through the northern sector of Red Rock County without mishap or more awkward surprises. After first happening upon Indians in a dry wash and then confronted by Mrs. Alma Juliette Collins on the dirt floor of her cabin, the rest of his patrol was uneventful. For once he welcomed dull routine.

Cale introduced himself to far-flung ranchers and cowhands by following wheel ruts and livestock tracks—dim signatures in desert terrain. To one and all, he delivered his message about an organized band of cattle rustlers.

"Hang the thieving bastards."

That sentiment toward rustlers was uniform, Cale discovered, after a rancher named John O'Reilly offered his terse view in a voice thick with brogue. Cale figured this unity of opinion was buttressed by the fact that no town was close at hand. Until now, this part of Colorado lay beyond the reach of the law. It was every man for himself until Gilmore sent deputies to patrol the region. Even so, one deputy could hardly cover it.

In this remote sector daily life was tenuous, mirroring the lawless frontier of a time gone by. Whether a lack of services offered by a town within wagon-team distance was the reason or not, O'Reilly echoed the outlook of Mrs. Collins: No mercy for thieves. No mercy in a land where folks barely scratched out a living by running a few head of livestock and hand-watering fenced vegetable gardens. The niceties of sworn testimony in a jury trial were too good for bandits, whether the thievery was cattle, horses, goats, chickens, or a slab of last year's beef jerky nailed to the wall of a shed out of coyote reach.

"Maybe we oughter put up a few signs in this here end of the county," a rancher named Ely Willis suggested to Cale. Squinting, Willis framed his idea in weathered hands, and pretended to read aloud: "Found guilty by honest men, lynched by the same danged gents."

The next day Cale heard another rancher vigorously agree: "A bandit dancing at the end of a noose will make others turn tail."

Cale finished scouting the barren terrain without learning of any sightings or discovering signs of rustlers. He turned the mare and backtracked. With frequent rest stops, plenty of grain, and ample water from a canteen or a seep in the earth, he knew this horse was good for twelve-hour days.

Counting the hours between here and Red Rock, Cale made a hard ride, camping under the stars. He gave the Collinses' place plenty of room, and headed for the Rainbow Ranch on the wagon road to Ute Creek. There was no sign of Indians, but hoof beats suddenly told him that he was not alone.

Off to his right, some seventy-five yards away, he spotted a horse. It was the roan from the Rainbow Ranch charging now at full gallop, black mane and tail flying. The horse that had been Thomas Pauls's favorite slowed to a trot on a parallel route. Cale's mare pranced. She tossed her head, eager to join a compatriot set free.

Cale yanked on the reins as a reminder of her servitude. Presently the roan veered away, galloping out of sight over a bare, rocky ridge. The mare watched that big, running horse—wistfully, Cale thought. After all, the stallion was gelded and the mare enslaved.

To the tune of creaking saddle leather and clinking bridle chains, Cale had dreams of his own. He nurtured an idle hope that he might bump into Eddie during a visit to the home ranch. The Pauls brothers had informed him of their collective decision to rent the sheriff's house, and outlined Eddie's plan to stay with their mother in town for a spell. Cale remembered that conversation. In all likelihood Eddie was in town, not on the ranch. She could not leave her mother alone in the house for long. Even so, Cale thought, a man can hope. . . .

When he arrived at the Rainbow Ranch, he learned Eddie was not on the place. Just as well, he figured now. Gamey and weary from the ride, he was so weak that he staggered as he tended his horse. Even though he could sit a saddle for hours, he still was not at full strength when it came to wrestling tack.

Cale readily accepted the hospitality offered by Roger and Alex, and lingered on the ranch. Inserting a well-placed hint in a conversation, he agreed to stop by the sheriff's house in town to relay messages to their mother and to their sister.

Roger: "Tell Mother all is well on the home place except for Alex's cooking."

Alex: "Tell Eddie about that saddle mount, Charley, going loco on us."

Cale rested all of one evening and into the morning of the next day. With the mare saddled and bridled, he led her out of the corral, swung up, and bid the brothers good bye. He made the ride to Red Rock in six hours. Stabling the mare in Wade Powell's livery, Cale went to his room. Then, with clean clothes under his arm, he hiked to Dave's Tonsorial Parlor on Broad.

Cale took a long look at himself in the barber's oval

mirror. The abrasion on his chin was nearly healed. While the cut on his jaw was plain to see, it was scabbed over and closing now, no longer oozing blood. Dave's hand was steady as he wielded a straight-edge sharp enough to split a hair, and shaved around the wound.

Cale came out of the place looking presentable. He was again reminded he was still as weak as a cat. The exertion of merely walking several blocks in boots meant for stirrups had fatigued him.

In daydreams he came upon Eddie on a street in Red Rock. Reining the mare to a halt, he greeted her with a gentlemanly tip of his hat. She smiled up at him, clearly admiring a man on horseback. Cale dismounted, hat in hand, and so began their conversation.

Life is cruel, and he did not happen upon the woman of his dreams. In Red Rock, he walked to the sheriff's house, paused at the gate to let butterflies settle in his stomach, and ascended a plank walkway slanting to the porch. At the door he reached out and turned a brass handle. The bell ringing on the other side of the door sent butterflies fluttering in his stomach again. One long moment stretched into two before the door opened. Eddie Pauls appeared there. At first surprised to see him, she greeted him with a cheery smile.

"Why, hello," she said. "Cale. Cale Parker . . . isn't that your name?"

"Yes, miss," he said, yanking off his hat as an afterthought.

"My friends call me Eddie," she said.

"I know."

"You do? How?"

"From your brothers," he replied.

"Oh, yes, of course," she said, cocking her head as she smiled again.

"I'm here to tell you," Cale began, "uh, well, I stayed over at your ranch last night."

"Did you?" Eddie asked.

"Yes, miss," he replied, stuck for the moment as he was mesmerized by her gaze.

"And?"

"Well, uh, Roger and Alex, uh, they asked me to tell you and your mother, uh, they're doing fine."

"I am glad for that."

"Except for Alex's cooking. Roger says it's killing him."

"Poor child."

Cale grinned, or tried to. He knew he sounded like some saddlebum talking around a mouthful of cold molasses. He swallowed, and cleared his throat. None of his rehearsed conversations had gone like this. At the moment he could not recall any of the silken phrases he had rehearsed, alone, in the saddle far from here.

"Uh," Cale went on, "Alex wanted you to know about that big roan gelding your father rode."

Her smile faded. "Charley? Did something happen to him?"

"He was banged up considerable," Cale said, "from trying to bust open a corral. Your brothers turned him out and set him free."

"Set him free," Eddie repeated in surprise.

Another voice came from inside the house. "Who is there, Edna?"

Eddie backed up two paces. She invited Cale in. He entered the house, and she closed the door behind him. Mrs. Marietta Pauls called out again as she wheeled herself down a narrow hallway toward them.

"Oh, it's you."

Cale looked past Eddie. No welcoming smile from her mother, he noticed as he greeted her.

"It's the deputy we met on the ranch road," Eddie answered. "Mister Cale Parker."

"I remember." Marietta halted the wheelchair, and looked up at Cale. "You sneaked up on us from behind like some road agent. Involved in a common brawl, weren't you?"

"Mother . . . ," Eddie said as though speaking to a rude child.

"Well, now that you're here," Marietta asked, "what do you want?"

"Mother."

"He must want something, Edna," Marietta insisted, "or he wouldn't be standing here, hat in hand."

Eddie cast an apologetic glance at Cale for the remark implying he was no more than a saddle tramp. She turned to her mother. "Deputy Parker spent last night on the ranch," she said. "He was kind enough to bring messages from Roger and Alex."

"Messages? What messages?"

"Roger despises Alex's cooking," Eddie said, "but he won't cook for himself."

"I am not surprised to hear that," Marietta said. "You've done everything for those two boys ever since my accident. . . ." Her voice trailed off. "Just because I wasn't able to wash and cook and clean did not mean you had to go and spoil them like you did."

Clearly a well-worn dispute between mother and daughter, Cale looked on in silence as Eddie changed the subject. "And something about Daddy's horse."

"Charley?" Marietta said, stiffening. "What about that outlaw?"

Eddie turned to Cale. "You said it was the roan, didn't you?"

"Yes, miss."

"Well, what happened?" Marietta demanded, earning another pained glance from Eddie.

Mother and daughter listened intently while Cale recounted events he had witnessed at the corral, and went on to describe the impromptu vote that had resulted in freedom for the horse. He concluded by telling them about his later sighting of the gelding galloping across the desert.

"Big and wild, strong as a stallion," Marietta said. "I was always afraid of what the beast might do to Tom. Let him run. Let him run until wolves bring him down. Good riddance, that's what I say."

Cale smiled. The words were different, but he heard the same tone in Marietta's voice that he had heard in Alex's when they had first met at the horse corral.

Bidding Eddie and Marietta good day, Cale went to the door. Eddie unexpectedly moved ahead of him. He pulled back as she opened the door. They stepped outside. On the porch, she quickly reached back and closed the door.

"You'll have to forgive my mother," Eddie said in a low voice. "At least, I hope you will."

"Looks like she has a notion of running me off," Cale said.

Eddie ducked her head, embarrassed.

"Reckon she has your interests at heart," Cale went on. "She's got me pegged for a hardcase. She wants to protect you."

Eddie lifted her gaze.

In that moment Cale feared he had said too much, that his words were interpreted to mean Marietta was right about one Cale Parker, and Eddie should stay away from him. He was surprised by her next comment.

"My father would have liked you."

"Why do you say that?"

"Because you are blunt," Eddie said. "Blunt and to the point. He was, too."

They gazed at one another until Marietta's plaintive voice reached them. Eddie backed to the door and turned, her hand coming to rest on the handle.

Cale's mind raced, leaving fear behind. Somehow he knew if she opened that door and went into the house without a word from him, he would lose her. "I want to see you again, Eddie."

She smiled over her shoulder.

"Maybe, uh, maybe we can take a buggy ride to the creek," he said. "And a picnic basket."

"Maybe," she said, and opened the door. She stepped inside without looking back at him, and closed the door.

Cale's stride was feather-light and swift when he headed for Broad Street. Eddie had not said yes to his invitation, but neither had she used the word men fear most from a woman—no. Was he dizzied by her attention and dazzled by her smile, or had her expression and tone of voice offered encouragement?

Maybe.

Cale thought about that, recalling her every word in the last few minutes. He even tried to calculate the meaning of that feminine gesture of tilting of her head when she smiled. The more he thought about it, he figured she was testing him. If so, there could be only one reason. Eddie wanted to find out if this suitor had the fortitude to stand up to her mother.

"Parker!"

Startled out of his reveries, Cale looked back. He halted and turned. Buster Baldwin came striding up the street behind him, scowling.

"What the hell are you doing, Parker?" Baldwin demanded when he drew closer.

"I'm on my way to the sheriff's office," Cale replied, "to report to you."

"The hell," Baldwin countered, halting.

Cale stared at him, his anger rising.

"I saw you," Baldwin said. "Don't think I didn't."

"Saw me," Cale repeated.

"Saw you waltz out of that house the Pauls women are renting," Baldwin said. He gave him a once-over. "Looks like you paid a visit to the barbershop and got yourself fancied-up before you went calling on the ladies."

"I brought messages to them from Roger and Alex . . . ," Cale began.

Baldwin interrupted: "Your job is to follow orders, Parker. Follow my orders. Nothing more."

Cale eyed him in silence.

"You ride where I tell you," Baldwin said, "when I tell you. Report to me ever' time you come back to town. There won't be no fancy flirting with the ladies. Understand?"

Cale continued gazing at him, a fist clenched. He understood all too well. If he had ever met a man he disliked more, he could not remember the gent.

Red Rock Signal

ATTACKS BY WAMPUS CATS
Livestock, Pets, Small Children
Endangered By Ferocious Predators

Sightings are rare, but few among us doubt the existence of this ferocious predator of our Western deserts and plains, the Wampus Cat. Small and quick, the breed is thought to be a

wolf-badger-wildcat cross, a vicious beast capable of taking down a calf one day while outsmarting gate latches to the chicken coop the next. The Wampus Cat is said to be short-haired with gray-brown coloration, almost invisible, fast as a bullet. With razor-like front claws and long, pointed teeth, the beast is unquestionably nature's most perfectly designed predator.

A word to the wise, dear readers. Keep your wits about you, and a sharp eye.

"This is what I warned you about, Edna. This is exactly what I warned you about."

"What is?"

"You don't know?"

"No, Mother, I don't."

"First," Marietta replied, drawing a deep breath before delivering the litany, "it was that disgusting deputy who's taken to calling himself sheriff. Now, it's that other deputy sniffing around here . . . both of them grinning like overheated dogs. Edna, listen to me. The sooner we move to Denver, the better."

Eddie started to protest, but her mother waved her quiet.

"If you stay long enough in Red Rock County," she said, "you'll end up marrying a filthy braggart or a beat-up deputy or some local bumpkin. Mark my words."

Eddie silently marked them, but not in a way her mother would have approved.

"You're a beautiful girl, Edna, beautiful and intelligent, and you deserve better. You truly do." With those parting words Marietta turned and wheeled herself down the hallway to her room.

Eddie leaned back against the wall, eyes slowly closing. Her mind filled with thoughts of Cale Parker. Love at third sight, she supposed, a smile crossing her lips. Perhaps one day she would tell him. . . .

Tell him what? That something strange and powerful had happened to her on this day? That some force, invisible and beyond words, had overtaken her?

When Cale had spoken to her minutes ago, that mysterious force sent her emotions surging. She knew that much. And from countless frigid winter days spent curled up with a leather-bound book on the settee in her father's library, she knew something about the mythology of ancient Rome. Cupid was the son of Venus, the goddess of love, so the ancient Romans believed. Perhaps one of the infant archer's arrows had found its mark—her heart. It was, she thought now, an explanation as good as any.

In those moments Eddie searched her mind. She had not felt this way after her encounter with Cale on the ranch road. And she'd certainly had no feelings of love toward him when their eyes had met during the funeral procession on Broad Street. That day, his face horribly bloodied, she had seen a tramp barely able to sit his saddle. But now it was different. Everything was different. For one thing, Cale's insight toward her mother had surprised her. His remark revealed a level of perception that she had never seen in a man before. For another, his plain-spoken manner did, indeed, remind her of her father. And there was something endearing about the way Cale had blurted out his invitation to a picnic. His manner had been shy, yet strong.

Cale. Cale Parker. Eddie yearned to say his name, even to shout it, and at once worried she would blurt out—"Cale Parker!"—where her mother would hear. Eyes still closed, she visualized him. Wound and all, he was handsome.

While not tall, he was muscular, broad-shouldered, narrow at the waist. She yearned to stand at his side, to be with him, to touch him.

As much as Eddie desired to see him again, soon, instinct told her to hold back, to be restrained. The same man who is fascinated by a woman's lowered gaze, she had often heard, is frightened by her stare. She must fascinate Cale without losing his respect. And to allow him to prove himself a worthy suitor, she would have to mask her feelings. She would wait for him to summon his courage and declare his love for her. For that was what a man must do to earn a woman's hand.

Eddie had glimpsed a certain, lingering look in his eye, and had no doubt Cale would act . . . but when? A pleasant sensation washed through her. The prospect of their courtship thrilled her.

"Parker! Parker!"

Cale was awakened in the night by shouts. Then a fist pounded on the door to his room. He sat up in darkness, feeling a familiar stab of pain in his ribs. Leaving his bed, he staggered across the room, and opened the door. Framed in starlight outside, Buster Baldwin stood on the landing, grasping a repeating rifle in both hands. He ordered Cale to get dressed and saddle up.

"Taylor sent a rider," Baldwin said.

Still foggy with sleep, Cale asked: "Taylor? Rider?"

"Rustlers!" Baldwin exclaimed. "Rustlers are moving a hunnert head due south along the Río River." He thrust the Winchester at him. "Griff Monroe's riding with 'em."

In the corral adjoining Powell's livery barn, Cale shook hands with Luke Scanlon, the T-Bar-H rider who had brought the message. Like most cowhands, Luke was lean, soft spoken, bowlegged. He and his saddle partner had seen five riders herding steers off T-Bar-H range. Too far away for brands to be identified, the drovers were southbound, moving fast.

"You sure one was Monroe?" Cale asked.

Scanlon nodded. "Nobody sits a big white horse like Griff does."

Even though weary from a long night ride, Scanlon was determined to join the posse. After Baldwin made a mark on a voucher authorizing expenses, Powell brought out a fresh horse with a ration of oats. The three of them took to their saddles. Riding through darkness to a brilliant dawn and the rising heat of morning, they reached the T-Bar-H before noon.

Henry Taylor furnished a hot meal and supplied rested saddle mounts. Buster Baldwin adopted a booming voice of authority when he suggested recruiting riders from the neighboring Circle M. Taylor opposed it. Identities of the rustlers were unknown, he pointed out, except for Monroe. They might be Circle M hands. Whether they were or not, Taylor added, time was wasting and the thieves already had a jump on them. Jaw clenched, a silenced Buster Baldwin turned away. Taylor joined the posse himself, along with three more T-Bar-H riders, all of them armed with rifles and side arms.

In silent determination under a hot sun, the seven-man posse made a hard ride through barren terrain. Cutting west, they rested on the bank of the Río River. Then they followed the course of the river as it wound southward toward New Mexico Territory. Tracks were clear. Five horsebackers trailed and flanked a large herd of cattle, well over a hundred head by Cale's estimate.

Long after sunset, the posse made camp at water's edge.

Building no fires, they opened tins—"saddlebag fare" cow-hands called the grub—and ate quietly. Cale had started thinking about what would happen when they caught up with the thieves, and he figured the other riders had, too. Lost in their own thoughts, they slept on the ground, and pushed on the next day at first light.

Herding steers was slow work, Taylor pointed out, and expressed his hope of overtaking the rustlers on the Colo-rado side of the line. His hope was renewed later in the day when they came upon a lame steer. The critter was branded T-Bar-H. Rather than being slowed by a crippled cow, the rustlers had left this one behind.

Dung was fresher as they neared the state line, but still they had failed to close the distance. At the boundary Taylor halted and dismounted. Along with the others, Cale swung down and led his horse to water. He arched his back and stretched his legs. The posse was soon joined by an-other T-Bar-H rider, Bill Dixon, who came splashing across the Río River from his hiding place among the thick wil-lows.

Cale learned Dixon was the cowhand paired with Scanlon when the two of them had spotted Monroe and the other rustlers. Dixon had followed their dust cloud from a safe distance while his partner galloped back to the home ranch for help. Now Dixon reported the thieves had passed this way, experienced drovers making good time as they crossed the border into New Mexico Territory.

Buster Baldwin took a long drink from his canteen. His initial disagreement with Taylor had silenced him until now. Corking his canteen, he gazed at the horizon ahead. "This is where my jurisdiction ends, Mister Taylor."

Baldwin seemed oblivious to the long silence that fol-lowed his statement. The nearest hand was Luke Scanlon, and he stepped back as though expecting an explosion.

Cale was reminded of an old saying: Beware the patient man who has lost patience. He had never seen a flash of anger in the gentlemanly demeanor of Henry Taylor, but he saw it now. The rancher turned to Baldwin, his long, angular face flushed.

"Playing it safe?" Taylor asked quietly.

Caught off guard, Baldwin did not have a ready answer.

"Is that what you're paid to do . . . play it safe?" Taylor asked. He added pointedly: "Sheriff."

After studying the ground, Baldwin slowly lifted his gaze. "Sheriff Gilmore, he always told me . . . 'Buster, don't you cross that line.' So I'm just telling you, Mister Taylor, what Joe always told me."

If he was invoking Gilmore's name to deflect Taylor's rage, Cale thought, the tactic was not working.

"You're aiming to be sheriff of Red Rock County, aren't you?" Taylor asked.

"Reckon so," Baldwin answered.

"Reckon so?" Taylor mocked him. "Is that all you can say for yourself?"

Other than a scowl, Baldwin had no answer for the challenge.

"You call yourself sheriff," Taylor said. "So I hear. That's true, isn't it?"

Baldwin nodded once.

"Now you're telling me, you'll be first to turn tail when the going gets tough."

"No sir," Baldwin said, "I'm not telling you that." He cast a troubled glance at Cale.

Cale answered the silent plea for help. "Sheriff Gilmore told us federal marshals cover New Mexico Territory. State authority ends at the line."

"Yeah, that's what Joe always said," Baldwin echoed. "Federal marshals enforce laws down in the territory."

"What the hell do you mean?" Taylor demanded. "Stealing is stealing, here or in the territory. No line changes that, does it?" The rancher drew a breath. "We all know U.S. marshals are sitting in the shade down in Santa Fé, *señoritas* waiting on them hand and foot. If we want anything done in Caliente, we'll have to do it ourselves." He faced Baldwin. "You riding with us?"

Buster Baldwin studied the ground at his feet while the other riders stared at him.

"Let me ask you this," Taylor went on. "If you aim to be sheriff of this county, will you need the support of Red Rock ranchers like me?"

Baldwin uttered a subdued reply. "Yes, sir."

"Then I'll make this simple for you," Taylor said. "Real simple."

Baldwin cast an uneasy look at the rancher. Taylor reached out and unpinned the sheriff's star from his lapel. He held it up for all to see.

"Without this little piece of pressed tin, you're a citizen like the rest of us. Citizens form posses and administer justice as they see fit."

Baldwin eyed him.

"Like I said, mister. Simple."

"What is?" Baldwin asked, eyes narrowing.

Taylor thrust out the badge as though proving an obvious point to a child. "You are Buster Baldwin, the citizen. Are you riding with us, or are you turning tail?"

The men of the posse watched in silence as Baldwin slowly reached out. He took the five-pointed star from Taylor's hand. Eyes downcast, he slid it into his pocket.

"Good man," Taylor said in a tone of voice that could

have been reserved for petting a dog. He turned to Cale. "From what I hear, Parker, you've got reason to go after Monroe. What's your deal?"

Cale took off his badge. "Let's ride."

"Gentleman," Taylor said, striding to his horse, "hit the saddles."

Cale was aware of Taylor's gaze as he moved to his mount. He thrust a boot into the stirrup and swung up. Taylor waited until everyone was mounted, and signaled Cale to take point.

Cale led the way at a walk. Spurring his horse to a canter, he turned in the saddle and looked back. Taylor had mounted now. Bringing up the rear, the rancher followed Buster Baldwin as they crossed into New Mexico Territory.

Chapter Eight

Eddie learned of the midnight posse from Ben Pittock, who in turn had heard about the pursuit of cattle rustlers from Wade Powell. Once determined never to be the dedicated worrier her mother was, now Eddie found herself conjuring up all manner of calamities that could possibly befall a group of men pursuing thieves, Cale Parker in particular. She did her best to push these thoughts away, knowing worry had never solved anything. Worry only brought misery to the bearer.

"How long will it take them to ride to Caliente and back?" she asked.

The newspaperman first eyed her, and then rubbed ink-stained hands on his apron. "Depends on whether they recover stolen cattle or not." He paused in thought. "Well mounted and on the prod, I suppose they could cover that ground in two days, maybe three. On the return trip with cattle? A week, maybe longer. Why?"

"I was just wondering when they might be back in town," Eddie said as though her inquiry was an idle question.

To Ben Pittock, no question was idle. "And why is that?"

Flustered, Eddie felt her face grow hot even in the stale air of this print shop. She looked at Pittock. The drooping mustache covered his mouth like the lower half of a mask, but she caught a twinkle in his eye.

"My profession," he explained, "requires me to ask questions . . . rude questions, polite questions . . . many,

many questions. But don't worry, Miss Edna Pauls, I'm not the village snoop. I won't ask you to name which man in the posse you are sweet on." The mustache lifted slightly when he grinned, clearly enjoying her discomfort. "I won't print any unfounded rumors. Only founded ones."

Rumors. Gossip flying through this town like mad hornets was chief among the reasons Eddie felt homesick for the ranch. She and her mother had discovered Red Rock teemed with rumors—some harmless, others vicious.

Mrs. Rose Waldron and half a dozen other upper crust ladies had seemed gracious at first. Only later did Eddie see through the transparency of their high-toned manners. From such a lofty position in the highest social strata in all of Red Rock, these ladies looked down their collective noses and spun tales about the behavior of selected victims.

"Didjahear?"

"No! What?"

"Do tell!"

"No!"

"Yes, it's true!"

"Good gracious!"

The stories ranged from amusing to cruel, from innocent to risqué. Ruth Anne, the fifteen-year-old daughter of Robert and Sarah Haynes, had left town for three months. Didjahear? She gave birth out of wedlock. No! Yes, it's true.

Why else would the girl depart abruptly? According to whispers, the infant had been adopted out of state. At various times the father was said to be Jonathan, Oscar, Daniel, Tomás, Jorge, and numerous other men of Red Rock, married and unmarried, a priest among them. The fact that no one had actually seen a baby, or even Ruth Anne showing, did nothing to dampen rumors. The family's tale of caring for an ailing relative in Illinois was dismissed by the town's whisperers, the all-knowing women concealed behind good graces.

According to whispers within the clique, Mrs. Hazel Everts's husband, Joshua, vice president of the Red Rock Bank & Trust, stole from the vault. It was a crime he had been committing for years. A respected member of the community and a Red Rock County commissioner—clever accounting covered embezzlement. Everyone knew. How else could plain Mrs. Everts afford silk dresses from a New York shop, a dozen wildly plumed hats, double-strand pearl necklaces, a fire opal ring, two diamond brooches from Tiffany & Company, and all the other finery exhibited so shamelessly from her carriage on the way to church or a social obligation?

Then there was squirrel-toothed Sharon Mae Yount across the tracks from the water tower. She entertained male callers, wandering husbands named in whispers, long after midnight, while trusting wives and children slept the sound sleep of innocence.

Eddie found herself yearning for the familiar cycle of chores on the ranch. Up to her elbows in soap suds to scrub laundry on a ribbed washboard was straightforward, honest work. So were the timeless and humble tasks of cutting firewood and tending animals. Town life allowed for more leisure than ranch life, but with idle time came malicious rumors.

Leaving the print shop, Eddie walked along the boardwalk past the mercantile. She paused at the plate-glass window. Inside, displayed among bolts of cloth and sample dry goods stocked in the store, was a Sears & Roebuck catalogue. The volume lay open to a page picturing a flowing wedding gown, floor-length, with a snug bodice and lace trim across the bosom. Eddie halted. She stared, as though heeding a sign from above. In truth she had never given a thought to the details of the gown she would wear on her wedding day.

Wedding!

In her mind, marriage was a vague event cast far into the future, vaporous as a dream. The unexpected appearance of this illustration of a white dress with a train brought the prospect of marriage to her mind as never before. While she stared, a realization came to her. On her wedding day, her father would not be there. Eddie had not thought of it until this moment. She would not take his arm to be walked down the aisle of the chapel with family and friends looking on. . . .

Tears came suddenly. Eddie turned away, hand to her mouth. Lunging headlong across Broad, head down, she rushed to Seventh Street with the fervent hope that no one had seen her crying.

From the crest of a cactus-studded rise, Cale noted all roads, cart tracks, goat and burro trails, cow paths, and footpaths led to Caliente. Railroad tracks swept past the village in a straight line. At the S&RG station, Cale saw the twin rails of steel shining under the setting sun in their seemingly endless course from horizon to horizon.

Taylor lifted a hand. The men of the posse halted, squinting against the last rays of daylight. Seven had grown to eight after Bill Dixon had joined them at the Colorado line. Now they peered down at the village.

Caliente stretched out from clustered dwellings to outlying farms. Platted in a tradition from Mediterranean Europe, the center of the village was marked by an open square. Long ago Spaniards had used it for more than parades and a gathering place for holiday celebrations. Disobedient slaves came under the lash here, and Indians who had dared defy government or church authorities were publicly hanged.

The whipping posts and gallows were long gone, the cries of agony long silenced by the winds of time. Now the community well and numerous benches shaded by cottonwood trees were surrounded by businesses. Modest residences stretched out from the center of town. These simple structures were squat, built of adobe blocks stacked and covered with stucco, topped by flat sod roofs. Cool in summer and warm in winter, the building material of sunbaked mud mixed with straw or wool was well suited to this climate of seasonal weather extremes.

Chimneys trailed wood smoke, Cale noted, and a scent of burning sage filled the air. At suppertime few people moved about. In the town square Cale saw men in widebrimmed sombreros with rainbow-like colors on the blankets worn over their shoulders. Children played while burros wandered narrow streets like beggars. Someone rang a dinner bell.

Peaceful as it appeared from a distance, Cale knew of Caliente's reputation for lawlessness and violence. Federal marshals passed through on patrol, never lingering. They headed south, taking their leisure in Santa Fé, as Taylor had suggested. In the absence of peace officers, the law of the fist, the knife, the gun prevailed in Caliente.

The riders bunched around Taylor. Baldwin held back. Cale saw him take off his hat and run a hand through sweat-plastered hair while casting furtive glances left and right. The men were silent, sensing the confrontation that had brought them here was imminent.

Cale looked past them. Downslope from this rise a barn

and complex of corrals stood alongside S&RG railroad tracks. A switch led to a siding and the slanted planks of loading chutes. Cale saw cattle milling in the corrals down there, too far away to read brands.

Taylor pointed to a small clapboard office between the siding and the main line. "The railroad agent, Stanley Harrison, is either in that shack, or he's home for supper. A good man, Stanley. He's honest. Can't say the same for the wheeler-dealers. Those crooks buy livestock day or night, cash, no questions asked even if the bill of sale is chicken tracks on a sheet of paper." Taylor drew a breath and expressed his long-standing grievance. "After paying freight charges to Harrison, the wheeler-dealers ride with the cattle cars to the Chicago stockyards. They sell beef on the hoof to slaughterhouse reps, and scoop up a quick profit."

"What's the going price per head, Mister Taylor?"

Cale saw Henry Taylor turn to the man who had spoken. Heck Jones was a raw-boned, lanky cowhand. A new hire on the T-Bar-H, he rode an unbranded horse loaned by Taylor.

Cale was not surprised to see the rancher shrug in reply. As a businessman, Taylor played his cards close to his vest. "I can tell you the wheeler-dealers make a hell of a lot more money than ranchers do . . . with half the sweat."

"Same story up in Cheyenne on the UP line," Jones observed. "Laramie, too. I know Wyoming stockmen who ride in cattle cars all the way to Chicago, shoving out the middle man altogether."

Cale had been introduced to Heck Jones. Dour-faced and scrawny as a post, he was good-humored. He had performed chores with quiet efficiency on the trail and in camp, clearly a seasoned cowhand. He had recently turned up on the T-Bar-H, and Taylor hired him. Now this cowhand was caught up in a posse with men he did not know.

"That can be done if you're close to the main line," Taylor answered him. "I'd lose three weeks out of every year if I made that trip from Caliente." He paused and eyed the cowhand. "Does Griff Monroe know you?"

"Nope," Heck said. "Why?"

"I was just thinking," Taylor said. "None of the Circle M riders know you, do they?"

"Never laid eyes on a man among 'em," Heck said. Deadpan, he added: "Fact is, Mister Taylor, all you suntanned desert rats look alike to me . . . fried by the sun like sowbelly in a skillet."

The cowhands grinned, welcoming levity.

Taylor paused in sober thought. "That scrubby range horse won't attract much notice."

Cale looked at Heck's mount. In this region wild horses were descendants of Spanish runaways, small in stature, but fleet and savvy. Only the strongest and smartest mustangs survived in an unforgiving land, and ranchers often bred them with larger American horses in search of the best traits of both breeds. This recent catch from a rope trap on T-Bar-H range, a mouse-gray stallion, was more or less saddle-broken, not yet burned by a hot iron.

"Whatcha got in mind?" Heck asked.

"Ride down there to those corrals and read a few brands for me."

Heck thought about that, and lifted the reins. "Reckon I can do that little job for you, Mister Taylor."

"Take your time," the rancher cautioned him. "Roll a smoke, and go easy like any saddle tramp passing through. Make a swing around the town square. Keep an eye peeled for saddle mounts branded Circle M . . . and watch for one big white stud in particular."

"Yes, sir," Heck said.

Taylor sent him on his way with a single nod. Heck touched spurs to his horse, and moved downslope toward the town and distant corrals. The rancher signaled the others to pull back. Cale reined his horse around with them, dropping behind the crest of the rise until Caliente was out of sight.

"What's your thinking on this thing?"

Cale heard Taylor pose the question. He did not know the rancher was addressing Buster Baldwin until he looked around and saw him shrug in reply.

"Well, now," Taylor said. "As a lawman, this is your line of work, isn't it?"

Buster Baldwin conceded the point with a nod.

"When we run up against those thieving bastards," Taylor went on, "what do you figure we ought to do . . . rush them, guns blazing? Or should we steal our own cattle out of those corrals down there, and high-tail it for home by the light of stars?"

"I dunno."

Taylor studied him. "Just what do you know?" Jaw clenched, he glowered in silence as the men of the posse looked away, studying the horizon. "Well?"

"Mister Taylor," Baldwin said, exasperated, "I done seen my share of gun play from Red Rock County, Colorado all the way to Dodge City, Kans-ass. I ain't a-scared, if that's what you're driving at. As long as I worked under Joe Gilmore, he never ran a posse. I've got no experience in this type of work. That's why I'm letting you call the shots."

Taylor turned away, barely concealing his disgust for the man. "Gents, looks like we'll make our plan as we go along. Check your weapons. Be ready to ride when I give the word."

When Heck returned, Cale listened intently to his report. He noticed again every man in the posse was silenced by the anticipation of something about to happen, something deadly, and there was no turning back.

"Just like you figured, Mister Taylor," Heck reported. "Sloppy work with a running iron. Circle M and T-Bar-H steers are penned down there. I seen a few wearing Diamond Bar, Circle C, and others with some kinda triple half-circle brand."

Cale was surprised to hear that. "Rainbow Ranch."

Taylor nodded agreement.

"Sheriff Gilmore told me the rustlers might range farther north," Cale said, "and it looks like they did."

Baldwin added with an air of importance: "That's what Joe said to me, too. Yes, sir. It's the reason I ordered Parker to patrol up north. . . ."

Taylor silenced him with one sharp look.

"That big white Circle M horse you talked about," Heck went on, "is tied at the rail in front of a *cantina* in the town square. Four other Circle M mounts are tied there, too."

"How about saddle horses branded USA?" Taylor asked.

Heck shook his head. "Can't say I eyeballed that one. Why?"

"U.S. marshals ride government mounts marked USA," Taylor replied. He turned to the men. "Seems we are on our own, gentlemen . . . a citizen posse, legal and above-board. It is up to us to hand out justice."

Baldwin's horse pranced, and tossed his head. The animal fidgeted, and suddenly hopped backwards as though sensing tension—or perhaps emulating the rider's state of mind. Baldwin cursed too loud and reined the horse down, too hard.

Cale saw Taylor take all this in. The rancher shook his

head once, and turned to his posse. "We're losing daylight, gents. Let's ride."

Casting long, darting shadows, they crested the rise and swept downslope, bunched, with Baldwin bringing up the rear. Instead of heading for town and mounting a frontal assault on five men in a *cantina*, Taylor angled toward the railroad tracks. He led the posse behind the barn and drew rein.

"Wait here," Taylor said to them as he dismounted. "Keep your horses quiet and your guns ready. Parker, toss the reins to Jones, and come with me."

Surprised by the request, Cale did as he was asked and fell in beside the rancher. They stepped over the tracks and strode to the S&RG agent's office between the main line and the siding used for loading livestock. On this hot evening the door to the shack stood open.

"Harrison," Taylor said. "You in there?"

Cale heard a gruff voice from within. A shadow moved when an egg-shaped man filled the doorway. Hatless, he wore a vest over his white shirt, a loosely knotted tie, and sleeve garters.

"Yeah. Who is it?" Stanley Harrison answered his own question from the doorway. "Mister Taylor! What're you doing down here, south of the line?"

"Chasing stolen livestock," he replied, "all the way from my T-Bar-H."

"Stolen," Harrison repeated in alarm.

"A hundred and some-odd head," Taylor said. "Prime stock stolen off my range and other ranches by a hatful of rustlers."

Bald as a cue ball and clean-shaven, Harrison's forehead wrinkled as he pondered the information. "How many?"

"Five thieving bastards," Taylor answered. "Well

mounted, experienced cowhands. Beat us here by a few hours."

"I saw that bunch, Mister Taylor," Harrison said. "Five, all right. They looked like ordinary cowhands driving trail-weary steers into the corrals."

"One gent on a big white horse?"

Harrison nodded slowly. "He collected money from a cattle buyer while the drovers headed for the nearest *cantina.*"

"Bill of sale's no good," Taylor said.

Harrison studied him. "What's your plan?"

"We're going after them," Taylor said. He added: "Stanley, I need your help."

"You do?"

Taylor nodded.

"To do what?"

"I'd like you to step into that *cantina* and tell the drovers there was a miscount."

"Miscount," Harrison repeated.

"Tell them more money's due them," Taylor said, "and they can collect from their buyer at the sale barn. *Pronto.* Can you do that?"

"Yes, sir."

"Now, as soon as you deliver that message," Taylor went on, "I want you to go home. Go straight home and stay there."

Harrison swallowed hard.

"Can you do that, Stanley?" Taylor asked again.

"Yes, sir. Uh, you mean, right now?"

Taylor nodded. "Deliver that message to the drovers right now, Stanley." He turned to Cale. "This young gent is Cale Parker."

Cale shook the agent's hand, cold and clammy on a hot

evening. He was amazed by Taylor's next remark.

"Parker is my *segundo*. He'll speak for me if there's a need."

Harrison nodded once, eyes opened wide now.

Cale did not grasp the implications until Taylor spoke to him on the way back to the barn. "I appeal to you as a duly appointed officer of the law, Parker. If anything should happen to me, you take over. It will be up to you and other survivors to drive the cattle back to Colorado."

Survivors. Cale glanced at the rancher as they stepped over the tracks.

"I don't trust Buster Baldwin," Taylor went on. "I trust you. My last will and testament is in a bank vault in town. Like I said, if something happens to me, well, Josh Everts at the bank will handle matters from there."

Taylor left no time for elaboration or discussion. Reaching the rear wall of the barn, he quickly organized the posse, preparing them for a confrontation with five armed men.

Cale was ready, but Taylor's last words to him still ran through his mind.

Eddie drove the ranch wagon out of Red Rock on the northbound road that followed the winding course of Ute Creek. She took it slow to save the horses. In late afternoon, the earth radiated heat like a pot pulled out of a stove.

Inhaling deeply, the mingling scents of horse sweat and warm leather made her remember trips to town with her father. Now with a load of supplies in the bed of the wagon, she planned to stay overnight on the ranch, cook tomorrow, and come back to town the next day or perhaps the day after. In truth, she wanted to stay longer.

Eddie had left her mother in the care of Hilda Bulla, a widowed German immigrant whose husband had succumbed to a rattlesnake bite years ago. Hilda tended a small dairy herd on the outskirts of Red Rock. Eddie had asked several people about her. Living outside of town, Hilda had escaped the rumor mill. Big, strong, capable, the woman was known locally for her fresh cream and the white and yellow cheeses made from Bavarian family recipes. Responding to common words of English and a great deal of gesturing, she agreed to look after Mrs. Pauls. Eddie welcomed the chance to set her own schedule for a few days.

Not that this was a frivolous trip to the Rainbow Ranch. Far from it. Eddie could almost hear her father's commanding voice: No good is served by leaving our wagon in town to gather dust. Every blamed day our team stands idle in Powell's high-priced livery barn is a waste of money. Might as well be stabled in our own blamed barn, like all the king's horses. Now get a move on. At home Eddie planned to stock the larder and cook for her brothers. Either Roger or Alex could take her back to town with a few more furnishings needed by Marietta, and then return with the empty ranch wagon. That was her plan.

Overjoyed by Eddie's visit, Roger and Alex raised a whoop when they came in off the range that evening and spotted the ranch wagon. Later, with supper on the table, they dove in, eating their fill of beef stew and fresh biscuits for the first time since their sister had left the ranch.

Mouth full, Roger accused Alex of trying to poison him. Alex replied in kind, saying that if he had put his brilliant mind to the task of concocting a gut-burning potion, he could have easily sent his ugly brother to the Great Beyond—a service to all mankind, he noted.

Eddie changed the subject. She mentioned Cale Parker's visit to the house in town. Her brothers fell silent, exchanging a startled glance. Then they stared at her. Alex broke the silence.

"You . . . you let that man into the house?" Alex asked. "With our defenseless mother. . . ."

Roger broke in, barking an urgent question of his own. "You're packing that little pistol I gave you, aren't you, Sis?"

"Is . . . is something wrong?" Eddie said, alarmed. She received no answer until she repeated her question, louder.

"Wrong?" Roger said. "No . . . uh . . . what could be wrong?"

"We'd better tell her," Alex said.

"Tell me what?"

Roger avoided her gaze.

"She'll find out sooner or later," Alex said.

Eddie demanded: "Find out what?"

"Cale Parker is . . . ," Roger began.

"Is what?" Eddie asked.

"Well, the man is a. . . ."

Alex finished the painful sentence. "Sis, he's a murderer."

Shocked, Eddie stared at her brothers.

"He murdered six children in a Methodist Sunday School," Roger said. "With an axe."

Alex corrected him. "Baptist. And it was sixteen children, not six."

"Methodist," Roger insisted. "Six little bright-eyed children, as pure and innocent as dawn."

Alex turned to Eddie. "He's a madman who took a meat

cleaver to sixteen children in a Baptist Sunday school class."

"Oh, the screams from those little Methodist mouths," Roger said. "The church basement ran red with blood that day."

"Ankle deep in blood," Alex said.

"Sis," Roger demanded, "why are you running with a man like that?"

"I wish Father was here," Eddie said, "to punish you for tormenting your sister."

Roger glanced at the empty chair at the head of the table. A long, silent moment passed.

"It still seems strange, doesn't it?" he said. "Father not being here, I mean. I keep thinking he'll come into the room, bellowing orders like nothing ever happened."

After a moment of silent reflection, Alex turned to Eddie. "Now, what's this foolishness about Cale Parker?"

"You two wouldn't make up lies about him if you didn't like him," Eddie said. "You think he measures up. That's the truth, isn't it?"

"Question is," Roger said, "what do you think of the axe murderer?"

"None of your blamed business," Eddie said, imitating their father's vocabulary.

"That's her way of saying she's in love," Alex said to his brother.

"Our sister's in love, all right," Roger said. "I knew it would happen sooner or later."

"Hopelessly in love with killer Cale," Alex said with a nod of finality, a set expression on his face reminiscent of their mother.

Eddie pushed her chair back. She left the table, turning away to prevent them from seeing her smile.

Red Rock Signal

A notable event from the grassy plains of Montana has recently transpired, one worth recording in the annals of the West, methinx. The Celtic bards of old might well have branded it a cautionary tale. It comes to us from a town called Drake in Phillips County, Montana. Read closely, dear readers. Judge for yourselves, and measure your opinions against the real events recorded herein.

A family with a criminal bent of mind, two mean sons sired by a reprobate named Saul Gaines, was finally brought to justice, or so it seemed. A trail of murders brought a rapid and true verdict. The Gaines boys and *paterfamilias* would hang, so sayeth the jury foreman. The benefit of hindsight reveals one certainty: Had the lawful sentence been carried out as swiftly as the jury had delivered it, three vicious killers would not have had the time or the opportunity to get the drop on a deputy and steal his key.

Shackled, the Gaines boys burst out of the cell-block in search of handcuff and leg-iron keys in the office. Confronted by the town marshal there, they overpowered their next victim and strangled him with their chains. The fracas was not without murderous cries and curses, and brought townsmen running. To a man, they correctly guessed the Gaines boys were making a break. Discovering the crime that had left the marshal dead on the floor of his office turned these townsmen into a mob.

Thus, it came to pass that the Gaines boys found themselves face to face with twenty men thirsting for blood. Readers of this account may anticipate a quick execution, and readily celebrate swift justice. After all, what would be the fate of three mad dogs?

Think anew, dear readers, for a strange turn of events took place in Drake, Montana, as the mob and the Gaines boys stared eyeball to eyeball, the shackled killers snarling and boasting of their prowess, never once denying their guilt. At any given moment the townsmen could have gunned them down. Yet they did not take such action. Why?

It seems, dear readers, that some mental alchemy overcame these townsmen, a transition from madness to sanity that prevented them from committing murder and thereby lowering themselves to the base level of the convicts. Even in their mob state, the townsmen made a distinction, thin as it was, between gunning down shackled murderers and hanging those same men in the presence of a judge with the citizenry looking on.

Your faithful editor offers this factual account as documentary evidence of the purity of pioneer character, a unique trait now consigned to the annals of history. For it is true. Mr. Saul Gaines and his two sons were lawfully hanged the next day at noon, immediately after the funeral of the town marshal. Thus, methinx, justice was served in Phillips County, Montana.

Chapter Nine

With restless steers milling in the Caliente corrals, the sounds and pungent odors reminded Cale of his days of working in the livery in North Platte. The similarity ended there. Now he stood hidden behind the back corner of the sale barn, Heck Jones at his side. Close behind them, two other men of the posse waited, all of them with guns drawn.

Cale glanced to his left. At the opposite rear corner of the barn Henry Taylor stood with Buster Baldwin, Bill Dixon, and Luke Scanlon. By Taylor's plan, they were to stay out of sight from the village. Their wait was not long. Cale saw Taylor peer around the corner, and quickly lean back. He lifted his hand in a silent signal to the others.

Cale waved to confirm it. He checked his handgun. So did Heck.

"Looks like we've got 'em dead to rights," Heck whispered. "They're out-foxed and out-gunned."

Cale eased around the corner far enough to see squared, adobe buildings. In the half light of dusk now, he made out four bowlegged drovers coming toward the barn from the village. Little more than shadows, their drunken laughter carried across the distance as the rustlers staggered toward a pay-off.

At Taylor's next signal, the men of the posse stepped out from behind the barn. They swiftly formed a line of four on each side of the structure, guns cocked and leveled.

"Stop right there!" Taylor shouted at the approaching men. "Get your hands up! Hands up!"

Cale had always thought of Taylor as a quiet man, but

now the rancher's booming voice broke the silence of the evening. In the next instant a shot was fired. From where or by
whom, Cale did not know, but immediately after that report,
thunderous gunfire erupted. The explosions from separate
pistols ran together like the roar of a beast, a violent voice silenced only when the revolving cylinders were emptied and
the night air was thick with the acrid smoke of gunpowder.

Taylor shouted to his men: "Reload! Reload!"

Cale pressed the release on his heavy handgun and let
the cylinder swing open. He expected to eject spent shell
casings, but discovered six live rounds. He stared at the
brass ends of the rounds. Not one had detonated.

"What's wrong?" Heck asked him.

Cale shook his head in reply. Baffled, he figured he had
not pulled the trigger. Not once. He could not even recall
what he had done while the other men fired at the approaching thieves. He must have stood as still as a statue,
frozen while the others blazed away, emptying their guns in
the space of a few seconds.

Hands shaking in the aftermath now, Cale shoved the
cylinder shut. Then he moved forward with Heck and the
other two men following. They kept pace with Taylor and
the armed cowhands on his side of the barn. In another
sidelong glance Cale saw Baldwin bringing up the rear on
the other side.

Cale looked ahead, straining to see in the rapidly failing
light. He made out forms on the ground. The four rustlers
were down. One sobbed in pain. The others were still, arms
and legs akimbo as they lay sprawled in awkward poses of
death.

Cale holstered his gun as he drew near the three corpses.
A dozen paces away, he halted. Judging from their boots
and garb, the men were obviously cowhands. A search of

their pockets by Taylor produced a few coins, folding knives, chaw.

The wounded man convulsed and cried with a child's plaintiveness. Edging closer, Cale saw blood seeping through the man's fingers where he clutched his abdomen. Eyes squeezed shut, his mouth was stretched open in agony. Taylor knelt at his side.

"Where's Monroe?"

"Oh, God . . . oh, God, you have killed me."

"Where's Griff Monroe?" Taylor repeated, louder.

"Dunno."

"He was in that *cantina* with you, wasn't he?"

"Yeah. . . ."

Taylor pressed him: "You ride for the Circle M, don't you?"

He did not reply.

"You'd damned well better answer me," Taylor said. "Tell the truth while you've got a breath left in you."

"Yeah . . . Circle M."

"Where's the money you got from a buyer?"

"In Griff's saddlebags . . . we aimed to divvy it up tonight . . . ride out afore dawn . . . oh, God, you have killed me. . . ."

While the men of the posse looked down at him and the others in those minutes, the wounded man's voice thinned to a whisper. Presently he quieted, fell still, as though he had drifted off to sleep.

A wave of nausea ran through Cale, and then a shuddering chill. He had never witnessed killings, never stood this close to a man dying. The sight of four cowhands sprawled on the ground, bloodied and motionless, left him sick to his stomach.

A year ago he had seen the remains of a UP switchman

who had fallen under the wheels of a locomotive. By the time the coal car, a line of freight cars, and the caboose had dragged him and passed over him, the corpse was barely recognizable as human. But now with blood seeping through bullet-punctured clothing, these bodies at Cale's feet were all too human.

Unnamed emotions surged through him while he stood with seven other men, all of them staring down at the carnage they had wrought. Hatless, one man had been shot through the left eye. The malleable lead bullet had flattened on impact, crashed through bone, and opened the back of his skull like a hammer blow from within.

"Damn your worthless hide, Baldwin."

Cale turned to see Taylor confront the stocky man, both men with fists balled. "You fired before my order."

"No, I never shot first. . . ."

"Don't lie to me," Taylor interrupted. "You got trigger-happy."

"Not me," Baldwin said. "I wasn't the one."

"Lie again," Taylor said, "and I'll have these men whale on you until they knock the damned truth out of you."

"I'm telling the truth," Baldwin muttered.

Taylor turned to Scanlon. "Is he, Luke?"

"No, sir."

Taylor pointed to Bill Dixon. "Is Baldwin lying?"

Dixon nodded once. "Yes, sir, he's lying."

Taylor faced Baldwin. "Four men are laying here dead because you got trigger-happy. If that wasn't enough, you held back while the rest of us moved on the rustlers."

Baldwin shook his head in stubborn denial.

Taylor said: "You lying son-of-a-bitch."

Baldwin straightened and squared his shoulders. "I won't take that off you, Taylor."

"You'll take it," he said, "if I have to shove it down your throat."

Buster Baldwin did not reply. Glowering, he turned and headed for the barn.

In the moments that followed, Cale grew aware of a disturbing fact. Only two of the rustlers were armed, their revolvers still holstered. The other two carried sheathed knives on their belts, one with a broken handle. With clothes patched and worn boots held together by strands of wire, Cale judged they were men who could not afford a side arm, much less an ammunition belt and holster.

Taylor was probably right, Cale thought. Faced with eight men, guns drawn, they might well have surrendered if given the chance. Baldwin had taken that chance away from them.

Taylor asked no one in particular: "Where do you reckon Griff Monroe ran off to?"

When no one answered, Heck Jones offered a theory. "I don't know the gent, Mister Taylor, but maybe he spooked when that railroad man came hunting for him and the others."

Taylor nodded. "Monroe's as crafty as a coyote. If anyone could smell trouble, it would be him."

"Going after him?" Jones asked.

Cale saw Taylor reply with a shake of his head. In a brief discussion, a search of Caliente was ruled out. With nightfall closing in, Monroe would be nearly impossible to locate in a maze of adobe structures. Besides, they all knew a force of armed *gringos* riding into that village would hardly be welcomed.

"Without Monroe," Taylor said, "we can't return the money to the buyer who got himself cheated in this transaction. All we can do is finish the job we came here to do . . . herd those steers back to their rightful owners in Colorado."

Cale saw Taylor gaze at the village. The rancher spoke again after a long moment of silence.

"Looks like our one-sided shooting match got folks in Caliente hunkered down. We'd better hit the saddles before the cattle buyer on the short end of the stick figures this thing out and comes after us with a posse of his own."

Hoof beats drew their attention toward the barn. Cale heard Taylor curse. A lone horsebacker emerged from the night shadows. He saw Buster Baldwin riding at a fast canter into the gathering darkness, a solitary rider headed north.

"I never trusted him," Taylor said. He turned to Cale. "Did I, Parker?"

Cale shook his head.

"Well, good riddance to him," Taylor said. "He's finished here, and he'll be finished in Red Rock when I get back and call a meeting of the county commissioners."

The men of the posse worked fast to open the corrals. Whistling shrilly and waving their hats, they drove livestock out and bunched them, forming a trail herd. They drove them away from Caliente by starlight.

Looking back, Cale saw villagers venture out of their adobe houses. Quiet as shadows, women and children halted while grown men and older boys edged closer. All of them peered at four corpses sprawled on blood-soaked ground. The men pulled off their sombreros and bowed their heads.

Taylor set a northerly course along the drainage of the Río River. Riding point with him, Cale saw rippling water reflect star shine like liquid silver. With drovers flanking and trailing the cattle, the long night passed when silver turned to gold under the first rays of sunrise. The posse crossed into Colorado with no sign of pursuers from New Mexico Territory.

* * * * *

Eddie sat beside Alex on the bench seat of the ranch wagon, the rough ride cushioned by a stack of discarded saddle blankets. The vehicle bounced and shook, jarring them all the way to town.

They arrived in Red Rock under the hot sun of midday. From the brick residence still known locally as "the sheriff's house", Alex drove Hilda Bulla to her cabin on the edge of town. He returned as Eddie was faced with an urgent question from their mother.

"I want to convince Hilda to move to Denver with me," she said. "That woman is hard-working and cheerful, even though she barely makes a living from her dairy herd. I want her to go to Denver with me, but she won't leave here."

"I'll talk to her," Eddie said.

Marietta seemed dissatisfied with that offer. Tight-lipped, she listened to Alex's report. He confirmed his own well-being and Roger's good health, along with prosperity on the Rainbow Ranch. He brought her up to date on sightings of the outlaw gelding.

"We've seen Charley running wild, tail high," Alex informed her. "He wanders along Ute Creek for water and graze. Reckon that outlaw's getting enough to eat on his own. We put out feed, figuring we could lure him into a corral that looked familiar to him. No dice. All that horse wants to do is run. He runs, but he always returns. He circles the home place, tossing his head and stamping a hoof. I still think that locoed horse is looking for Father, waiting for him to come back." Alex paused and added: "Sometimes I think we all are. . . ."

Marietta listened absently. She reminded her son of her wish to move to Denver as soon as possible. "If you believe you can stall me here until I change my mind," she said, "you are sorely mistaken."

Eddie saw Alex lower his gaze, a loyal son who could not lie to his mother, at least not out loud.

"I have no wish to live out my days in this low-class burg," Marietta went on, waving a hand toward the doorway of the house and the town at large. She turned to her daughter. "Frankly, I don't believe you do, either, Edna."

Eddie knew her mother abhorred the town's gossipmongers as much as she did. Disgusted by small town women hissing like vipers, Marietta routinely declined recent invitations to club meetings and social events. "If they are downgrading other ladies," Marietta had said to her daughter, "what are they cackling about us behind our backs? Are they saying we are ignorant hayseeds? And what are they saying about you, a single woman?"

"Mother," Eddie said now, "I intend to live out my days on the ranch."

"You're too young to be talking that way," Marietta said. "Your life lies before you with twists and turns no one knows."

Eddie saw a certain set to her mother's face when she drew a deep breath. She braced herself. A speech was coming.

"Your life as a tomboy might have suited you in the past," Marietta said, "having been raised by a father you adored. Tom encouraged you to ride horseback like a boy and play rough and tumble with your brothers. Edna, I did not approve then, and I still don't. Girls need to develop their femininity in the proper ways. I was unable to guide you after the accident. . . ." Her voice trailed off as she fought tears. "But those days are gone," Marietta went on. "We all need to face that fact. You need to be thinking about marriage, Edna. Think about marriage, and think about starting a family. You can't very well do that in this little town, now, can you?"

I can, Mother, Eddie thought, *and I have thought about marriage. . . .* She did not mention Cale's name aloud and, like her brother, lied by her silence.

She did not dare look at Alex for fear of somehow revealing her innermost thoughts. Her feelings toward Cale Parker were secret, a private treasure held dear. Her brothers had made a shrewd guess, and she did not want Alex to spout off about Cale Parker now.

"We gave our word," Eddie said. She turned to her brother. "We will keep our promise as soon as we can. Won't we?"

Alex nodded stiffly.

"When?" Marietta demanded, slapping the arm of her wheelchair. "When?"

Henry Taylor held his posse together long enough for the men to herd the stolen cattle to three ranches in the southern sector of Red Rock County—the Diamond Bar, Circle M, and T-Bar-H. Sam Aiken was overjoyed by the recovery of his steers, and offered to pay a reward to each man in the posse. In this end of the county it was common knowledge Sam and Chipeta lived on the knife-edge of starvation, and the men declined his offer. Besides, as Taylor reminded them, the riders would receive a stipend from the county.

At the Circle M, Rollie received stolen livestock on behalf of the absentee owner, Aaron Miller. With Griff Monroe's unexpected departure, the ranch cook had added foreman to his list of duties. Now he confirmed Taylor's theory when he said four more riders were gone from the bunkhouse. He promised to send a written report to Mr. Miller in Denver, explaining to the owner the thefts and the vigorous pursuit of rustlers by a posse all the way to Caliente.

Cale had never questioned Rollie's honesty or doubted his competence. After a lifetime in the saddle, this gimpy man knew the art and the business of cattle raising inside and out. His new rôle as foreman seemed to be a good fit, and Cale hoped the owner had enough horse sense to make the promotion permanent.

Taylor listened in silence while Rollie confirmed there had been no sign of Griff Monroe in these parts, but at some time the man must have made a clandestine plan with the four missing riders. Now with cash bulging in his saddlebags, Rollie speculated the erstwhile foreman was long gone. Taylor was inclined to agree.

At the T-Bar-H, the riders peeled off sweat-stained, high-smelling vests, shirts, trousers, long handles, and socks. Bare-headed, naked men sprinted for the horse troughs. A scrubbing would be followed by a hot meal and well-deserved shut-eye in the bunkhouse.

Noting Cale wore his badge now, Taylor took him and Heck Jones aside. "I've noticed you two work together without a hitch. If I provided fresh saddle mounts from my string, would you gents be willing to drive the remaining livestock? They belong to the Rainbow Ranch and the Circle C. It's a two-man job, and I figure you're the right pair to get it done."

Cale and Heck exchanged a glance.

"As a bonus to the stipend," Taylor added, "I'll see to it that the county throws in a shave and hot bath in Dave's Tonsorial Parlor for the both of you. Deal?"

"Deal," Cale said after Heck nodded agreement.

Taylor added an enigmatic request. "Soon as you're done, gents, meet me in town. Both of you. You'll find me at the Colorado House."

Following Ute Creek, Cale and Heck drove the stolen cattle to the Rainbow Ranch. At his first sight of the irrigated fields, Heck let out a whistle. He had never seen the spread before, and marveled over a stream-fed pond and crops flourishing in the desert. The shining surface of the water behind the dam was neatly dimpled by trout rising to water-borne insects.

Leaving the livestock there, Cale led the way to the ranch house. He introduced the Pauls brothers to Heck Jones, and advised them of the return of the stolen steers bearing the Rainbow brand. That night the four of them played no-money poker, drank rye-spiked coffee, and swapped tales. Without naming names of ranchers or towns, or even confiding his own legal name, Heck Jones revealed a piece of his back trail.

In Wyoming he had thrown in with the wrong bunch. A shooting war flared between homesteading newcomers and established ranchers. Nesters had been shot or hanged, their livestock stolen or slaughtered. After witnessing the lynching of a homesteader while the man's wife and sobbing children looked on, Heck had waited until nightfall. He had led his horse and pack animal away in darkness, heading south.

Camping by day and riding by starlight, he had crossed into Colorado. He did not know if he had been pursued by hired gunmen, but a number of wealthy ranchers had reason to fear his testimony if participants in the range war ever came to trial. Heck knew other witnesses who had disappeared, and took no chances.

In time he reached the T-Bar-H in "this here awfulest desert country knowed to man," and figured he had left range wars behind. Instead, he hired on just in time to be pulled into Taylor's posse.

"Wherever I go," Heck said, "it's more of the same."

"What do you mean?" Alex asked.

Heck demonstrated bunkhouse accuracy when he spat into a brass spittoon six feet away. He turned to Alex.

"Cowhands getting theirselves killed," Heck answered. "Killed over what? Over brown-eyed, four-legged, bawling critters wanting nothing more than water and grass. Killed over horses. Killed over water claims. Killed over fenced range. Killed over unfenced range. Killed over what? I'm asking you. Killed over what?" Heck paused, struggling to squeeze his thoughts into words. "Plenty of good men have lost their lives in this raw land . . . hell of a thing when you think about it."

With a third shot of rye under his belt, Cale unburdened himself of troubling thoughts of his own. He figured Heck knew he had not fired his revolver in the Caliente fight, and decided it was time to get it out in the open.

"Reckon I froze," Cale concluded.

"Fact is," Heck said, "I never noticed. I was too busy thumbing fresh rounds into my own gun to pay any mind to yours."

Alex grinned. "Should 'a' kept your mouth shut, Cale. Nobody would have known."

"I'm the one who knows," Cale said.

Roger studied him. "You naming yourself a coward?"

Cale did not answer immediately. "I know what happened, and I'm not proud of it."

Roger and Alex turned to Heck.

"All hell busted loose in the blink of an eye," Heck said. "If those rustlers hadn't folded, you'd have done what needed to be done."

"I appreciate that," Cale said. "Something still bothers me, though."

"What?" Heck asked.

"Only two of them were packing pistols," Cale replied, "and they had no time to defend themselves. . . ."

"They were thieves," Roger interrupted. "Weren't they, Heck?"

Heck Jones nodded, and said: "They done proved it by staggering out of that *cantina,* skunk drunk, and laughing about how they was gonna grab up some more money."

"Don't drag yourself through hot coals over it, Cale," Roger went on. "Those men made their choice long before the posse caught up with them."

Heck spat again. "Once I heard a preacher rail against sinners grabbing up their filthy lucre. Sinners lust for it, he claimed. Oh, how he blistered folks who lusted after ill-gotten gains and filthy lucre." He paused. "Cale, that's what them gents down in Caliente got . . . paid in full."

The discussion ended there. Cale felt a measure of relief, but still could not rid his mind of the image of unarmed men dying on blood-soaked ground. He knew it was a sight he would never forget.

In the morning Cale and Heck bid the Pauls brothers good bye. They set out on the dim ruts left by wagon wheels, driving the last of the stolen livestock to the Circle C.

In the kitchen Eddie dropped her mother's favorite teapot. The thin porcelain vessel shattered at her feet while the voice of Henry Taylor droned on and on in the parlor.

"A long time ago, Missus Pauls, I was widowed. Yes, ma'am. I know the sorrow that strikes deep into the heart of the bereaved. Yes, ma'am, I do, and for that very reason I never figured on marrying again. But lately I've given it some thought. I've been thinking . . . well, I've been thinking, Missus Pauls, if you're the marrying kind. . . ."

That was the statement Eddie had overheard, the words hitting her with enough force to knock the teapot from her hands. Fashioned in England and designed with a gently curving spout and delicate handle, it was hand-painted in a floral pattern. Now the teapot lay at her feet in a thousand pieces.

If you are the marrying kind. . . .

Traveling to Red Rock from the T-Bar-H, Taylor had come calling, ostensibly to report on the return of stolen cattle to the Rainbow Ranch. He sat with Marietta in the parlor while Eddie heated water for tea. Wearing a clean brown suit and a starched white shirt, he carried the scent of cologne all the way from Dave's Tonsorial Parlor to the sheriff's house.

"Fact is, Missus Pauls, your boys are too young to be running a big spread," Taylor went on. "There's more to the job than tending cattle and forking hay. There's the finances. My guess is your late husband kept track of Rainbow finances in a ledger book, and he read his numbers and notations like the Holy Word itself. If the budget isn't watched and handled just so, steers have to be sold off out of season at a loss, and, well, those boys could lose the place before you knew anything was amiss. So I've been thinking . . . I figured if the day comes when you would consider marriage, well, we could join forces . . . in a manner of speaking."

Porcelain shards crunched underfoot when Eddie rushed out of the kitchen. She lunged down the hall to join her mother and Taylor in the high-ceilinged parlor, clearing the doorway in time to hear her measured reply.

"Now, Mister Taylor, I am flattered by your attentions, I truly am, but the Rainbow Ranch belongs to my children. They are doing all the work now. If they decide they want to sell, you can talk to them. . . ."

"I will save you the trouble," Eddie broke in.

Taylor shot her a hot look.

She saw the man's anger flare, but did not allow him to stare her down. "We won't sell the ranch," she said. "Now or ever."

"Well, a man can't be faulted for trying," Taylor said with a forced smile.

Maybe not, Eddie thought, showing a false smile of her own, but a man can be faulted for not knowing when to shut his blamed mouth. She had believed this matter to be settled. If Taylor came back again, she promised herself to tell him exactly that.

The marriage proposal had caught Eddie by surprise, but it had stunned her mother. As she later found out, Marietta had not even heard the crash of her teapot when it burst into pieces on the kitchen floor.

Red Rock Signal

EXCITING NEWS FROM CALIFORNIA
Great Diamond Hoax Exposed
Wild Tales of Gems Equal In Size To A Pigeon Egg
Stampede Of Miners Unabated

Word comes to us from distant California of a great hoax finally exposed. A vast field of glittering diamonds has been rumored out there since the Rush of '49. Guy Dean O'Boyle, a self-appointed mining engineer, claims to have mined by placer techniques nearly 700 small diamonds from a field 3,000 acres in size. He shipped $1,000,000 in diamonds to the House of Rothschild in London for evaluation and sale.

Prominent among the gems was a single diamond of matchless purity the size of a pigeon egg, a fine and mighty rock said to be valued at $500,000.

Dear reader, methinx this to be not the work of nature in all her blazing glory, but a mining engineer's opium fantasy. Just as winged fairies do not fly silently through magical forests of perfumed flowers, no such field of diamonds sparkles under the sun "somewhere in California." No one on this continent has actually seen the storied pigeon egg diamond, or any other such gem. Cornered at last, the perpetrator of a grand myth finally admitted his deception. Too easily, some say.

For is this not a strange function of the human capacity for nurturing dreams of easy fortune as a motive for continuing the search? Such pointless treks occur in California to this day. Bands of ill-trained miners hunt for a field of gems, an array of wealth seen only by the infamous Mr. O'Boyle. It will come as no surprise to those of us in possession of rational minds that O'Boyle is still engaged in the nefarious practice that fueled his primary motive—the sale of shares of stock in his venture.

Dear reader, fantastic as it may seem to us, dreams of limitless wealth were only heightened by O'Boyle's widely published admission of perpetrating The Great Diamond Hoax. Believing THIS claim to be a clever ploy, a machination designed by O'Boyle to mislead and thereby conceal the location of his treasure, hundreds of gullible folks crave to be privy to The Secret, and continue buying shares of stock.

Methinx idle investors and wandering fools in California should be informed of the hoax visited upon us a few years back. Some of you may recall purchasing tickets to gain entry into a walled tent where the viewer gazed upon the horizontal figure of the Great Petrified Man. This fossilized gent turned out to be chiseled stone, nothing more than common gray granite. The crude statue was presented to the trusting folks among us as a fossilized human male seven and a half feet tall, eyes closed, lips forever curled in a smile of ridicule.

While composing his column, Ben Pittock heard the shrill whistle of a locomotive. Bell clanging as the hissing steam engine slowed to a halt at the water tower beyond the depot, he muttered irritably at this intrusion into his concentration. No train was scheduled for this day, yet here it was, belching smoke into the sky.

Finished, Pittock was preparing to run his first proof when he was interrupted again, this time by insistent rapping at the back door of the print shop. He put down the sheet of paper.

It was unusual for anyone to knock on the door that opened to the back alley. Wiping his hands on his apron, Pittock moved around the press to see about it. He opened the door, only to glimpse two burly men the moment before a fist slammed into his face. Driven back, another punch sent him reeling to the floor.

Chapter Ten

Sleek and swift movement caught Cale's eye. He looked downward and glimpsed a rattlesnake slithering away from the hoofs of passing cattle. With Heck on point, Cale rode drag. They drove nine scrawny steers bearing the Circle C brand on bony left hips, the animals' hides mutilated where brands were blurred by a hot running iron in a careless or hurried hand.

Amid the churning dust now, Cale saw the diamondback. It was a big one, four or five feet in length by his quick estimate, and thicker than a blacksmith's forearm. With a thin tongue darting from its mouth, the creature fled to safety in a clump of rabbitbrush.

Cale wore a bandanna tied snugly over his mouth and nose. Raising up in the stirrups, he peered through the sifting dust at a sage-studded ridge ahead. The ranch was not far beyond it. After peering left and right, Cale checked their back trail. He and Heck had come this far from the Rainbow Ranch without catching sight of Indians or the outlaw gelding once ridden by Thomas Pauls.

Cale did not know what sort of reception to expect when the ramshackle sheds of the Circle C came into view. He had not confided to Heck the details of his previous encounter with Alma Juliette Collins. But he had formulated a plan, simple as it was.

With the steers herded to the mud-ringed sink hole that passed for a well, Cale called out to Mrs. Collins. By his plan, once the reason for their visit was explained to her, he and Heck would turn back, their task finished. They would

149

make a beeline for the Paulses' ranch, use it as a stopover, and then head for Red Rock.

That plan was abandoned the moment the distant report of a rifle reached them. Cale ducked, even though he knew it was too late. The bullet had whined past his ear, a chunk of lead that did not have his name on it. He caught a glimpse of Heck leaping out of the saddle. Landing in a crouch, the cowhand reached for his revolver.

"Damn, Cale!" Heck exclaimed, his wild-eyed gaze swinging left and right. "Wisht you'd told me these folks ain't the hospitable type!"

Cale hurriedly dismounted. Three surly dogs approached him from the shady side of the cabin, teeth bared as they growled. A moment later the door swung open. Shotgun in hand, Mrs. Collins appeared there. Cale saw her halt, scowling. Standing perfectly still, she was framed in the doorway like the subject of a bizarre portrait. Then she moved. Thrusting the shotgun's butt plate to her shoulder, she brought the barrel up, swiftly aimed, and pulled the trigger.

A blast of buckshot pelted two of the dogs and peppered Cale's boots and trouser legs. Both ranch dogs fled, howling. Behind him, his mare reared.

"Want me to drop her?" Heck shouted.

In a glance to his right, Cale saw him draw aim on the ranch woman. "No!" Cale waved urgently at her. Pulling down his bandanna, he identified himself. He ducked again at the sound of rifle fire, and another bullet whizzed overhead. He heard Heck swear again.

"You'd better let me kill someone around here," Heck said, swinging his handgun toward the lingering puff of powder smoke in the distance, "and damned quick."

Cale saw Mrs. Collins lower the shotgun.

"Oh, hell," she said. "It's you. Deputy Scarface. What the hell you doin' here? Who's that with you?"

Before he could answer, she stepped through the doorway and lifted the shotgun over her head, swinging it left and right in a signal.

"That's my Colly doin' the shootin'," she said, lowering the gun. "Likely he's been a-watching you through the telescope on his rifle. Probably figures you're thieves, what with you wearing that mask and driving our cattle. What in the name of hell do you think you're doing, anyhow?"

"We're returning stolen Circle C livestock, Missus Collins," Cale said. "Rustlers burned over your brand. . . ."

"Stolen!"

"Yes, ma'am."

Cale recounted recent events in Colorado and the expedition from Red Rock into the northern reaches of New Mexico Territory. He learned from Mrs. Collins that Colly had not yet discovered any Circle C steers were missing.

Nothing unusual about that, Cale figured. As he had learned from other ranchers in this region, the driest of the dry desert, domestic cattle were far-flung, gathered in small herds. The animals barely survived summer drought or winter cold, sometimes beating great odds with the weather only to die from a lack of nutrients. Keeping track of the wandering critters was full-time work for one rider, as she had explained during Cale's first visit, and her man had little time to spend at the home ranch.

"Colly just rode out a while ago," she said. She added: "Being the bashful type, he won't come no closer until you strangers are gone. Or dead."

"When are we leaving, Cale?" Heck asked.

"Right about now," he replied.

"Suits me," Heck said. Holstering his revolver, he

caught his horse and swung up.

Cale joined him. As they turned their mounts, he saw Heck cast an uneasy glance toward the hidden rifleman.

"I tell you, Cale," Heck said, "I don't like taking that, not off any man."

"Taking what?"

"Potshots from a chicken-shit bushwhacker laying on his belly somewhere out there," Heck replied. "I've got a notion to circle him. Move in behind him and take him down . . . beat the livin' hell outta him . . . that's what I oughta do."

"Good idea," Cale said.

As they rode away, Heck gave it up. "Reckon we oughta head back to town, though . . . Taylor wanting to talk to us, and all . . . what do you think, Cale?"

"Yeah," Cale said, knowing Heck was a man who had to talk wild notions out of his system before he calmed down.

Cale looked back. Alma Juliette Collins still stood in front of her cabin, not exactly pretty as a picture with her shotgun in hand as she stared after them. Heck turned, too, following Cale's gaze.

"She winged her own dogs," Heck said. "Did you see that? Shot her own danged dogs."

Cale nodded. "She'll be digging buckshot out of their hides for a spell."

"Speaking of hides," Heck said, pointing to dark spots on his boots and trouser legs left by shotgun pellets. "What about yours?"

"I'm all right," Cale said.

"You sure?"

Cale nodded. "Did you hear that shotgun go off when she pulled the trigger?"

"Yeah," he replied. "What about it?"

"Not much louder than a kid's popgun."

"What're you driving at?"

"Missus Collins skimps on everything," Cale replied. "There wasn't enough gunpowder in those hand-loaded shells for the buckshot to hurt me."

Heck thought about that. "All I know is, that was one poor thank you for risking our necks over Circle C steers. The bitty never offered supper, or even to grain our horses. Nary a drink from her well, neither."

"If you'd taken a good look at the scummy cow piss in that well," Cale said, "or smelled the inside of her cabin, you'd know we escaped with our lives just by riding out of here in one piece."

Heck grinned.

"Mister Newspaperman, this here message is from the good folks at the S and RG . . . be a mite respectful next time you write about the railroad.

"Right now, you feel like a plow horse walked on you. Isn't that right? Thought so. If we have to come back to teach you another lesson in manners, you'll feel like a locomotive ran you down.

"Remember your poor old ma's advice. If you can't think of something nice to say, don't say nothing. You clear on that, Mister Newspaperman?"

Ben Pittock remembered nodding in reply. Lying on his back on the paper-strewn floor of his print shop, he stared at the circular pattern in a pressed tin ceiling, a view he had never taken in before.

He had tried to speak, to bellow, to fight, to curse—but with the air knocked clean out of him, he could not draw a breath, much less hand the railroad toughs the lashing they deserved. Instead, he had meekly acknowledged their threats while his eyes teared and he tried to gasp for air. For good measure, his attackers administered kicks to his ribs and belly before departing through the back door.

The goons were right about one thing, Pittock thought now. He felt like he had been trampled by a horse. Pain surged through his chest with every breath he took. And with every breath he plotted revenge.

Eddie left the house on a secret mission. Telling her mother she was going to town for a brief shopping trip, she walked hurriedly from Seventh Street to Broad. Crossing the main street, she passed false-fronted store buildings and the cavernous frame structure housing **Red Rock Signal & Job Printing, Benjamin Pittock, Prop.** With a casualness that did not come easily to her, she sauntered to the window of the mercantile next door. The object of her secrecy was still on display there, in plain view of passers-by.

Eddie gazed at the Sears catalogue. It was still open to the page picturing an elegant wedding gown with tapered leg-of-mutton sleeves and a stand-up collar, open at the throat. Never in her life had she been beset by such tumultuous thoughts and wild notions. Now she could hardly get the images of her wedding day out of her head. Day and night she thought of that dress, snug and silken, elegantly trimmed with fine lace, veiled. . . .

Movement on the other side of the glass gave her a start, as though her secret had been discovered. Perhaps it had. Peering through her own reflection, Eddie looked into the store. She saw a thick-bodied woman inside and glimpsed a smiling face under the curled brim of a long-plumed hat. It was Mrs. Rose Waldron. She carried a shopping basket on her arm—and she had been watching.

With a quick smile of greeting, Eddie turned away. She

walked swiftly along the boardwalk, ducking into the recessed entryway of the print shop as though important business had brought her here, not to the mercantile. She felt
awkward and foolish, knowing full well the next topic of
local gossip would be Edna Pauls swooning over the Sears
illustration of a wedding gown. One wedding in particular
captivated her, folks would soon be whispering, the ceremony every young woman dreamt about. And just who is
the man of her dreams? Mrs. Waldron might well be posing
that question right now. A man already married? A priest?
Didjahear? No! Yes!

Thus began, Eddie supposed, the turning and churning
of Red Rock's rumor mill. Her thoughts were interrupted
when the door opened behind her. She turned, uttering an
involuntary gasp.

Eddie stared at Ben Pittock. His bulbous nose was bent,
swollen, purpled. Her hand went to her mouth, first in surprise, then out of concern for his well-being. She barely
heard him ask how he could help her today.

"Mister Pittock, you're hurt. . . ."

He shook his head once. "I'm all right."

"But what . . . what happened?" she asked.

"Nothing worth discussing," he said, and changed the
subject. "I saw you standing here. A printing job brought
you to my door, Miss Pauls?"

Remembering horseplay between brothers a time long
ago, Roger's fist had landed squarely on Alex's snout. She
remembered the damage, and knew beyond doubt what had
happened to Mr. Pittock. "Who hit you?"

"I ran into a door. Clumsy of me. . . ."

"What was the door's name?"

His walrus mustache lifted when he smiled. "I guess I
had that one coming." He paused. "If you must know, Miss

Pauls, it was a stout cottonwood. The deciduous monster leaped upon me, branches slicing the air like whips as I ran into a stout trunk. You'll read all about the monumental battle in the next Methinx column. . . ."

"Mister Pittock," Eddie interrupted.

He drew a breath, grimacing with the effort. "All right, all right. Truth of the matter is, I found myself on the receiving end of a message from S and RG bigwigs."

Eddie looked at him curiously. "I don't understand."

"The bigwigs sent a couple of toughs to Red Rock," he explained, "for the purpose of influencing the editorial content of my newspaper."

Eddie's eyes widened as the meaning of his words sank in. "The S and RG hired two men to beat you up because of what you wrote about the railroad spur?"

He nodded. "Heavy-handed, wouldn't you say?"

"Report this to the sheriff, that's what I'd say . . . ," she began.

Pittock shook his head. "No need to bring lawmen into the matter. I can handle it myself."

"Mister Pittock," Eddie said.

"Believe me," he said, "I can handle this little dispute."

Eddie paused in exasperation. "You sound just like my father."

"Young lady," Pittock said, "you know I take that as the highest compliment. . . ."

The newspaperman was interrupted by the rumbling of wagon wheels, a popping of whips, and rough voices. Eddie turned toward Broad. She watched a caravan of mule-drawn ore wagons pass by, a dozen or more heavy vehicles. The cacophony of rolling wheels, driving hoofs, and profane shouts of teamsters nearly drowned out one other voice that reached her ears.

That voice was familiar. It brought a catch to her throat. A moment passed before she saw him. Like ghosts, two men on horseback emerged from the dust cloud stirred by the passing wagons. The pair of riders angled across the street toward the print shop. One man she did not know. The other wore a badge—Cale Parker.

"Eddie!" Cale called out again. "Eddie!"

She saw him lift a hand to the brim of his hat, and smiled as she greeted him.

Cale remembered the dream. While making his rounds of desert cattle spreads, he had daydreamed of a chance meeting with Eddie. The happenstance occurred in Red Rock. Impeccably dressed, he saw himself as the gentleman on horseback speaking to the woman he loved. Never mind the clothes from his war bag were patched and threadbare, that he wore cowhide boots with run-over heels—somehow the outfit was transformed while he courted the most beautiful girl in town.

Now with a glance at Heck Jones, reality expunged the dream. In Heck, he saw a reflection of himself. Far from the gentlemanly demeanor of his imaginings, he, too, was caked with trail dust and grime, both men showing the effects of a hard ride out of the harsh desert of northern Red Rock County.

Eddie left the recessed doorway and moved to the edge of the boardwalk. She gazed up at Cale. "Two men attacked Mister Pittock . . . hardcases sent by the S and RG Railroad."

Cale looked past her. Benjamin Pittock stood still, mute. Cale saw the man's bruised nose, as well as an annoyed look in his eyes.

"What happened?" Cale asked him.

"Nothing to involve lawmen," Pittock replied tersely.

With Cale and Heck looking on, Eddie filled in the blanks, recounting her conversation with the newspaperman.

"Is that true, Mister Pittock?" Cale asked when she finished.

"Of course, it is," he replied. "Miss Pauls would never lie. But as I told her, I will handle the matter myself. No need to involve you or any other gendarme."

"Gendarme," Cale repeated.

"Translated from the French," Pittock explained, "I refer to an officer of the law. In a word, Deputy . . . you."

Cale thought about that. "I don't know anything about French, but from what Eddie's saying, looks like you're outnumbered."

"I admit the goons caught me by surprise," Pittock said. "It won't happen again."

"Are they still in town?" Cale asked.

"After their fun with me," Pittock replied, "they very likely departed on the next out-going train. I won't lodge assault charges against anyone, if that is what you're hinting."

Eddie cast another exasperated look at him.

"I'm thinking about something else, Mister Pittock," Cale said, with a glance at Heck.

"What would that be?" Pittock asked.

"If you see that pair in town, let me know."

"For what purpose?"

He glanced at Heck again. "We'll even the score."

"Thank you, Deputy," Pittock said, "but that won't be necessary." He turned, and stepped into his shop, closing the door behind him.

Cale saw Eddie look after him, slowly shaking her head.

"Are all men mule-stubborn," she asked, facing him, "or just the ones I happen to know?"

Cale dismounted. "All good men are stubborn as mules, Eddie. The others are jackasses."

"Some choice," Eddie said.

Cale motioned to his saddle partner. "I'd like you to meet this stubborn gent . . . Heck Jones. Me and Heck, we just got back from returning stolen steers to the Rainbow herd."

"Mother and I learned some of the details from Mister Taylor," Eddie said. "I've heard talk of a shooting down in Caliente." When Cale did not offer details, she went on: "I am glad you are all home safe and sound. I owe you a word of thanks for returning our livestock. I hope my brothers expressed their gratitude properly."

"One did," Cale said, "one didn't."

"In what way?"

"Heck beat Alex in poker," he replied, "but we all lost to Roger."

"Roger has a way of coming out on top," Eddie said. "Alex hates him for it."

"So do I," Heck said.

"Me, too," Cale chimed in.

Eddie smiled. Her eyes moved from Cale to Heck, and back to the man she loved. "Tomorrow I'm baking a batch of lemon-iced cookies. Stop by the house for lemonade and the best cookies you ever sank your teeth into. . . ."

Cale broke in: "Eddie?"

"Yes?"

"A long time ago," he said, "we talked about a picnic down by the creek. I spotted a stand of willows that will give us some shade down there . . . if you're still interested."

159

Cheeks coloring, she bowed her head.

Cale was mystified by her silence, but Heck caught the hint.

"Pleased to make your acquaintance, Miss Pauls," Heck said. Turning his horse, he headed for Dave's Tonsorial Parlor across Broad and down half a block from the Colorado House.

"Sorry if I embarrassed you," Cale said to Eddie now. "Reckon I got a little over-eager with my invite. Seems like I trip over my own boots every time I get my eyes on you."

"How about today," Eddie said. "Sundown?"

Cale was too flustered to string the right words together. "Today . . . uh . . . for a . . . for a picnic?"

She answered with a laugh. "That's what we're talking about, isn't it?"

Cale nodded. Feeling slow-headed, he thought a moment. "I'll round up some grub. . . ."

"Oh, our pantry is loaded to the gills," Eddie said. "Living in town, I've found it's awfully easy to buy too much food when you're used to ranch life. I'll load the basket with odds and ends, and make a jar of lemonade. Just bring your appetite when you pick me up at sunset."

After a shave from Dave and a scrub in his tub, Cale and Heck left the tonsorial parlor, both sporting clean clothes, brushed hats, and polished boots. At noon they met Henry Taylor in the lobby of the Colorado House. He came down the stairs, greeted them with vigorous handshakes, and escorted them into the hotel restaurant.

With luncheon entrées ranging from sirloin steak to fresh trout to venison and oysters, the menu surpassed Cale's desert fantasies. So did the prices. Several offerings were equal to a day's wages. Cale was surprised when Taylor insisted they order anything on the menu that caught their fancy, and then told the waiter to pile it high.

"To tell you the truth," Taylor said, "I have a request to make of you gents, and I aim to make you feel beholden to me."

Cale and Heck looked at him curiously.

"After a fine midday dinner," Taylor went on, "you'll be more inclined to say yes than no."

Cale wondered about that remark, but not enough to slow him down. Heck, either. Both men ate their fill, plates loaded. Afterward, over coffee and brandy, Taylor leaned forward on his elbows and made his pitch. "Gentlemen, I have been authorized by the Red Rock County commissioners to offer an important position to each of you."

Cale repeated: "Position?"

"The positions of sheriff and deputy sheriff," Taylor said.

Cale and Heck stared, momentarily stunned by his words.

"As you both well know, the job is not without danger," Taylor went on. "But it pays almost twice what you'll make on any ranch in the county. I'm recommending you, Parker, for the position of sheriff, while Jones pins on the deputy's badge."

Cale and Heck exchanged a glance, both men still speechless.

Taylor must have sensed doubt in the gesture, for he went on: "I consider myself to be a good judge of horseflesh and men, and last night I advised the county commissioners that you two are the best candidates for these positions." He paused. "My suggestion is simple. Get acquainted with your duties. Make your final decision in thirty days. No matter what happens, you'll both be paid for your time."

"What about Buster Baldwin?"

"That two-legged jackass throws his weight around," Taylor said, "telling everyone who will listen that he's sheriff of Red Rock. He carries that article from the *Signal* like it's some kind of diploma. Fact of the matter is, if you two accept the offer from the commissioners, Baldwin will be relieved of his badge . . . first thing tomorrow morning by all the commissioners." He slapped his hands together. "Well, what do you say?"

"Mister Taylor," Cale said, "there is something you should know. . . ." His voice trailed off.

"About you?"

Cale considered mentioning his failure to fire his revolver in the gunfight, but decided against it after he thought back over his previous conversation with Heck, Alex, and Roger at the Rainbow Ranch.

"Well?"

"When Sheriff Joe Gilmore interviewed me last year," Cale said, "I lied about my age."

"Did you, now?"

"Yes, sir."

"Would you be surprised to learn," Taylor asked, "that I do not give a royal damn how old you are?"

"Reckon I would."

"As I mentioned," Taylor went on, "I consider myself to be a sound judge of men and horses. In my experience with the human critter, some are men and some are boys. Boys never grow up. No matter what the calendar says, they are forever boys. Don't get me wrong. Boys have their place in this world. They make good drinking buddies, obedient soldiers, and fair cowhands. But a kid with a gun backed up by a badge is bad business." He drew a breath. "I recall talking to Joe about you, Parker. You grew up in a hurry, perhaps when you lost your parents and found yourself on your own at an early age. Is that about the size of it?"

Cale did not answer immediately. He well remembered striding away from row upon row of freshly dug graves in the North Platte cemetery, head bowed, tears hot on his face. Two of the newest graves from the epidemic were the final resting places of Jonathan and Wilma Parker. From that day forward, Cale had been too busy earning his keep to give much thought to the subject of growing up or not growing up. He had not been offered a choice.

Now he said: "That may be so, Mister Taylor."

Taylor turned to Heck. "While we are on the subject, any dirty laundry you want to air out?"

"Well," Heck said slowly, "over the years I've played both sides of the law."

"Plenty of good peace officers can make that claim," Taylor said. He asked: "Any reward dodgers with your name on them?"

Heck shook his head as he thought about the question. "I never killed nobody, never robbed a train, never held up a bank." He added thoughtfully: "But I've bunked with men who have done one or more of them things."

"If you don't mind my asking," Taylor said, "what brings a seasoned cowhand like you to this desert in the back corner of Colorado?"

"Don't mind your asking," Heck replied. "Not much to it. Range war up in Wyoming. Hanging trees bore fruit, as they say. I got my fill of it. Rode out before the hanging rope or a bushwhacker's bullet found me."

"Subject closed," Taylor said. "Now tell me, can you swear in good faith to uphold the laws of the state of Colorado. Both of you?"

Cale and Heck looked at one another again, and replied: "Yes, sir."

"That's all I need to know, gentlemen," Taylor said. He pushed his chair back, eyeing them before he stood. "I get the feeling you two need some time to go over my offer. I have business in town. Meet me in the lobby of the Colorado House . . . say, nine tomorrow morning?"

Cale and Heck nodded.

"I'll have a fresh pot of coffee and a plate of pastries on hand," Taylor said. "We'll go from there."

A wicker picnic basket loaded with fried chicken, sliced summer sausage, cold potato salad, a brick of aged cheddar cheese from Hilda Bulla, and biscuits with butter and jam not only made an appealing picnic supper, but the occasion also provided an opening for Marietta's criticism.

"He's a rough one," Marietta said.

"Who?" Eddie asked, even though she knew.

"Carl whatever-his-name-is," she said, and shuddered. "I keep thinking about that bloody scar on his face."

"Parker," Eddie said. "*Cale* Parker."

"Whatever name he's using," Marietta insisted, "he looks like a filthy outlaw. Acts like one, too, sneaking up behind innocent women like he does." When Eddie did not rise to this bait, she added: "He wants only one thing from you, Edna."

"Mother."

"Let's be honest," she said.

Eddie turned to her. "You start."

"I see carnal desires in his eyes when he looks at you," Marietta said. "Soon as he gets what he wants, he'll be gone. . . ."

"Mother!"

"It's the truth," Marietta said. "He's a saddlebum."

"Mother," Eddie said, "who did you marry?"

"What in the world are you talking about?" Marietta asked. "You know who I married."

"But when you first met the man you married," Eddie said to her, "he fit that description. Didn't he?"

"You know better than that," Marietta said. "Your father was a gentleman. A fine gentleman. . . ."

"But when you first met him," Eddie broke in, "he was a cowhand camping by the river. He had no roof over his head and few prospects. After he started the Rainbow Ranch and dug out the reservoir, you saw his strength and determination. You saw 'grit mixed with a full measure of loco.' Mother, you've said those very words to me a hundred times."

Marietta did not reply.

"Father made his way in a hostile land," Eddie said, " 'one blamed steer at a time,' as he used to say. That's the truth, Mother. You know it is."

Marietta lowered her gaze.

"All I ask is that you give Cale a chance," Eddie said.

Chapter Eleven

As one who paid cash or did without, Cale found himself short of money in a pivotal moment of his life. His policy of never-a-borrower-be had been handed down to him from a Scotch-Irish background on his mother's side. Maybe it had been grounded in wisdom in Britain, the land of her birth, but here, in the American West, ranchers, miners, and loggers survived in a cycle of borrowing and repayment to banks and shop owners. Now Cale was left without a line of credit in any of Red Rock's stores.

Owning nothing of value to sell or swap, he confided his dilemma to Wade Powell. With the simple act of signing a hand-written IOU, the liveryman advanced ten dollars in cash, the carriage deposit and horse rental fees—expenses charged against earnings due Cale from the county for his service in the posse.

"A safe loan, I'd say," Powell stated in answer to Cale's expressions of gratitude. He added with a conspiratorial grin: "Just don't tell Josh Everts or anyone else I have ventured into the loan business. Bankers hate competition."

Driving Red Rock's finest one-horse carriage, Cale splurged and bought a new hat and a blue neckerchief in the mercantile on Broad. With the kerchief knotted at his throat, he drove to the sheriff's house on Seventh, head held high. Mounting the front porch planks with his new hat in hand, he reached to the door and turned the bell handle, just then realizing the hour was well before sunset.

Early or not, Eddie must have been watching. The door opened immediately. Stepping out, she closed it and greeted Cale cheerily. He took the basket by the handle with one hand, and clapped the stiff hat on his head with the other. Then he bowed slightly and held out the crook of his arm in the manner of high-hatted gents he had seen escorting ladies in their finery.

With a gentle laugh, Eddie slipped her arm through his, and they walked stride for stride to the carriage. Cale wondered if they were being watched, but did not look back to find out. He did not want to give Mrs. Pauls the satisfaction.

The significance of Eddie's hurried actions back there had not been lost on him. It was a safe bet mother and daughter had argued, and now Mrs. Pauls refused to sanction this picnic by her presence or any gesture of good will. She did not approve, Cale figured, any more than she approved of the prospect of a ruffian alone with her daughter. He took heart. For if he was right about that, it meant Eddie wanted to be alone with him.

The weather heaped disapproval upon them, too. Summer rainfall was rare in this region, and Cale smelled the storm before he saw it. Upon reaching the outskirts of town, a low rumble of thunder drew his attention skyward. Clouds bulged into towering cumulous domes above—innocently white on top, dark and menacing on the bottom edges—as though poised to launch an attack.

More growls of thunder sent the horse hopping, head bobbing up and down nervously. Cale could have turned back, and perhaps he should have in the interest of safety, but he did not want to flee with the prospect of earning another I-told-you-so from Eddie's mother. Holding the horse under a tight rein now, he was determined to win this fight.

One man's determination to be alone with his girl proved to be a weak defense against Mother Nature. Moments later the storm came charging on a high wind breaking before a wave of driving rain.

While the horse pranced, Cale looked left and right. He spotted the ruins of a homestead cabin, and made a quick decision. He swung left and drove toward a weathered Conestoga wagon. Wheelless and resting on its side, the prairie schooner lay on a weed-grown track like a beached shipwreck with shredded sails. He drove past it to the abandoned cabin, and drew up. Jumping out of the carriage, he helped Eddie down. Like the old wagon, the cabin was a derelict, too, with north-facing log walls listing away from years of battering by winter winds. He tied the horse while Eddie took shelter under a section of sod roof that had not yet caved in. Cale joined her there, his new hat splotched by rain.

The brunt of the storm hit hard. Heavy raindrops sent up puffs of dust like bullets until the ground was soaked. Then rivulets of muddy water slithered away while lightning crackled overhead.

Cale and Eddie smiled at one another. He did not know how to put his thoughts into words, but there was a measure of security in the two of them standing close together while observing the storm from a position of safety. Summoning up his nerve, he put his arm around her shoulders. She did not pull away. To his great surprise, she reached around his waist and drew closer. He felt the soft warmth of her body. A dizzying, unnamed emotion coursed through him as though that lightning bolt had found him. If ever a desert fantasy had come true in his life, this was it.

Standing side-by-side, they watched a fierce rainfall slanted by wind. When the storm blew through, a lingering rain smell carried the scent of sage. The wind abated and the hard rain let up. Diminished to a sprinkle, soon the squall was gone.

Cale and Eddie stepped out of the cabin, silently emerging from the ruins of an unknown pioneer family's hopes and dreams. Cale looked around. The failed homestead was marked by weather-split, sun-bleached logs, a caved-in dirt roof, and the ruined wagon.

"I wonder what brought settlers to this place," he said.

Eddie pointed to a break in brush, marking the banks of Ute Creek fifty yards distant. "They may have planned to irrigate. A ditch would bring water here . . ." Her voice suddenly thickened with sorrow. "Oh, Cale, I miss my father so much. I think about him every day."

Cale put his arm around her and drew her to him.

"He probably knew why this homestead was abandoned," she went on, "and, if he were here, he could tell us." She looked around, blinking away tears. "Settlers might be buried on this place, somewhere . . . in forgotten graves."

Cale listened as she repeated accounts of homestead families, stories she had heard from her father. In that era emigrants trekked West with no more than an overloaded Conestoga, a few head of livestock, and the clothes on their backs. They came to hew cottonwood logs for a cabin, to hunt and to fish, to garden, to tend animals—to make a home. A grueling westward journey brought them to a marginal existence here.

Where Thomas Pauls succeeded, most failed. Pauls had the foresight to dig out a reservoir long before water rights were ruled by statute. His vision of the future was rewarded. Stored water gave him a margin of safety unknown to other ranchers, now unattainable by any of them.

Cale and Eddie, two intruders in the after-storm silence of this funereal site, looked up at a full rainbow curving over the eastern horizon.

" 'Seven colors of the spectrum arch high into the sky'," Eddie quoted a favorite poem, " 'to chase away earthly gloom, drab and dry'."

Cale was still mulling over tales of the pioneers of her father's generation when she recited the verse. He looked at her questioningly.

"I read about rainbows in a book of science from my father's library," she said. "Somehow, I don't know how, the colors are intensified by the heat of summer."

Cale thought about that as they gazed at bands of bright colors in a perfect half-circle—a symbol of hope, he thought, amid the ruins of a homestead where all hope had been lost. He looked over his shoulder. To the west, the setting sun blazed.

"Fire in the rainbow," he said.

Eddie nodded slowly, and then smiled at him a moment before they embraced.

Cale drove the carriage away from the old homestead to the wagon road. He turned north. Rutted tracks on this stretch of road paralleled the creek. A mile and a half farther, he pulled off to the side. He climbed out and helped Eddie down. Their hands clasping, she held on a moment longer than necessary. They smiled, and once again glanced skyward. In the last few minutes the rainbow had faded and disappeared.

Carrying the picnic basket, Cale led her to the clearing he had seen earlier from the road. The site was a sandy bend in the creek, a private place sheltered by a stand of chest-high willows. Now they discovered teepee rings and a lean-to shelter fashioned from woven willows.

"Looks like someone else favors this campsite," Eddie said.

Cale conducted a brief search. He saw no signs of ashes or bones. "Not lately," he said.

Spreading an oilcloth tarp he had found under the seat of the carriage, Cale covered the rain-dampened sand at the water's edge. Ute Creek flowed slowly here, sending out soft ripples to reflect the sky. In the aftermath of that sudden and violent storm, the air was still fragrant with the pungent scents of desert sage and wet soil.

Eddie knelt. She opened the wicker basket and took out a red-checked cloth. Spreading it on the tarp, she brought out matching napkins and flatware, placing them with care as though setting a fine table.

Cale reclined on an elbow. He watched her until she became aware of his attention.

"Something on your mind, Cale?"

"You."

"Flattery," she said with a dismissive wave of her hand. She gazed at him. "Something is worrying you."

"Reckon so," he conceded, a bit unsettled to hear his mood so readily named.

"What is it?"

Cale pursed his lips while framing his reply. A moment passed before he told her the reason for an elegant noon meal hosted in the Colorado House by Henry Taylor.

"Cale!" Eddie exclaimed. "Cale, that's wonderful!" She studied his face, her own expression sobering. "But it's troubling you, isn't it?"

"I keep thinking about Joe Gilmore," Cale said. "Those are big boots to fill. Bigger than mine."

"Oh, Cale," she said. "Don't compare yourself to him."

"Other folks will," he said.

"Sheriff Gilmore had to start somewhere, didn't he?" she asked. "Cale, don't you worry. As soon as you get your feet on the ground, and people see that badge on you, they'll forget all about Joe Gilmore." She added: "Sheriff Cale Parker. I like the sound of that."

Cale shook his head slowly. "Folks in Red Rock miss Joe. They're still calling your rented house 'the sheriff's house'."

"I know," Eddie said. She thought a moment. "Cale, when I first heard the news Sheriff Gilmore was leaving Red Rock, I went to Mister Pittock. I wanted his opinion."

"Opinion? About what?"

"I wanted to know if Cale Parker would be considered for the position," she replied, "over Buster Baldwin."

Cale studied her.

"It's true," she said. "I did ask him . . . exactly that."

"I believe you," Cale said. "What did Pittock say?"

"He told me it was a foregone conclusion," she replied.

"What was?"

"That the sheriff's badge would be handed to Buster Baldwin," she said. "That's what Mister Pittock said. But I knew better, didn't I? And so did the county commissioners."

"All they know is Mister Taylor recommended me and Heck for the jobs. . . ."

"You will be a far better sheriff than Buster Baldwin," she said. "Deep in your heart, you know it is true. Don't you?"

He gazed into her eyes. He wanted to kiss her, but sensed it was too soon. He had never been energized by a woman's praise before, and his confidence soared. For the moment he was able to push away the feelings of inadequacy that had been clogging up his mind.

Too modest to say so aloud, even to Eddie, Cale knew she was right. He would make a better lawman than

Baldwin. Not that he did not have a great deal to learn—but that was true of any new job. His experiences of riding alone in the desert, and then making rounds in town with Gilmore added to his confidence. He remembered the sheriff telling him serious crimes in town were rare and arrests few, most related to drunken fist fights, husband-wife disputes, theft.

Cale reflected on all of that now. He would be accepted if he performed well as a lawman, as Eddie had said. In time he would earn respect. He breathed easier. The "position" that had towered over him had been cut down to size. He figured he could handle matters that came before him as sheriff of Red Rock, after all.

Eddie did her level best to avoid staring openly at Cale, but an overblown standard for feminine modesty seemed silly to her now—or worse, affected and pretentious. She found herself gazing at him while they sat beside the creek, and forced herself to look away. Water clouded by the downpour flowed by, gentle as a whisper. Their conversation had ended for the moment, and a comfortable silence settled over them.

They exchanged a smile. Eddie had never been kissed before, and found herself wondering what it would be like to be kissed by Cale—at once hoping he would not try, not yet, for that would only prove her mother was right about his intentions.

The scar on his face was still scabbed, she noted, but it was healing. In time the wound would be no more than a fine line crossing his jaw and cheek bone. It did not detract from the fact that he was a very handsome and vital young man.

Eddie's thoughts meandered like a stream coursing

through a meadow. She had never felt this way before, and yearned for the moment at hand to stretch far into the future. Just thinking about Cale was satisfying in a way she never could have imagined. Her experiences with eligible men were limited to talking to seasonal hired hands on the ranch—men her mother called "saddle tramps"—and brief, passing conversations with Red Rock townsmen during shopping trips to Red Rock. Even so, she recognized unique qualities in Cale.

Fire in the rainbow. She had seen him gazing at the rainbow, and knew he was giving thought to what she had said. He had voiced a keen observation. That was another quality she liked about him. He listened. After considering her words, he offered ideas of his own.

Above all, she sensed determination in him. The trait set him apart, a driving force emanating from within, just as her father's acuity and physical strength had separated him from other ranchers. Her mother had admired and honored those qualities in the man she had married. Why on earth did she fail to see the same traits in Cale Parker?

Today, before leaving the house, Eddie had made a decision. She decided to keep the unwanted attentions of Buster Baldwin to herself. She knew Cale would be thrust into a supremely awkward position if he were aware of Baldwin's crude pursuit of her. Now that Cale would in all likelihood be promoted to high sheriff, a confrontation between the two men could flare into violence. If Cale was drawn into a fight that she somehow triggered . . . ?

The possibility of it alone was more than she could bear. In that moment it occupied her mind so completely that she missed Cale's whispered words.

"What?" she asked, gazing at him as though just now awakening.

"I love you, Eddie."

She stared, trembling within. No man had ever declared his love for her. She had never shed tears of joy in a man's arms. Holding on for dear life now, she savored both in the strong embrace of the man she loved.

She pulled back, seeing his wild expression. In that moment she discovered something else about Cale—her tears frightened him. Despite herself, she smiled.

"What's wrong?" he asked in alarm.

"Nothing . . . nothing."

"You're crying. And laughing."

"I know," she said. "It's my way."

"Your way of what?"

Her emotions surging, she wiped her cheeks. "My way of saying it," she said, and gazed into his eyes.

"Saying what?"

"Oh, Cale, I love you, I love you, I love you." She moved into his arms again.

They held one another, neither speaking until he whispered: "I want to be with you forever, Eddie."

"Forever," she repeated, a word right for this moment. She cast a question to the heavens. "What am I to do?"

"About your mother?"

She pulled back. "Cale Parker, you are reading my thoughts without my permission."

"You've done that to me," he said, grinning.

"Sometimes I think we've known each a long time," she said. "It's a feeling I can't explain."

"Don't try," he said. "What about your mother?"

"I know her all too well," Eddie went on. "If I tell her we are in love, she will say we have not known one another long enough. It is infatuation, a puppy love soon to fade. That's what she'll say."

"Let's try to prove her right."

"What?" Eddie exclaimed.

"I know my love for you is real," Cale said. "Nothing can bust it. Your mother will know that, too, if we give her time to get used to the notion."

Eddie thought about that.

"Tell her we are courting," Cale went on. "Tell her you expect me to come calling."

"I know you are right," she said. "But this will be hard on her."

"Losing you?"

Eddie nodded. "That is how she sees it. Besides worrying about me, Cale, she lives in pain. Every day is a day of pain."

"Tell me what happened to her," he said.

Life for the Pauls family changed forever the day Marietta was thrown from her horse. Flung against the top rail of a pole corral, she tumbled to the ground where she lay as still and limp as a rag doll. That awful moment was forever fixed in their memories. From that day on, conversations among the Pauls were framed in one of two contexts—"before the accident" or "after the accident".

It had happened without warning or precedent. The tame mare had spooked. Whether the cause was a fluttering butterfly, a gust of swirling dust, a slithering snake, a leaping grasshopper—no one would ever know. Rearing and twisting, the horse had suddenly bucked, pitching Marietta. She had slammed into the rail and fell to the ground.

Carried gingerly into the house by her husband and Spud Jenks, she was placed in her bed and tended. She could not be comforted. Sobbing in her pain and paralysis, she wished for death. Her children cried.

Nothing had changed the fact that Marietta had lost all sensation from her hips to her toes. The only feeling ever to return was burning pain. From the day of the accident to this day, pain in her lower back was the one constant in her daily life. That, and the devotion of her eleven-year-old daughter.

Eddie's chief memory of the aftermath was her father weeping to exhaustion, a strong man bowed, inconsolable. A week later he left his children and the ranch in the care of Spud Jenks, and took his wife to doctors in Denver. From there, they traveled to Kansas City. The prognosis was unanimous. Damage to lower vertebrae was extensive, every medico reported after their tapping and pin-pricking examinations. Bruises and abrasions would heal, but nothing could be done to restore sensation in the lower half of her body. Marietta Pauls came home to the Rainbow Ranch in a wheelchair.

The knowledge that he had done all that could be done to mend her brought no satisfaction to Tom Pauls. He was a man accustomed to shaping his own trail in life, but this one defied him. Neither the strength of his body nor the force of his will made her whole again. A dark and cold sorrow came over him. In a sense, the paralysis of Marietta confined them all.

"Through those years," Eddie said now, "I cared for her. Then, after father died, she announced we were moving to Denver. I shouted at her. I didn't mean to. But I know my mother. She would devote her energies to climbing the tallest social ladder while searching for a suitable husband for me. In time I would marry and care for my own children with Mother looking on from her wheelchair, telling me what to do." Eddie drew a ragged breath. "Oh, Cale, I feel horrible about saying it, but . . . but don't I have the right to set my own course?"

He reached out, and took her hand.

"I've never said that to anyone," Eddie said, at once relieved and troubled. She leaned against him. "Not even to my brothers."

On the way back to Red Rock, she broke a long silence. "What are you thinking about?"

"You," he said, casting a quick smile at her.

"Why, Cale," she said in theatrical exaggeration, "you must think about me all the time."

"Every blamed minute."

"There you go again," she said, "talking like my father." She asked: "What else are you thinking . . . the truth this time."

"I was going over simple arithmetic."

"Arithmetic," she repeated. "What do you mean?"

"If my arithmetic is right," he said, "you and I share a birth year."

"You're seventeen?" she asked in surprise.

He nodded.

"I thought you were older," she said.

"So did Joe Gilmore," he said. "He thought I was twenty when I applied for the deputy's job."

"Lying to the sheriff," she said, shaking her head. "Cale, that's a crime."

"Keep it under your Sunday best hat."

She paused. "When were you born?"

"June Twenty-First," he replied.

Her eyes widened. "I was born on June Twenty-Fourth!"

"I'm older than you are," Cale said.

"I was raised to respect my elders," Eddie said, deadpan. "Don't worry. I won't tell anyone you lied to the sheriff."

* * * * *

Red Rock Signal

Methinx our neighbors to the south have good reason to believe a certain poisonous creature embodies nature's revenge for the brutal Spanish conquest of the region. The creature is feared by all. What is it? Can you guess? Read on, dear reader, to discover the identity of said monster.

In our modern era we know the golden arachnids by their Latin name, *centruroids sufferus*. The fossil record indicates they have skittered across the face of the earth for millions upon millions of years, slender pincers and deadly stinger unchanged. Simple residences in Mexico feature front porches and back steps paved with glazed tiles. These tiles are not merely decorative. Too slippery to climb, they are the first line of defense.

The next line of defense involves the necessity of shaking out one's boots every morning. Give your sombrero a firm slap, too. In addition, S&RG train passengers have learned by bitter experience to peer under the seats before sitting down. As we know, the ferocious sting of these insects can kill a child and inflict immeasurable pain on an adult.

With such power, comes great legends. One tells of the "death cell". In 1884 a certain Pedro De Baca of Durango, Mexico, was jailed for a horrendous crime—the murder of a child. He denied all guilt. Therefore, in accordance with local custom, he was placed in the death cell where no criminal had survived a single night. When morning came, his jailers were amazed to find him alive. Pedro De Baca had lived with killer insects all night, and thus at sunrise was declared to be innocent. He was set free. Such is the tale of justice south of the border.

Have you surmised the identity of this terrifying species? If you answered SCORPION, you are correct. Whether you believe the above account to be factual or fictional, beware of the scorpion's stinger. Faster than lightning and more potent than the desert rattler's venom, it is quite real.

While addressing mysteries of the natural world, let us now dispel two stubborn myths. Not true, modern science assures us, is the belief that owls hoot loudest at the crack of dawn for the purpose of awakening roosters, thus explaining why those domestic cocks crow at first light.

Secondly, the belief that birds high in the sky are merely the shadows of invisible birds is also false.

Cale took Eddie to her door, and drove the carriage to the livery. He helped Wade Powell put the horse up. They rolled the carriage into a covered shed alongside the black landau. All the while images of Eddie filled his mind. Vivid daydreams were interrupted when he was hailed by a man crossing Fifth Street.

"Thought we had this thing figured out."

Cale turned. He saw Buster Baldwin approach the livery. "Figured what out?" Cale asked.

"You get my meaning," Buster said.

"Do I?"

He drew up. "Hell, yes. I told you to stay away from them womenfolk, didn't I? I seen you and Miss Pauls in that high-wheelin' carriage, don't think I didn't. I'm telling you again. Stay away from Miss Pauls. Stay away, or you'll be out of a job, *pronto.*"

"One of us will be," Cale said. *"Pronto."*

"What the hell are you talking about?" Baldwin demanded.

Cale did not answer.

Baldwin moved a step closer. "Parker, if there's something I'm supposed to know, spill it."

Cale turned and walked away—or started to. Behind him, Baldwin lunged. One big hand grasped his shoulder. Cale tried to pull away. Boots tangling, his own momentum shoved him off balance. He was unable to duck a looping punch. Baldwin's fist grazed his jaw. Arms swinging to regain his balance as he staggered backwards, Cale went down. He landed on his backside, hard. He saw Baldwin standing over him, hands on his hips.

"To hell with you, Parker," Baldwin said. "Turn in your damned badge. Turn it in, and get out of Red Rock. If I see you in town after today, you'll be looking through the bars of a cell." He wheeled, and strode away.

Cale got to his feet. Brushing dirt from his trousers, he saw Wade Powell. The liveryman stepped out of the shed housing his carriages, a look of disgust lining his brow.

"Next time," Powell said, "keep your feet under you. Like this." He came up on the balls of his feet and raised his fists. "Get up on your toes, kid. Give that palooka a battle, not some kinda sissy shoving match."

Cale acknowledged the advice with a silent nod.

"To tell you the truth," Powell said, glancing down Fifth Street after Baldwin, "I don't think that lard-ass wanted a fight. He got in one lick, and marched off in a hurry. If you'd kept your feet under you, you could 'a' hammered him."

Cale made no reply.

Powell studied him. "You don't have one idea what I'm talking about, do you?"

Cale shook his head.

"Kid," the liveryman asked, "do you wanna learn?"

Cale thought about the beating handed out by Griff Monroe, and now his embarrassment over a poor excuse for a fight with Buster Baldwin. He knew Powell was right. Baldwin had practically run from him, as though fearful of what would happen when Cale got back on his feet.

"I want to learn."

In the privacy of the livery barn, Powell taught his student principles of the sweet science. First came posture, then footwork, then boxing techniques.

"Flex your legs at the knees," Powell said. "That's it. Now move from side to side, fists up, elbows in. Smooth, quick. Like this. Get comfortable. Don't worry about getting hit. Your opponent won't hurt you if you're moving away from his next punch. See how I'm up on my toes, knees bent? Just like a ballerina."

Powell paused, looking at Cale over his fists. "Hell, you've never seen a ballerina, have you? Didn't think so. Best athletes in the world. Smooth as oil, swift or slow, they move with complete control of their bodies. Boxers should take lessons from ballerinas."

Cale imitated Powell's moves as best he could. He was surprised by the grace of this man—and the quickness of his fists.

"Block a punch, sidestep a jab," Powell said. His fist shot out, followed by a right cross—both missing by an inch. "Take your opponent's haymakers on your arms or shoulders. Not much power in wild-ass punches. With a brawler like Baldwin, all you gotta do is step inside. Cut his range in half, and he won't hurt you. You may get bruised up, but you won't go down."

Powell moved closer to demonstrate. "Lean forward a little. Come on, get comfortable. Flex those legs. Move. Move inside. Closer. Come on, closer. That's it. Now plant your feet and throw an uppercut. Like this. Quick. Straight up. Now, go low. That's it. Follow the uppercut with a punch below his belt buckle. Put everything into it, and you'll knock the breakfast out of him."

By lantern light, Cale punched a feedbag suspended on a rope looped over a beam. He practiced until he earned some approval from the pugilist. "Practice, practice, practice," Powell said. "Work on your steps. Find your shadow on the wall, and practice some more."

Footwork was more difficult to master than punching, Cale learned, lateral steps more important than head-on charging. Power comes from the legs, Powell stated repeatedly, and if the feet were out of position, every punch was weak or misdirected.

"Work these moves on a palooka like Baldwin," Powell said to his sweating student, "and he'll eat dirt."

"Edna, are you doing this to defy me? Is that what you want? First, you forsake me. Now, you defy me."

Even though the tears were as predictable as her mother's reaction, Eddie wept, too, after announcing the pending courtship by Cale Parker. Seeing tears on her mother's lined face, Eddie struggled to control her own emotions. Above all, she wanted to avoid arguments and re-criminations. But did she have a choice? She wondered about that now more than ever. In the past her mother had set the agenda for every heartfelt discussion between them.

"No, Mother, I am not defying you. I love Cale. He loves me."

"Love! You're barely seventeen. What do you know of love?"

"I know what it means to me," Eddie replied. "And I know I'm in love with him."

"You know nothing of true love," Marietta insisted.

"If our love is true," Eddie said, remembering Cale's advice, "it will last. Our courtship will prove it. Isn't that what you have always told me?"

Outmaneuvered by that answer, Marietta was speechless for the moment. She had often advocated impossibly long, chaperoned courtships as a means of protecting her daughter from smooth-talking drifters and hired cowhands, men offering blue-sky promises to a girl who had never traveled more than a horseback ride away from home and hearth.

"This is the first time you have ever been alone with a man," Marietta said, "and now you want to marry him. What kind of sense does that make?"

"Cale and I plan to give ourselves time to get to know one another," Eddie went on. "Time for you to get to know him, too."

"Edna, believe me," Marietta said, "you're far too young to know what you're doing. He wants one thing from a pretty young woman like you, and one thing only. After he gets it, he'll leave you in a cloud of dust. Then where will you be?"

"Mother, you are wrong about Cale," Eddie said. "He is

a good man." She drew a deep, weary breath. "I've asked you before, and I'm asking again. Give him a chance."

"I've seen enough," Marietta said with a shake of her head, "to know Carl Harper's no different from all the other ranch hands drifting through Red Rock County."

"Mother, his name is. . . ."

Marietta drew a ragged breath and interrupted her daughter. "According to the gossipmongers of Red Rock, he doesn't even own a saddle horse and war bag. He arrived on the underside of a S and RG freight car. Tramps ride the rods, Edna. Tramps. Now that Joe Gilmore's gone, Carl Harper will return to a tramp's life. Mark my words. . . ."

"Mother," Eddie broke in, "his name is Cale, not Carl. Cale Parker. Not Harper."

"I don't care what name he goes by," Marietta said with a tone of finality. "I won't allow him to come sniffing around here, sneaking up behind us like he did on our ranch road. If he tries another stunt like that, Edna, I'll send him away. I know this is difficult for you to understand at your age, but it is for your own good."

"Would you say that," Eddie asked, "if you were talking about Sheriff Cale Parker?"

Chapter Twelve

"What the heck, Heck."

Heck Jones grinned. "Let's give this wild bronc' a ride, pard."

With a handshake and no more discussion than that, Cale and Heck made their decisions. They kept their morning appointment with Henry Taylor in the lobby of the Colorado House. There, fortified by mugs of coffee and half a dozen pastries, they accepted his offer.

Conditions of employment for the Red Rock sheriff and deputy sheriff positions included a probationary term of thirty days. Upon expiration of that time period, the commissioners were scheduled to meet for evaluation and review of the performance of both candidates. Following that, an official ruling would determine whether the appointments would be deemed permanent.

Joined by the banker, Joshua Everts, Cale and Heck mounted the staircase with Taylor. At the landing, a hallway to the right led to his suite. They followed him in, their footfalls muffled by thick carpeting.

Cale had been told by Joe Gilmore that suites on the top floor of the hotel were reserved. Finely appointed rooms were held for wealthy ranchers, railroad barons, and trophy hunters from back East. Signaling their approach by telegraph, adventurers touring the great American West from all points of the compass passed through this outpost of civilization on the high desert.

Cale figured Gilmore's descriptions had been exaggerated. But now he drew a breath. He had never seen the likes of it.

With walnut paneling, gold-plated fixtures, and elegant maroon wallpaper trimmed with gold leaf, the imposing silence here underscored the solemnity of the occasion. As though entering a sacred place nearly concealed in deep shadows, the far-reaching import of the moment sank in when Cale entered the suite. Heck came in a pace behind him, hat in hand as his eyes darted left and right, up and down, awestruck, too.

Three other commissioners waited there, cigars fired and brandy snifters in hand. With the door closed, five gents in their tailored finery eyed two ruddy-faced young men clad in the garb of ranch hands—simple cotton shirts, vests, and jackets and trousers of wool. After introductions, the men were silent amid posh, cushioned furnishings. Old doubts reared up as Cale came under their stares. He wondered again if the order was too tall, if he was too young and inexperienced for a position of this level of responsibility. The urge to flee surged through him.

He attempted to shove misgivings away, remembering Eddie's unqualified expression of faith in him. Her earnest sincerity had bolstered him then, and now he felt a measure of confidence as he recalled her words and even the sound of her voice. Besides, he thought, in thirty days he would decide if this job was right for him, or if he was right for the job.

"Are we ready, gentlemen?" Taylor asked.

Joshua Everts brought a Bible from an end table. He was a man of great, dark muttonchops, a bushy style of sideburns that emphasized his high brow and somber expression. He was dressed, Cale noted, in a pin-striped suit and a vest with a silver chain and fob.

Taylor stepped forward to administer the oath. As directed, Cale raised his right hand and placed his left hand on the black-covered volume. He vowed to uphold the laws of Colorado, even at his own peril. Then came Heck's turn. Using his full name, Beverly Hector Johnson took the same oath.

After handshakes and congratulatory comments were exchanged all around, Taylor made the next announcement. "Gentlemen, as you know, we have before us one last, unpleasant chore. No time like the present. We're agreed on that, aren't we? Good. Now, if you will accompany me to the sheriff's office, we shall dispense with this piece of business."

Taylor clearly held sway over the commissioners. With hardly a word exchanged between them, they left the Colorado House, new sheriff and deputy in tow. In bright sunlight they walked along the boardwalk on Broad, the cluster of well-known men drawing looks from residents, shopkeepers, and the drivers of passing wagons.

Cale saw Taylor unbutton his coat and pull it open, showing a holstered revolver. The chore awaiting, he realized as they drew near the sheriff's office and cell-block, was to inform Buster Baldwin of his official status—citizen of Red Rock. He was not the sheriff now, nor had he ever been, the glowing editorial in the *Signal* notwithstanding. Cale figured Taylor had planned a show of force. Strength in numbers gave these businessmen confidence. Their presence was meant to overwhelm hostility in a stubborn man when they marched into that office, guns holstered, but showing.

Looking to his left, Cale glimpsed Baldwin through the plate glass window. He manned the desk that had been Joe Gilmore's for a decade. On the glass a five-pointed star was painted in black, edged with gray. Past that emblem, Cale saw the seated figure of the man who would not be sheriff.

Taylor opened the door. The commissioners filed into the sheriff's office behind him. Cale and Heck brought up the rear.

Cale saw Baldwin look up, briefly startled by the sudden invasion. Then he stood. Scowling defiantly, he planted both hands on the desk top in a gesture of ownership.

"Mister Baldwin," Taylor announced, "our duty as commissioners calls for us to officially notify you of termination."

Baldwin's scowl deepened.

"Your pay envelope is at the bank," Taylor went on. "Pick it up at your convenience. At this time we are ordering you to remove the badge. Hand it to Sheriff Cale Parker. If you need a few minutes to gather personal items from the office. . . ."

"Bastards."

Cale saw Taylor stiffen.

"Mister Baldwin," Taylor said evenly, "follow my instructions. Your service is hereby terminated. You have no further business here. I advise you to take your leave peaceably."

"You bastards," Baldwin said again. He turned his attention to Cale, but made no move to unpin his badge or yield his position behind the desk.

"If force is required," Taylor went on, "you shall be placed in irons and locked in a cell. Is that how you wish to spend your last day here, Mister Baldwin?"

Buster Baldwin's gaze was lit by hatred as he turned to Taylor again. "You've had it in for me ever since I got roped into that damned posse. I never should have rode with you. It was illegal for a Colorado lawman to cross that border into the territory, and you knew it. You knew it before you murdered them men. . . ."

This was too much for Henry Taylor. "You bear full responsibility for those cowhands dying in Caliente, Baldwin. If you hadn't pulled the trigger before my order, we'd have taken them peaceably and left them hog-tied."

Baldwin cursed him again, his voice thick with rage.

"Take off that badge," Taylor repeated. When Baldwin did not obey, he raised his voice. "Take it off! Take it off, and get out of here!"

The rancher's outburst surprised Cale. Like the others, he kept his gaze on Baldwin. The stand-off lasted a full half minute. In that time no one spoke or moved. At last Baldwin reached to his lapel. He unpinned the sheriff's star, grimy fingers fumbling with the release. Finally pulling the badge free, he flung it down on the desk. It caromed off the top and struck a brass spittoon on the floor with a hollow *clink*. That must have given him an idea, for he stepped out from behind the desk and picked up the badge. Spitting on the star, he held it over the spittoon and dropped it in. With a last look thrown like a stone, Baldwin's gaze swept past the silent onlookers to Cale. "Fish your badge out of there, you back-stabbing son-of-a-bitch."

Cale realized Buster Baldwin saw betrayal in him and blamed him for all that had gone wrong. The threatening tone in his voice needed no other utterance to convey that message. Baldwin grabbed up his hat and stomped out, leaving the door standing open behind him.

Cale looked after him. Outside the doorway, a figure loomed on the boardwalk. Ben Pittock had observed the angry exchange, and now the newspaperman watched Baldwin's swift departure.

Eddie heard heavy footfalls resounding on the pine planks leading up to the porch. She stepped into the hallway when the doorbell sounded. Moving swiftly to the front door, she opened it. She was not expecting a visit from Cale, but she hoped to find him there. Her welcoming smile faded. She drew back. Her caller was Buster Baldwin.

"Don't shut the door on me," Baldwin said. He added: "Please."

Eddie gazed at him, trying to read his intentions. She had never heard a please or a thank you from him before. He had removed his hat, and now held it before him, eyes downcast in a pose of humility that was almost comical in its exaggeration.

"I know you don't think much of me, Miss Pauls," Baldwin said, "since we got off on the wrong foot, you and me, and I ain't here to ask nothing from you. I mean, I ain't gonna ask much from you."

"What is it?" Eddie asked.

"I need work," he replied. "I figured since your pa died you might could use another hired hand on the Rainbow. I've worked cattle on the biggest ranches in Kans-ass, and I know ever' ravine and water hole on your spread 'cause I have rode your land, top to bottom. I'd make a danged good outrider for the Rainbow Ranch. So I'm a-wondering, Miss Pauls, if you'd consider putting in a good word for me with your brothers, fine gents that they be."

Eddie was surprised to hear a note of sincerity in his voice. As they stood there facing one another, she realized Baldwin had very little understanding of the depth of her revulsion toward him. Now he stood before her, a man visibly unclean and ripe with foul odors, trying in his own way to make amends. This, even though an outright apology for his threatening behavior lay well beyond his comprehension.

"Next time I speak to Roger and Alex," she said now,

"I'll tell them you are seeking ranch work. Hiring and firing is up to them."

"Obliged, miss," he muttered. "Tell 'em I've worked cattle. Tell 'em I've worked steers aplenty. Your brothers, they won't ree-gret hiring me to ride herd on Rainbow stock. Not for one single minute, they won't."

"I'll tell them," Eddie assured him, and watched him turn and walk away, head still bowed. She closed the door.

"Edna, Buster Baldwin is the wrong man for you."

Eddie turned, only then aware of her mother's presence. Looking at her in the wheelchair stationed in the middle of the hallway, she saw a distraught look etched into a deeply lined face. As never before, Eddie realized Marietta had shifted her endless capacity for worry from fear for her daughter's safety to the prospect of her marriage to the next saddlebum who knocked on their door.

"I know, Mother. I know."

Red Rock Signal
LAND PURCHASE OF NOTE

Your faithful editor has learned of the largest range and livestock purchase in the history of Red Rock County. The source of the following information is one of the principals. All facts are confirmed, published exclusively herein for readers of the *Signal*.

Mr. Henry Taylor quietly struck a bargain with Mr. Aaron Miller. Both gentlemen are noted ranchers of the region. As longtime *Signal* readers will recall, Mr. Miller resided on his ranch until recent years when his family repaired to Denver.

T-BAR-H JOINS CIRCLE M

We are advised Circle M Ranch holdings are to be combined with the neighboring T-Bar-H, with all livestock running under the Taylor brand from this day forward. Terms of the sale are inclusive. All structures, land features, springs and seeps, and water rights now fall under the ownership of Henry Taylor. With this purchase, his T-Bar-H Ranch becomes the largest horse and cattle operation in the county, and no doubt one of the most significant land holdings in all of Colorado. . . .

Ben Pittock went to press, knowing this massive land deal had not even been whispered, much less rumored until details were completed, deeds signed over. Pittock had been awarded the privilege of breaking the story in the *Signal*, the biggest news lead to hit this county in a long time. He had been flattered when Henry Taylor came to his shop and confided in him. After the large-scale theft of cattle from the Circle M, Mr. Miller had reached an obvious conclusion. He simply could not manage the operation of a large ranch long distance without exposing his holdings to theft and, via telegraph, had agreed to sell to his neighbor, Henry Taylor.

In return for taking Pittock into his confidence, Taylor had asked him to keep the land deal secret until all parties were ready for a public announcement. The editor agreed, already calculating the number of extra copies he would print for an issue bearing dramatic front-page news.

In truth, Pittock was caught up in it. The more details he learned from Taylor, the more he was convinced this transaction was beneficial for the town and the county as a whole. Pittock learned Taylor was intent on protecting his holdings by demanding more law enforcement in the county. He was not alone. Cattle and horse thefts, and heightened fears of violent robberies in general, had led to calls for more lawmen. The calls had grown louder with the sudden departure of Joe Gilmore.

Pittock favored the plan Taylor presented to the county commissioners even though it included a tax hike. The added revenue made room in the county's budget for the hiring of more deputies—Bill Dixon and Luke Scanlon—in addition to Heck Jones.

"Good and fearless men," was how Taylor described the new deputies.

With Cale Parker serving as sheriff, Taylor went on, a total of four lawmen would provide outlying ranchers and local residents alike with more protection from the criminal element than ever before. Taylor also confided to Pittock his plan to send Circle M riders packing, along with the long-time ranch cook out there.

"A few rustlers might be riding with honest cowhands," he said. "The only sure-fire way to root them out is to clean house."

Cale gathered his three deputies in the sheriff's office—his office now, he realized as he glanced around the interior—and pointed to the county map on the wall while discussing assignments. With Henry Taylor looking on, Cale described his experiences while patrolling the south and north sectors of Red Rock County. He made no mention of his escapade with Alma Juliette Collins. On the subject of women, he figured every man for himself was the rule. For the rest of it, Cale wanted to be certain the newly appointed deputies understood what they were getting into when they pinned on the badge. It was lonely work, he said, and not every rancher, homesteader, or mustanger welcomed visits by a lawman. While a deputy's pay was greater by far than a cowhand's, so was the risk to life and limb.

Heck chimed in, citing the errant long-range shooting of Colly Collins as an example.

"Most folks are friendly enough," Cale said, and remembered a cautionary remark from Joe Gilmore. "But some will hate you on general principles." He went on to describe his encounter with Griff Monroe. Cale bore scars from the confrontation, and admitted he had not been prepared for violence. He should have been. Now he cautioned the deputies to be careful in their encounters—and to be on the look-out for Monroe, a wanted man.

"As far as we know," Taylor interjected, "Monroe left Caliente with his saddlebags stuffed full of cash. He's long gone by now, likely."

Neither Scanlon nor Dixon was dissuaded by the prospect of trouble on the open range. Both men accepted the badges Cale handed to them, along with a handshake from a new sheriff wishing them well. For now, Scanlon would ride the south sector, Dixon the north.

Cale turned to Heck. He outlined a revised scheme for dividing the county into law enforcement districts. He assigned Heck to a middle ground between the north and south sectors, a region that included the town itself. Heck was instructed to range freely in and out of Red Rock.

This plan came at Taylor's suggestion. In addition to covering outlying farms and homesteads, Heck would conduct regular patrols in town with Cale. If trouble erupted, both would be in reach. Two lawmen on duty would not only discourage troublemakers in Red Rock, Taylor pointed out, but would demonstrate the benefits of the new tax levied by the commissioners.

After the deputies left, Taylor said: "You've already grown into the job."

Cale turned to the rancher.

"Yesterday you were a deputy taking orders," he observed, "and today you're high sheriff giving them."

Cale shook hands with him, and they parted. Alone in the office, he still felt uneasy about the gunfight down in the territory. Once again, though, he had made no comment to Taylor. It was in the past. *Time to let go of it,* Cale thought. Pinning on the sheriff's badge meant he was taking on new responsibilities—not from yesterday, but from this day forward. He had battled uncertainties and self-doubts, taking heart when the new deputies had readily accepted his leadership. They had listened intently, respecting the fact that he spoke from experience. Cale was satisfied they could get the job done.

He spent much of the afternoon in the office. The place was dirty. After dusting with an ostrich feather duster, he cleaned the sooty lamp chimneys, and then swept the floor. He explored drawers and pigeonholes in a roll-top desk. After reviewing the Reward dodgers, he found the itinerary of the circuit judge, and posted it. He filed county and state forms in alphabetical order. The papers were impossibly jumbled, some upside down, others bearing crude marks in ink on the signature lines. He leaned back in the swivel chair. For the first time, he realized Buster Baldwin had a secret. The man was illiterate.

Cale inspected weapons chained in a rack mounted on the wall. After a search he found the key on a ring with the cell keys. He field-stripped and cleaned the bores of each rifle and shotgun, and took an inventory of stored ammunition. Finished with those chores, he faced one last task. In this dry climate, every door scraped, squeaked, or squealed. Finding an oilcan on a shelf under the gun rack, he lubricated locks, latches, and hinges, and carefully wiped off the residue. Then he washed the window. Afterward he inspected the cell-block, a windowless place bearing odors of chaw and soured vomit.

Show the tin. In the afternoon, Cale left the office to run an errand. Townspeople gazed at him. He realized this occasion marked his first patrol as sheriff of Red Rock. He was nervous, at once determined not to let uncertainty show. Following Joe Gilmore's example, he met stares and sidelong glances alike with a smile and friendly greeting. If he had not fully realized it before, he was aware now of Gilmore's words: Wearing the badge, he had said several times, changes a man's life. Cale caught an inkling of it now. Every passer-by seemed to know him. He sensed their expectations ran high.

"Half of this damned job," Gilmore had said on another occasion to Cale, "is letting folks see you. Make the rounds, show the tin, and folks sleep better at night."

Now Cale walked to Fifth and headed toward Wade Powell's livery. In his pocket were four Red Rock county vouchers, redeemable-by-merchant at the bank. Signed and neatly folded, one was endorsed to himself and three more covered his deputies. The county provided mounts and gear for the lawmen, and the current horse contract had been awarded to Powell. Cale discovered the paperwork was overdue, neglected since the departure of Gilmore.

"Parker!"

Cale heard that familiar, agitated voice, and looked over his shoulder. It was Buster Baldwin. The man must have been watching for him, Cale thought, noting the location of their earlier confrontation was nearby. Now Baldwin crossed the street, face flushed, neck bowed.

"You ain't gonna run me off," he said, clenching his fists. "No, you ain't."

Even at this range Cale smelled whisky on his gusting breath. "Pick a fight with me, Buster, and I'll have to decide."

"Decide what?"

"To run you off," Cale replied, "or lock you up."

Baldwin eyed him. "Big shot now, ain't you?"

"I'm the sheriff, Buster."

"You done stole my job out from under me," he said. "You and that damned Taylor. He's nothin' but a crook."

"Take your complaints to the county commissioners."

"Fancy-pants crooks, ever' damned one of 'em," Baldwin said.

"Crooks," Cale repeated, figuring any man Buster Baldwin disliked fell into the category.

"They dance to Taylor's tune, don't they?" Baldwin demanded. "Well, don't they?"

When he edged closer, Cale smelled a bitter odor of cheap whisky mingling with the stench of body odor.

"Looks like you're dancin' that jig, too, Parker."

"Walk away," Cale said.

Baldwin raised a fist, and moved a pace closer. Cale saw a drunken appetite for violence in the man. Primed for a fight, Baldwin was determined to take this feud to the conclusion he wanted.

Cale reached to the brim of his new hat, and tossed it aside. Baldwin did the same, flinging his floppy felt hat away. Growling, he advanced one pace and then another, his right fist cocked. A sudden squint in his bloodshot eyes gave him away.

Side-stepping the punch, a clumsy right, Cale bobbed away. He raised his fists, elbows in. He waited, watching those bleary eyes, and then ducked a looping haymaker, that punch telegraphed, too. Baldwin threw himself off balance with it, and staggered.

Cale quickly moved inside, legs bent at the knees. He took a glancing punch high on the shoulder. Bending at the waist, he planted his feet. After one feint, he let go with an uppercut. The short, swift punch had all the power of his upper body behind it in its upward drive. His fist connected to Baldwin's beard-stubbled chin. His head snapped back. Cale saw Baldwin's eyelids flutter. The man stood there like a stout target, blood trickling from his upper lip. His fists sank. This was the opening Powell had demonstrated while sparring in the barn.

Coming in low again, Cale positioned his feet. He cocked his right arm back, and drove his fist deep into Baldwin's soft abdomen. The punch below the belt drew a pained sigh, a deep, wounded sound Cale had never heard from a man before. He stepped back, lowering his fists. The fight was over. Baldwin's mouth hung open, lip bleeding. He stared helplessly at Cale. Dropping to his knees, he toppled over, moaning as he doubled up.

Cale picked up his hat, frowning as he inspected a smudge of dirt on the crown.

"Told you he'd eat dirt."

Cale turned. He saw Wade Powell step out of the livery barn.

"You took that palooka down," Powell said. "You took him down by the book, one page at a time, damned if you didn't."

Cale lifted his gaze to Powell. "He came at me like you said he would."

"Saloon brawlers are all alike," Powell said. "A pugilist can take a brawler apart any day . . . like you just did." He clapped a hand on Cale's back. "Ready for your next lesson?"

As Eddie had secretly hoped, Cale came calling after sunset on that hot day. In anticipation of his visit, she had made a batch of cookies and squeezed lemons. When she saw him coming on Seventh, she went to her mother's room and invited her to join them on the porch for cookies and lemonade. Marietta declined with a shake of her head.

Eddie and Cale sat outside on the shaded porch, both of them acknowledging the fact that neighbors would notice this pairing, that folks in town would talk now, and the rumor mill would churn and grind.

"Can't stop folks from talking, can we?" Eddie said.

Cale took her hand. "Let folks talk until they're blue in the face. I want Red Rock to know I'm in love with the prettiest girl of all. Now that I think on it, if they don't talk about us, I will."

Eddie smiled, and squeezed his rough hand.

They sat quietly. Noises drifted to them—the low rumble of passing wagons in town, a dog barking in the distance, a child's shout.

"Your mother knows I'm here?"

She nodded. "As you might guess, she disapproves."

"Of me?"

"You, me, us," Eddie replied. After a silence, she said: "Before the accident I worked at her side . . . we washed laundry . . . milked cows . . . churned butter . . . gathered eggs. . . ." Eddie breathed deeply. "Memories keep coming back to me, Cale. Once . . . I must have been eight or nine . . . I found Mother on the verandah. She watched Father working with a saddle mount in one of the corrals by the barn. I remember a certain look in her eyes. She loved him very much, you know. When I came to her, she cupped her hand at the back of my head, and drew me close. I remember her warmth . . . a child safe and secure with her mother."

Cale held her when she wept. "Through all these years, Eddie, she has been safe and secure with you. I would not want anything to change it."

Cale walked through town after midnight, up one boardwalk and down the other as he tested the locked doors of shops lining Broad. No vehicle or pedestrian traffic at this hour. On the far end of Broad, across the railroad tracks, he heard raucous sounds. Discordant music and raised voices drifted through the night air from saloons and dance halls.

Before accepting the job that required a badge, he wandered through establishments offering liquor, games of chance, the company of men at a bar, of women in rooms upstairs. Now he recalled Gilmore's words. *Wearing the tin brands a man. Don't set foot in a saloon after nightfall . . . unless you're summoned by a barkeep, a barkeep down on his knees, begging you to settle the issue.*

It's one thing to keep the peace, Gilmore had said on another occasion, but it's something else to go hunting for trouble where men do their drinking, gambling, fighting, whoring. Now Cale followed Broad back to the S&RG depot. Quiet here, he could hear water dripping from the tower a hundred yards farther down the tracks. Lamplight in the depot drew him to an open window. He spoke briefly to the telegrapher. Then he crossed the platform toward hand carts and a canvas-topped station wagon. Halting abruptly, he quickly knelt behind that short-coupled vehicle. Ahead something had moved. By starlight Cale had glimpsed a figure ducking down, or thought he had. Whatever or whoever it was, the figure disappeared in a tangle of shadows at the far end of the railroad platform. Cale drew his revolver, and eased back the hammer. He suspected he had glimpsed the stocky figure of Buster Baldwin.

After their fight, Cale had tried to help Baldwin to his feet. Still in pain, Baldwin had swatted Cale's arm away, roundly cursing him. Cale had stepped back and watched him stand. Hunched over from the punch to his solar plexus, Baldwin had wiped blood from his lip. He had picked up his hat and uttered one last threat before staggering away.

I'm a-gonna get you, Parker. Don't think I won't.

Now a chill ran up Cale's back. The shadow moved again, this time bumping into a wheeled cart. Cale leveled his revolver, not knowing if he had heard the rattle of a cart's axle or a gun cocked. In a split-second decision, he drew aim and squeezed the trigger. Instead of a bucking handgun and the immediate, ear-busting discharge he expected, Cale heard only a metallic *click*. Fear surging through him, his left hand swept over the hammer, swiftly cocking the single-action Whitney.

He aimed and pulled the trigger again. Another harmless *click*. In that instant Cale believed he was a dead man. Even in the dim starlight Baldwin could not miss at this range.

"Don't shoot! Don't shoot me!"

Cale heard the plea from the night shadows. That voice sounded familiar, but he could not place it until he saw a man emerge from hiding. The figure approached warily, hands up, walking in a gimpy stride.

"Don't shoot me!"

"Rollie?" Cale said. "Is that you?"

"Yeah, it's me," he said, coming out of night shadows. "Damned glad you didn't shoot."

Cale swallowed hard. "So am I."

In the span of a few seconds Cale had believed his day was done, that he had walked into Baldwin's ambush where death was one trigger pull away. In the next instant he had almost killed an innocent man. Sweat broke the chill coursing through his body. His deepest emotions seemed ready to explode with volcanic force. He could barely stand. He took one full breath, and then another, steadying himself. What if . . . ?

Cale managed to gather his wits. "What are you doing here, Rollie?"

"Waiting for the next night freight outta Red Rock," he replied. "I aim to ride the rods to Caliente, and then head north in a passenger coach . . . Wyoming, Montana, somewhere north."

"North," Cale repeated, mystified.

"I'm getting outta this desert country," Rollie said. "Outta the whole damned state. . . ."

Cale heard the man's voice trail off. "Why?"

"Didn't you hear the news?" Rollie asked. "I got fired. Me, along with all the other Circle M hands, drew our time."

"But you don't have to leave the state," Cale said. "Or even the county. Plenty of ranchers will hire a good cook. I'll have my deputies ask around for you. . . ."

Rollie broke in: "Cale, you don't understand. I gotta leave."

He could not read Rollie's expression. He sensed tension—and fear. He had never pegged Rollie for a fearful man.

"You're wearing the sheriff's star now," Rollie observed

when polished metal caught starlight.

"Yeah," Cale answered.

"Baldwin outta the picture?"

"Yeah."

"Taylor shoved him off the cliff, didn't he?"

"Rollie," Cale asked, "what's going on?"

The cook did not speak until Cale prodded him again.

"I saw them," he replied, as though that explained everything anyone needed to know.

"Who did you see?"

"Griff."

"Griff!" Cale repeated. "Griff Monroe?"

"Big as life."

"Where?"

"In the Circle M horse barn," Rollie answered. "I heard voices. I came in through the tack room. I saw them out there in the runway."

"Saw who?" Cale asked.

"Griff Monroe," Rollie said again. "Him and Mister Henry Taylor."

Chapter Thirteen

Eddie learned far more about the Circle M ranch cook than she ever wanted to know. For one, she learned Rollie snored with the rhythm and volume of a steam-powered saw. For another, instead of a steam engine's black smoke, he pumped green flatulence into the air.

Rollie was a man who traveled with a wad of refried beans, his saddlebag fare laced with roasted chiles and diced onions. This dark brown mass was packed in a lard bucket, the whole shebang wrapped in back issues of the *Police Gazette* and the *Signal*. Eddie learned these little-known facts not from personal experience with the man, but from Cale.

In the morning, she answered a knock on the front door and found Cale there, a worried look creasing his brow. Still in her nightdress, she grasped his arm and pulled him into the hallway.

"What's wrong?" she whispered, closing the door. "Cale, what's wrong?"

He recounted last night's events. He had talked Rollie into sleeping on the floor of his rented room—a loud and fragrant mistake he discovered too late. All night he dreamed of a sawmill amid stacks of lumber and mountains of beans, beans, beans. . . .

"Mister Taylor and Griff Monroe!" Eddie repeated. She shook her head in disbelief. "Is Rollie sure?"

Cale nodded. "He's sure."

"What on earth were they talking about?"

"Rollie doesn't know," Cale said. "But he's running

205

scared, I can tell you that."

"Scared?"

"Taylor told him no man should die this close to hell," Cale replied, "and Monroe shoved him out of the barn at gunpoint. Rollie rode out of there without looking back."

"What did you say to Rollie?" Eddie asked.

"Told him I'd help him," Cale replied. "But I have to do something quick. He won't stay in Red Rock. I figure when we hear the whistle of the next night train, we'll know he's gone."

Eddie still struggled to comprehend all of this. "Mister Taylor in cahoots with Griff Monroe? Cale, that can't be. Can it?"

Standing there in the sun-washed front hallway of the sheriff's house, they mulled over what they knew, and guessed at what they didn't. Cale heard for the first time about Taylor's persistent efforts to buy the Rainbow Ranch.

"I've told him twice the place is not for sale," Eddie said, "but he doesn't believe me. He doesn't believe Mother, either. He even offered to marry her . . . a business deal, as he said to her."

In the end, Cale and Eddie bumped up against imponderables. Were both Monroe and Taylor guilty of stealing cattle to sell at the Caliente stockyards? Did they conspire to send four men to their deaths? How did the purchase of the Circle M fit into an alliance between Griff Monroe and Henry Taylor?

Stymied, Eddie asked: "Cale, what will you do now?"

"That's the question that brought me to your door," he replied.

"What do you mean?"

"I don't know what's going on," he answered. "Not yet. But I might need witnesses later."

"You mean, Rollie?"

Cale nodded. "The Rainbow Ranch is short a cook. If Rollie was there, he could earn his keep. . . ."

Eddie finished his thought. "And lay low for a while?"

Cale nodded. "Rollie knows how to run a cattle operation. When he's not wrestling the stove, he could give your brothers a hand with the ledger book."

Eddie gazed at the man she loved. "You want me to take him to the home ranch, don't you?"

Ben Pittock accepted twelve tins of oysters in exchange for a subscription to the *Signal*. He took inordinate pleasure in this swap. A case of oysters had recently been stolen from an S&RG freight car. So he had heard. If anyone were to ask, of course, he had no knowledge of it. In Pittock's experience, barter was commonplace, part and parcel of the newspaper business. As a man with an eye for bargains, he enjoyed this aspect of his profession. A week ago one dozen eggs was the subscription rate paid by a homesteader. A pail of butter from a farmer was the price a month prior. Shoe repair made another good swap. The only item of value Pittock refused outright came from the telegrapher—an open ticket on an S&RG passenger coach. He would sooner walk.

Working from scribbled notes accumulated over several weeks, Pittock composed his next "Methinx" column. He set type, and discovered several column inches of blank space. It was axiomatic never to leave empty spaces on the page. This one had several holes. After muttering over it, he loosened the form and experimented with type positioning. Half an hour later the result was unlike any scheme he had ever seen. Not all the news fit to print, perhaps, but the print fit the news.

Pittock stepped back, eyeing his creation. He was proud of the imaginative flair, a design and headline meant to catch the eyes of readers.

NEW & NOVEL USES
For Back Issues Of The *Signal*
Our Treasured Fountain Of Information
In The Great State Of Colorado
County Of Red Rock

Starting the morning fire
Padding for hard bunks
Bustle enhancement
Window cleaning
Wiping soot from lamp chimneys
Applying boot polish
Shining up those darned boots for Sundays
Covering the floor of the chicken coop
Reading material in the outhouse
More reading material, anywhere, any time
Wrapping cooked food
Insulation on the north wall
Wallpaper
Derailing locomotives

No question about it. This arrangement of type was daring. The text was interesting, if Pittock said so himself. With the list capped by that humorous last line, folks in town would be chuckling and talking about it for a good long time. Some ladies might grouse over the bustle reference. Pittock might have to offer a public apology. So be it. In truth, he welcomed complaints, believing the only deadly fate faced by a newspaperman was to be ignored. The

greater the affront, the more attention to come his way—
and the more sales to follow. Let us find out what that rap-
scallion is up to now! was a cry of outrage from the literate
citizenry virtually guaranteed to sell more copies of his next
issue.

So went his theory. No matter how this column was received by *Signal* readers, printing "Methinx" at a crazy
angle would capture attention. An imaginative approach
might bring in more revenue—whether in cash for advertising space or swapping goods and services for subscrip-
tions.

Pittock concluded his column with a note. He addressed
Dear Readers in a deadpan request to bring their sugges-
tions for additional uses of the Red Rock *Signal*, New &
Novel, to his print shop.

A lesson in the pugilistic arts was interrupted when Heck
Jones returned to town. Sweating, Cale emerged from the
barn as Heck turned out his saddle horse in the corral at
Powell's livery. After Powell led the horse into a stall in the
barn, Cale and Heck engaged in the favorite pastime of
cowhands. Leaning on their elbows on the top rail, they observed the milling horses and pointed out strengths and
weaknesses of each animal. After every horse in sight had
been evaluated, Heck gave his account of patrolling ranches
and farms on the outskirts of town. He had introduced himself, and all had gone well with folks welcoming him on his
first patrol.

Heck paused. He gave Cale a deliberate once over,
noting the missing gun belt. "The most nakedest critter
walking the earth," he observed, "is a lawman without a
gun."

Cale agreed. He offered Heck makings. The deputy

shook his head. Cale talked while he rolled a smoke. "Monroe busted that old Whitney I've been lugging around. All this time it was about as dangerous as a claw hammer."

"Griff Monroe busted it? How?"

After leaving Eddie this morning, Cale had taken the revolver to the gunsmith's shop one block off Broad. The problem was quickly found—a damaged firing pin rendered the gun inoperable. It happened, as Cale told Heck now, when Monroe had yanked the Whitney from the holster on his cartridge belt and thrown the gun into the rocks. Cale fired the cigarette. It was an odd thing, he told Heck. He must have pulled the trigger six times during the Caliente fight, after all. In the heat of that one-sided battle, he had been too riled to know his gun had misfired. Damage to the weapon had never occurred to him. Later, the oversight had prevented him from gunning down Rollie.

Heck listened, reaching the obvious conclusion about a misfiring revolver. "Now that you're high sheriff, maybe you oughta go and buy yourself a new side arm."

Spending that much money ran against his upbringing. The Whitney would be repaired within the day. Even so, Cale acknowledged that he had given some thought to the purchase of a revolver.

"The gunsmith handed me a Colt fresh out of the box," Cale said. "Forty-Five caliber, blued steel, walnut grips, double-action smooth as pie. Best six-shooter ever made, that Colt is powerful enough to knock a man off his feet at fifty paces."

Heck said: "Reckon it's the ideal weapon for a man in your line of work."

"My line of work," Cale mused.

Heck eyed him, awaiting elaboration.

"I keep thinking about those four men lying dead down there in Caliente," Cale said at last. "Then I think about what happened when I drew on Rollie last night. I pulled the trigger, Heck . . . twice at point-blank range. I'd have killed him, sure. Now I'm thinking. . . ." His voice trailed off.

"Thinking what?"

"Being a lawman is not my line of work."

Heck was amazed he would even give voice to such a notion. "When it comes to wearing the sheriff's star, you're the man for the job. Everybody in Red Rock knows it."

"Not everybody," Cale said.

"You mean a yokel like Buster Baldwin?" Heck scoffed. "What about a gent like Henry Taylor? Or those other commissioners? They want you on the job, Cale. To a man, they want you behind that badge."

Cale dropped his cigarette. He ground it into the dirt with the toe of his boot, and faced him. "We need to talk about Taylor."

"What about him?"

A look of disbelief crossed Heck's weathered face when Cale repeated Rollie's account of events in the Circle M horse barn. Disbelief gave way to acceptance. Rollie had no reason to lie. If anyone was lying about the theft of cattle in Red Rock County, it was Griff Monroe. That supposition left Heck with the same knotted questions about Henry Taylor that Cale and Eddie had come up against.

"What are you gonna do now?" Heck asked.

Cale had felt haunted by that question ever since the incident with Rollie on the railroad platform last night. He faced the task of questioning Henry Taylor. When and where, he did not know. None of his haphazard training had prepared him for a dilemma like this one. Questioning a county commissioner in a criminal matter? Cale doubted that even in his ten-year career Joe Gilmore had ever faced a task like it.

Thinking of Gilmore gave Cale a glimmer of an idea. Leaving the livery, he walked alone to the telegrapher's window in the S&RG depot. He wondered if any warrants were out for Griff Monroe, and sent a query to Joseph Gilmore in care of the U.S. Marshal's office in Denver.

After confirming the message had been received, Cale made his decision. He looked for Henry Taylor, soon determining the rancher was not in the Colorado House or anywhere else in town. He caught up with Heck in a canvas-roofed café on the far end of Broad.

"I aim to ride at first light," Cale said, pulling out a chair as he joined him. "I'll be gone two days, maybe three."

"Where're you headed?"

"T-Bar-H."

"I'll ride with you."

Cale shook his head. "You need to make the rounds here in town . . . show the tin, as Joe used to say."

"You figure Taylor's out there on his ranch?"

"All I know is, he's not in town."

Heck thought about that. "What if you don't cut his trail out there?"

"Then I'll ride on to the Circle M headquarters," Cale said, "where Rollie saw him."

"That's it," Heck said suddenly, and pushed his chair back.

"Where are you going?"

"To tell Powell I'll need a fresh horse in the morning," Heck replied. "I'm riding with you."

"I appreciate your offer," Cale said, "but Red Rock needs a lawman. When I'm out of town, you're it." He added: "We swore to it, remember?"

Heck started to protest, but was silenced when Cale turned and signaled a waitress.

"Let's get some supper," he said.

Charley came back. That was the first thing Eddie noticed when she returned to the home ranch with Rollie. Ears perked at them, the big gelding looked no worse for wear as he stood alone in the sturdiest corral on the place. Charley whinnied and watched them ride past the corral, two horsebackers angling toward the oversize double doors of the horse barn.

Alex let out a whoop from the ranch house. Roger came behind him, shouting a greeting, too. Hatless, the brothers bounded down the stairs and jogged across the yard.

Eddie dismounted in the runway of the barn. She helped a grimacing Rollie out of the saddle, and introduced him. As she suspected, Roger and Alex knew him by sight from Saturday shopping trips to town over the years. Now they vigorously shook Rollie's hand to welcome him formally to the Rainbow Ranch.

Rollie gritted his teeth against pain in his knees. "I appreciate your friendly howdies. Looks like you fellers are stuck with me for a spell. Your sis can sit a Western saddle all day, but this here spot where we're standing in this here barn is as far as I can go without resting up for a few days. Pitiful, ain't it?"

Leading the mounts into empty stalls, Roger and Alex pulled off saddles, blankets, and bridles. They listened while Eddie recounted the events that had brought them here on horses rented from Wade Powell. The gazes of her brothers abruptly swung to her, both of them struck silent.

Taylor?

She saw the same look of disbelief on their faces that Cale must have seen on hers. The notion of Henry Taylor in cahoots with Griff Monroe was a hard one to swallow. Yet no one disbelieved Rollie. He was an honest man, one who obviously feared for his life.

"I always knowed he was a damned crook! Didn't I tell you? Taylor's nothing but a damned crook!"

Eddie turned in surprise. Amid a steady stream of curses, a stocky figure emerged from a horse stall at the far end of the runway. He had been shoveling manure, and now he threw his shovel down, cursing again as he stomped toward them. That end of the barn was nearly dark, but there was no mistaking the man behind that voice.

"Clean up your mouth, Buster," Roger said. "There's a lady in the barn."

"I heard what you was saying," Buster Baldwin announced when he reached them. "Ever' damned word proves Taylor's a crook. Don't you see? Taylor and Monroe sold off stolen cattle. How else could Mister Henry Taylor scrape up enough cash to buy the Circle M?"

Eddie listened in amazement. Baldwin's lip was swollen around a deep cut, not yet scabbed over. He had been in a fight a day or two ago, she figured. Now Baldwin's bitter accusations, laced with profanity, were bizarre, too wild to be true. That was her first thought. She had to admit on second thought that his theory explained recent events in Red Rock County.

Breaking the silence, Baldwin bellowed: "Don't believe me, do you? Hell, let's get this whole deal out on the table. I know what you Pauls think of me. Don't think I don't. Shoveling manure and chopping firewood for a meal or two . . . that's what I'm good for now that I ain't wearing the badge. That's how you Pauls think of me, don't you?" He drew in a breath. "If you're so damned smart, you tell me."

Alex asked with an edge in his voice: "Tell you what, Buster?"

"The reason Taylor stocked the sheriff's office with men beholden to him," Baldwin said. "You don't know? I'll tell you. The bastard done it so's he can ramrod law enforcement in this county, that's why. . . ."

Eddie had heard enough. She cut him off. "The new sheriff is an honest man."

Baldwin cast a sarcastic look at her. "Sweet on him, ain't you?"

"Listen to me," she said evenly. "Sheriff Cale Parker is honest. He'll go by the law. That's all you need to know."

"Well, I reckon he'll have a chance to prove that," Baldwin said. "Plenty of chances, if my guess is right."

Folding his arms across his chest, Roger spoke up now. "What guess is that, Buster?"

"Hell, it's plain as the nose on your face," he replied. "Mister Henry Taylor ain't done. He'll make another deal as crooked as a coyote's back leg."

Roger pressed him. "What are you talking about?"

"Now that the famous Tom Pauls is gone," Baldwin said, "Taylor aims to get his hands on this spread, water rights and all. Then he'll own just about every acre of irrigated land from here to hell-and-gone."

Rollie had listened in silence. Now he turned to the Pauls brothers. His gaze swept past Roger and Alex, landing on Eddie.

"Has Mister Taylor tried to buy this here ranch since your pa died?"

Eddie nodded.

Baldwin barked out a harsh laugh. "What did I tell you? Huh? What did I just tell you?"

"I reckon we gotta give Buster a mite bit of credit," Rollie said when no one else spoke up. "That new sheriff oughta go after Taylor."

Riding from dawn to sunset, Cale drew in sight of the T-Bar-H headquarters. He paused before urging his mare forward. Smoke plumed from the stovepipe in the roof of the cook shack. A few horses were in the corral, tails switching and ears perked, all of them looking at the approaching rider. Cale expected to see Henry Taylor come out of his house, warmly greeting him as he had in the past. This time he did not. No one else came out, either. Cale rode past the ranch house. He reined up at the door to the cook shack and mess hall, and hailed the place. A stove lid clanked inside. Floorboards creaked, and the door opened.

A red-faced, paunchy man stepped out, soiled towel in hand. Taylor had introduced him months ago. Cale did not recall his name, but he recognized the T-Bar-H cook, a well-fed gent with a tangle of gray hair on the top of his head.

"Sheriff," the cook greeted him.

"I'm looking for Mister Taylor," Cale said.

"Ain't here."

"Where is he?"

"He don't tell me where he goes."

"When was the last time you saw him?"

"Dunno," he said. He paused, and then refined his answer. "Maybe four, five days ago."

"And you don't know where he is now?"

He shook his head.

"Is he riding with T-Bar-H riders?"

"That's none of my business."

"Looks like it is your business," Cale said.

"How's that, Sheriff?"

Cale jerked his head toward the stovepipe. "Looks like supper's on, or getting ready to be."

"Sheriff, if you're hungry," the cook said, "I'll fry up steak and spuds for you."

Cale eyed him. That was not what he meant, and he figured they both knew it.

"Don't bother," Cale said, turning his mare. "I'll wait a spell over yonder."

Riding toward a stand of cottonwoods, he felt certain the cook's terse answers to his questions covered lies, or half truths at best. Dismounting in a patch of grass, Cale thought about possible reasons for the man to lie. If he was lying, that probably meant Taylor had told him to. For the first time Cale wondered why the rancher had never invited him to stay overnight in the bunkhouse. Perhaps it meant no more than it seemed—all the bunks were taken. If Cale was the suspicious type, though, he would consider another answer. Taylor did not want a lawman mingling with his riders. Why? As Joe Gilmore had once said, a fair number of men in these parts worked as cowhands, but in truth they had ridden the Outlaw Trail to get here.

Cale heard horses. A pair of cowhands rode in from the north, and presently another trio cantered in from the southeast. Two more riders hazed an injured steer, probably for slaughter. Over the next hour Cale saw more horsebackers arrive, his view dimming in the fading twilight. He counted a total of nine men, all of them looking toward him as they filed out of the horse barn to the mess hall where the cook served their supper. Taylor was not among them. After nightfall pale lamplight glowed in the bunkhouse windows, and Cale figured T-Bar-H hands were in for the night at the home ranch.

He rode away, recalling a distant campsite he had used while on patrol. A luminous night, the light of a three-quarter moon easing over the horizon helped him find it. After tending his horse and hobbling the animal, he bedded down on his blanket with his saddle for a headrest.

Cale arose before dawn. Leaving the T-Bar-H behind in night shadows, he made a hard ride to the Circle M. It was a long, hot day in the saddle. When the ranch buildings came in sight, he pulled back. He drew rein behind a sage-studded rise and dismounted, telescope in hand. Lying prone at the crest, he watched the place, occasionally observing through the magnifying lenses of the brass telescope. There was not much to see. No horses were in the corral, and one barn door stood half open. Nearby, the chicken coop was empty. On the south side of the house, the leaves of plants in a fenced vegetable garden were wilted.

The sweltering heat forced him off the desert hardpan. His mare needed water, and so did he. Idly wondering how sage and thin grass could survive here, he stood. Closing the telescope, he thrust the instrument into his saddlebags. He took the reins and led his mount to the ranch buildings. He turned her into the corral. At the nearby pump, he raised and lowered the handle, the mechanism shrilly squeaking and squealing until water gushed into the trough.

While the mare drank her fill, Cale walked through the main house and outbuildings. His footfalls resounding on bare floorboards, he confirmed his first impression. The house was empty, the cupboards bare, furnishings gone. In the barn, stalls stood empty, too. No sacks of grain were in the mow, and only a scattering of hay and straw was left behind.

Returning to the corral, Cale took off his hat and put it

on a corral post. He pulled off his shirt, boots, trousers, and long handles, and draped the dusty and sweat-stained clothes over the top rail. He lowered himself into the trough and leaned back in this great luxury in the desert. He plunged his head underwater, and came up blowing. The mare approached, sniffed at him, and moved away as if to say: You expect me to drink that stuff, cowboy, after you washed your stinking carcass in it?

Cale stood and looked at himself. He examined the faded bruises and lacerations on his chest and ribcage. The pain in his upper body had receded to the point where he no longer thought about his injuries every waking moment.

Mosquitoes found him. Slapping at the insects in gathering dusk, he vaulted out of the horse trough. He dressed, and then pounded trail dust out of a hat no longer new. He clapped the hat on his head, pulled a slice of jerky out of his saddlebags, and wandered around the place again, chewing.

A certain quietude had settled over this abandoned ranch. While he was not spooked by tomb-like silence, he decided against bedding down in the empty house. He had slept in the great outdoors from the time his parents had died to his first week on the job with the Union Pacific in North Platte, Nebraska when he finally had enough money to rent a room. In that time he had come to terms with the loss of his mother and father, and now sleeping under starlit heavens held an appeal that he felt but could not name.

Cale found a spot just beyond the pole corral where the mare stood, asleep on her feet. He had no sooner pulled off his boots and stretched out and he was asleep, too. From a great distance, so it seemed, the mare pranced and whickered.

"You ain't got much savvy, kid. You sure as hell don't."

Cale awakened, roused to a voice he had not heard for a

long time, a voice all too familiar. He opened his eyes. Night had passed. Looming out of a dawning sky, Griff Monroe stood over him, revolver in hand.

"I've been watching you since first light," Monroe said. He paused. "That's a good scar on your jaw. Want another one like it?" He drew his boot back, and kicked Cale in the ribs. "Do you?"

Cale rolled away, crying out against the surging pain. Memories coursed through his mind, agonizing remembrances of pain and humiliation. He tried to stand, but Monroe came after him. Placing a boot in the small of his back, he sent him sprawling.

"That's for starters. What's it gonna be? A kicking, or another pistol whipping?"

Cale looked up at him. More than a blast of pain, he had never felt such rage. "Fight," he said now through clenched teeth.

"Huh?"

"Fight me."

"What are you cryin' about?"

Cale got up on his knees. "Put the gun away, Griff, and fight like a man."

The challenge drew a smirk. Monroe tried to kick him again, but missed when Cale hastily crawled away on all fours. Hardly a dignified retreat, the maneuver brought a laugh of ridicule from Monroe.

Cale came up on his feet. Facing Monroe, he felt puny under the glowering stare of a thick-necked, broad-shouldered man he knew to be as strong as an ox. An idea came to him in that moment of wordless confrontation. His ribs hurt where he had been kicked, but the pain was not as severe as he let on. Wincing in an exaggerated way, he clenched his jaw and taunted Monroe.

"Afraid, Monroe? Afraid of a fight?"

Griff Monroe swore. He holstered his gun. Unbuckling the cartridge belt, he hung it on a corral post. In the next instant he spun around and rushed him.

Cale had expected a move like that. Saloon brawls were often won or lost by the first punch. On his toes, Cale brought his fists up and bobbed away. Monroe rushed past him like a goosed bull. When the big man caught his balance and turned, Cale was there. He connected with a quick punch to Monroe's jaw.

Every move comes off the jab. That advice in the art of pugilism was Cale's latest lesson from Powell. Sting your opponent's face, he had instructed him, and bloody his nose with your jab. When he comes for you, mad as hell, fade away. Fade, and you'll take the power out of any punch.

Powell had been right about that. In short, stinging jabs to the face, Cale's knuckles broke his skin. Monroe wiped the back of his hand across his mouth and gingerly touched his nose. Seeing bright red blood, he looked at Cale in disbelief. Then came rage.

Cale back-pedaled, escaping his charge. Monroe was not fast, but his fist came hard. Cale absorbed a heavy blow on his forearms. He nearly went down from the force of it. No matter what Powell had said, a blow from Griff Monroe hurt. Monroe was a barroom fighter who expected his man to go down. His expression showed surprise when Cale danced away. Monroe lunged again, one fist cocked. Cale faked, and side-stepped him. Half turning then, he set his feet and threw a short, hard right. The blow to Monroe's temple knocked the look of surprise off his bloodied face and sent a hint of fear into his eyes.

"Had enough, Griff?"

Monroe swore and came for him again. This time he did not mount a blind charge, but moved slowly. He was intent on using his strength to manhandle Cale and shove him to the ground where he could administer another kicking. He discovered, too late, the hand speed and footwork Cale had learned from his mentor.

Cale's jab lashed out, his left fist tattooing Monroe in quick blows that splattered blood across his broad face. Baffled by this rapid-fire attack, Monroe halted, still alert, but confused. Cale saw the opening. He moved in. The price he paid was a looping punch on his shoulder, a blow lacking the power of Monroe's previous punch. Cale bent at the waist. He set his feet in the balanced stance Powell had taught him. He uncoiled his upper body like a spring wound tight, the force of it unleashed all at once. His fist caught the underside of Monroe's chin.

Cale saw his head snap back. Knees buckling, Monroe staggered, struggling to stand now. Hurt by the uppercut, the big man was unable to defend himself. Even though he saw it coming, he could not move to avoid the next punch. He watched helplessly as Cale reached back with his right arm and let go with all the strength he could muster.

Cale's fist drove into Monroe's abdomen below his belt buckle. Just like Buster Baldwin a few days ago, Monroe groaned and softly cried out. He went down like a sack of feed rolled off the back of a wagon. Bloodied while he lay at Cale's feet, Monroe's mouth stretched open in agony. He ate dirt as he labored for his next breath.

Chapter Fourteen

Red Rock Signal

After due deliberation and consideration of this matter, the soundest editorial judgment is, methinx, to withhold the name of the town in question. Some of you may have come to Red Rock from this place and will not wish to be reminded of a past life best left to the silent shadows of time. Those of you who have relatives living there may not wish to be associated with them. Either way, a number of you will recognize the following characterization instantly. None of you, methinx, will readily confess or even admit how you came upon such rude knowledge.

In this unnamed town every structure facing the S&RG railroad tracks, whether canvas or frame, is a saloon or gambling house, or worse. A carnival at full blast, these establishments wring currency from drunken men all night and every day. Faro, poker, chuck-a-luck, wheel of fortune, keno are the games played with $20 gold pieces for chips and the roof for a limit. So they claim.

The elements of this town are diverse, a tapestry of conflicts preventing harmony of any sort. Drunken cowhands and high-smelling buffalo hunters leap at one another's throats with the slightest provocation. Soldiers at the nearest outpost are scrappers, men in blue with nothing to do but drill or fight. Railroad graders hate freighters. Result, dear readers? Boot Hill is fully occupied in this town.

Public hangings are carried out weekly. One particularly notorious and murderous criminal demanded the attending preacher hang instead of him, and, when the subject came under further discussion from onlookers, the outlaw's argument nearly carried the day. Seems this preacher had lusted and coveted with greater frequency than anyone had previously known. The trap door no sooner dropped than the preacher skipped town.

The worst of it, though, involves the matter of water. Water? Yes, water, the lifeblood of desert and jungle. For it was known to all that the gent who drove the water tanker into the city limits was a saloon hopper. One barkeep pitching him into the street only sent our man lurching on to the next deadfall. The act was repeated in saloons open all night and every day until this gent had acquired a snootful.

Erratic at best, some water deliveries were never made at all. One lady discovered the driver reclining in the shade of his tanker, fast asleep in a drunken stupor amid clouds of flies. A former teacher of arithmetic (among the classics and other subjects) she knew what to do: Reduce the problem to a mathematical equation. Thus, the solution was numerical, readily solved.

How can this be? you may ask. First, she recruited assistants. The ladies on the gent's water route calculated the cost of cheap whisky, per ounce. Then, based on observation of their bleary-eyed subject, they calculated the quantity required to finance his binges. That determination made, the solution was reduced to a simple matter of re-scheduling home deliveries over a period of twelve days. Adjustments and re-calculations were factored into the formula, and from that day forward our man was prevented from accumulating enough cash any given day to pay for his next bender.

Now he could afford but a few drinks at a time, just enough rotgut to take the edge off his humor. He scowled and hung his head in a dog's misery, but with a brain pickled in alcohol the poor fellow never comprehended the calculations that broke his cycle of drunken binges. In short, this unnamed gent residing in an un-named burg served by the S&RG Railroad never knew what had been done to him. He knew only his misery.

"That cook farts out the gawdawfulest stink," Buster Baldwin said. "Smelling up the place like he does, what the hell's his chow like?"

Eddie overheard Baldwin complain to her brothers of rumbling flatulence from Rollie. The stench filling the bunkhouse, he reported, was as dangerous as methane in a coal mine, this foul effluvium a hundred times more offensive.

"I'm telling you boys," Baldwin said, "that stink will

knock an ox plumb off his hoofs. I sure as hell won't share no bunkhouse with him. A man could die."

Eddie marveled at the heartfelt sincerity of Baldwin's complaint, wondering how he could possibly separate his own reeking body odor from the gaseous by-product of refried beans mixed with onions and fire red chiles. Perhaps one stench neutralized the other in some bizarre chemical clash unknown to science.

True or not, she would hear no more of it. In the ranch house she spoke privately to her brothers. "Buster Baldwin has no place on the ranch."

Roger and Alex eyed her for a long moment.

At last Alex spoke. "Is there something we need to know, Eddie?"

"No," she said.

Roger asked: "Has Baldwin ever . . . ever done anything to you?"

"No."

Alex pressed her. "You sure, Eddie?"

"I'm sure," she said.

Roger and Alex gazed at their kid sister. Neither brother questioned her further. Baldwin did not belong here. That was that, even though the decision left them short-handed. The Rainbow needed an outrider, and the brothers considered posting a note on the board at the train depot.

The next subject to come under discussion was the hiring of a ranch cook. Not only on the home place, but a chuck wagon cook would be needed during fall roundup when seasonal hands were hired. If the candidate passed that test, he would be in line for year-'round employment.

The brothers respected Rollie's experience at the stove as well as his detailed expertise in the cattle business. They welcomed his advice regarding everything from compilation of tally sheets to weekly ledger book entries.

Thomas Pauls had always sweated out the pencil work himself, often working by lamplight late at night while his children slept. He never got around to schooling any of them in the art of budgeting and record keeping. He himself had learned from Spud Jenks.

As to Baldwin's complaint, the brothers sought Eddie's counsel. She urged them to hire Rollie, suggesting his diet would change once he exhausted his supply of pinto beans. In time he would find his way around the cook house kitchen and pantry, eliminating the problem of thunderbolts from dark, colonic depths.

Thus it was decided. While a range rider was still an unfilled position on the ranch, they all agreed Buster Baldwin was not the man for the job. Tomorrow he would be paid two dollars for the chores he had completed, fed a hearty breakfast, and sent on his way.

The next day Eddie rode one horse and led the other to Red Rock, returning both mounts to Powell's livery. After turning them out in his corral, she did not go straight home. She walked to Broad, turned, and went to the sheriff's office. Finding it empty, she backtracked, making her way toward Seventh until she was hailed.

She turned. Heck Jones came after her on foot.

"I was down the street a ways when I saw you heading away from the office, Miss Pauls," he said. He halted, and pulled his hat off his head. "Anything I can do for you?"

"I was looking for Cale."

His dour expression broke into a quick grin. "Figured as much."

"Can you tell me where he is?" she asked.

Perhaps she should not have inquired. She listened to Heck, and then bid him good day. Trudging to the house, tired and saddle sore from a long ride, she found herself worrying about Cale. Her mind conjured up gunfights and rattlesnake bites, any number of deadly situations that could be faced by the man she loved. By the time she mounted the slanting planks to the front door of the sheriff's house, she laughed at herself, or tried to. There was no denying it. Among other traits inherited from her parents, she possessed her mother's boundless capacity for worry.

Cale searched Griff Monroe's saddlebags. In one he found wadded clothes and spare ammunition for the Winchester rifle and revolver the man carried. Monroe cursed wildly when Cale appropriated the weapons and bullets. In the other saddlebag, among meager possessions—strips of beef jerky, tins, and a sharpening stone—was a blue Mail Pouch tin.

Cale stepped back. On a hot day, this discovery sent a chill up his back. Tracks left by a shod horse indicated Monroe had ridden in from the south. That meant he had come from the direction of the Diamond Bar. Cale turned to him.

"Have you taken up chaw, Griff?" he asked.

Monroe lay on his side on the ground, a big man bloodied, beaten. Hands bound in wrist irons behind his back, all he could do was curse Cale, and he was not yet done with that job.

Cale grabbed a muscular arm and yanked Monroe to his feet. "You favor *cigarillos,* don't you?"

Monroe swore at him again.

Cale said: "I figure you took this tin off Sam Aikens."

"You can figure any damned thing you want," Monroe said in a denial laced with more profanities.

"There's one sure way to find out," Cale said. "I'll take a

ride down to the Diamond Bar and ask Sam Aikens if he's missing this tin of chewing tobacco."

Cale heard Monroe swear with renewed passion when he shoved the tin into his own saddlebag. He turned to his prisoner. "Sam's all right, isn't he? Him and Chipeta?"

When Monroe answered with more curses, Cale went on: "Reason I ask, you seem to like hurting people. I figure you might have beat up an old man and his woman if they had something you wanted."

Monroe let go with a renewed string of profanities, this time his invective mixed with threats. Even with his hands bound behind him, the fight had not gone out of him, not all of it, for he lowered his head and charged, trying to head-butt Cale.

Dodging away, Cale allowed him as much room as he would a bull on the prod. When Monroe halted, cursing at the futility of further resistance, Cale moved in. He hooked a boot heel behind Monroe's foot and shoved him. He fell to the ground, landing on his backside.

Cale gazed down at him. "I'll leave you tied to that water pump. When I get back, we can talk about you and Mister Henry Taylor."

"Taylor. What about him?"

"You tell me."

"I ain't telling you nothing."

"Where is he?"

Monroe did not answer.

Cale glanced skyward. "I'll give you a couple days out here to think that over."

"Chain me in this damned heat," Monroe said, casting a desperate look at him, "and you'll be leaving me for dead."

"Seems fair," Cale said, "considering how you left me."

"I never left you for dead," he said. "You had water

and a horse . . . and shade."

"You didn't know if I was alive or dead," Cale said, "when you rode out that night."

"Hell, you was breathing," Monroe protested. "If I'd wanted you dead, you wouldn't be standing here, jawing at me." He added: "You can take that to the bank."

Cale studied him. "Griff, what do you have against me?"

"You're nothing but a cocky kid hiding behind a badge," he said. "Too damned high and mighty for your britches."

"Is that all?"

"Ain't that enough?"

"No, it isn't," Cale replied.

"I got nothing else to say to you," he said. His bloodied face screwed up when he added: "Except one thing."

"What's that?"

"You whupped me," Monroe replied. "Dunno how you done it."

"I used some pugilism," Cale said.

"Huh? Pugilism. What's that?"

"Want a re-match," Cale replied, "so you can find out?"

Monroe cursed him.

"If you whip me," Cale offered, "you can ride out a free man. Deal?"

"Go to hell."

"I'll let you blaze that trail," Cale said. He looked past the corral at the iron pump. "With jerky and a bucket in reach by that pump, you'll have food and water . . . enough to tide you over until I get back. From here, you're going to a jail cell in Red Rock. Then you can tell me about Taylor. I want to know about the money from Caliente, too."

"I said I ain't telling you nothing," Monroe said.

Cale rode out. With a glance back, he saw Monroe sitting on the ground where he had left him, wrist irons and leg irons secured to the pump. With some effort, Monroe would be able to get up on his knees and work the handle to draw water. He would be miserable, Cale figured, not only from that awkward position and the heat, but having to relieve himself where he sat.

Cale made a hard ride. When he drew in sight of the Diamond Bar, he stood in the stirrups to look ahead. He was wary of what he would find there. Monroe was a violent man, and Cale figured Sam Aikens, even though well past his prime, would not duck a fight or back down from anyone—over a tin of Mail Pouch or anything else. It was a bad mix.

Cale stared. Out of place on the Diamond Bar was a smoke-gray saddle horse in the corral. He watched the spirited animal high-stepping in a circle. Cale had never seen this one before, and wondered if Sam had purchased or swapped the mount from a passing trader.

He was much relieved when the cabin door opened and Cyclone sidled out, tail slowly wagging. Sam Aikens moved through the doorway behind his dog, lifting a gnarled hand as he called out to Cale.

"Howdy, young 'un!" Sam said.

Cale drew rein and dismounted as Chipeta edged into the doorway behind Sam. Cale approached the cabin until he saw Chipeta step aside. A third figure appeared there. Cale halted. He was surprised to see the tall, angular man who came out. Dressed in a dark, vested suit powdered with a coating of trail dust, Henry Taylor greeted him with a smile.

" 'Evening, Sheriff Parker."

Eddie baked a batch of sourdough biscuits, fried links of venison sausage seasoned with sage, and scrambled four eggs. Then she heated water for tea. With no animals to tend, she had overslept, awakened by calls from her mother. After helping her through her morning routine, Eddie wheeled her into the dining room and served a late breakfast.

This was not the first time she had awakened to see the sun on the wall. It was a slothful habit by ranch standards, one she had acquired from too much easy living in town. Following breakfast, she washed dishes, and cleaned the kitchen. Eddie felt restless, at once aimless. At the ranch there had always been plenty to do.

She told her mother of an unnamed errand, and walked to town shaded from the sun by a parasol. On Broad, she found Ben Pittock sweeping the boardwalk in front of his shop. She crossed the street and stopped there, noting his bruised nose. Then she demanded to know the name of the town he had written about in his latest "Methinx" column. Deadpan, Pittock refused to name either the town or the soused driver of the water tanker. He was clearly pleased by her interest, until she asked how a newspaper could possibly derail a locomotive.

"I figure the right folks will get the message," Pittock said.

Eddie left it at that and wandered closer to the mercantile window next door. She paused to gaze at the illustrated wedding gown, the real reason she had come here. As one who had scarcely given a thought to her wedding day, she was now preoccupied by it. Trying to imagine every detail of the ceremony, she could not stop thinking about "her day". She knew the reason for this fascination—Cale. Every time she thought of him, an eagerness swept through her body like a physical force. She felt certain Cale would ask for her hand in marriage, and she was equally certain of her answer.

"Making plans, Miss Pauls?"

Startled, Eddie jumped. She had been immersed in thought, too far gone to be aware of Ben Pittock's broom strokes bringing him close enough to look over her shoulder. She shook her head now, and faced him, cheeks hot.

The newspaperman had guessed correctly, of course. He knew it, too, she figured, for his great mustache lifted when he smiled at her. Embarrassed, Eddie tried to make small talk before bidding him good morning. She turned away, and crossed Broad again. On the other side of the street she headed down the boardwalk, parasol twirling over her shoulder.

She knew Cale would not be in town yet, not unless for some reason he had turned back and made a night ride to Red Rock. With that remote possibility all but ruled out, she hoped to catch Heck in the sheriff's office. It was a long shot, but perhaps the deputy had learned something about Cale's pursuit of Henry Taylor.

The office stood empty, door locked. She walked on, strolling to the S&RG depot, unoccupied, too, except for the telegrapher. She halted there. Her eyes went to the message board. She stepped closer. A folded sheet of paper bore Cale's name, the first time she had seen it written out with his new title—**Cale Parker, Sheriff**. She wondered what it could be, and decided to inform Cale the moment he returned to town.

Across the way the saloon district was quiet at noon. No doubt Heck was still asleep after a night of making his rounds and pointing drunks in the general direction of their beds.

Eddie lingered for several minutes. The railroad tracks pointed south where the barren plain stretched beyond Red

Rock to the far horizon. Cale was out there, somewhere, and she hoped he was all right.

"Mister Taylor, he done told me you're sheriff now," Sam Aikens said to Cale. "I was fixing to go to Red Rock to fetch you or one of your deputies. Scanlon came through a week ago. He wasn't here when I needed him."

"What happened?" Cale asked, his gaze moving from Sam Aikens to Henry Taylor, and then back to Sam.

"I done lost better'n half my herd to rustlers, that's what," Sam said. He added: "You tried to warn me thieves might come back. I should 'a' listened. Reckon I should 'a' bunked with steers instead of chickens."

Cale watched as Sam drew a ragged breath, an aged man on the verge of shedding tears. Sam went on to say that he had known something was amiss when his cattle scattered. In his search, he found earth churned by the hoofs of bunched steers. Twenty-five or thirty head were cut from the Diamond Bar herd, including breeding bulls, the heart of his livelihood.

"Mister Taylor, he done offered me a loan," Sam said, with a glance at the rancher. "I appreciate that, and I jest might have to take him up on it. Don't wanna go bust and sell out." His voice quavered. "What would I do then?"

Sam turned his head. He spat a thin, brown stream that missed Cyclone by a foot. The dog sniffed it, and backed away, tail between its legs. Chipeta watched from the door.

Henry Taylor had listened quietly, an expression of sympathy lining his brow. Now he turned to Cale.

"Raise a posse, Sheriff," Taylor said. "Run those marauding rustlers to ground like we did that bunch in Caliente, and maybe you'll recover Diamond Bar beeves before they're sold and loaded into cattle cars bound for the Chicago stockyards."

Taylor's gaze was steady, his deep voice confident, self-assured—and condescending. Cale nodded slowly in a perfunctory reply, for the first time knowing full well he was in the presence of a liar.

Chapter Fifteen

Uncertain of his next decision, Cale decided to play his cards cautiously, revealing one ace at a time. He figured Diamond Bar steers had been stolen by Griff Monroe, and Henry Taylor was somehow involved. Proving they committed the crime was another matter.

If Diamond Bar steers had been herded through the barren hardpan Cale had seen at this end of Circle M range, they would be difficult to track. It was guesswork, but, if Griff Monroe knew of a hidden spring out there, a small herd would virtually disappear from sight in the vast terrain. Monroe could tend the steers, and still use the abandoned headquarters of the Circle M Ranch as a place to meet secretly with Henry Taylor. When he was ready, he could drive them to Caliente with altered brands.

Now Taylor presented himself as a benefactor. Sam Aikens had no reason to doubt him. Cale did not have to be a banker, though, to see things differently. At this point, a subsistence loan to Aikens was little more than a down payment, leverage guaranteeing Henry Taylor acquisition of another ranch in the Río River drainage.

Cale turned to his mare. He opened his saddlebag and pulled out the blue tin of Mail Pouch tobacco. He held it up for the old rancher and Taylor to see.

"I arrested a thief at the Circle M," Cale said, and saw a fleeting look of alarm cross Taylor's face.

"Thief," Taylor repeated.

"Griff Monroe," Cale said.

Sam exclaimed: "Monroe!"

Taylor asked matter-of-factly: "What exactly did you arrest him for, Sheriff?"

"Assault on a lawman," Cale replied.

"You took a beating from him while back," Taylor said. "But I thought you just now called him a thief."

"He stole this tin from Sam," Cale replied. "I figure he rustled Diamond Bar steers. In my book that makes Griff Monroe a thief. . . ."

"Hold on there, young 'un," Sam interrupted. "Monroe never stole that tin from me."

"This is the one I gave you, isn't it, Sam?"

"No, it ain't."

Nonplused, Cale asked: "How do you know?"

Sam Aikens jerked his thumb over his shoulder toward the cabin. " 'Cause the one you gave me is setting on a shelf in there."

"You're sure?" Cale asked.

Aikens nodded. "Still got tobaccy in it."

Cale stood still for a long moment, feeling foolish. His ace had turned out to be a deuce. Worse, under the stares of Henry Taylor and Sam Aikens he felt like a child among adults. Now he mentally sorted through this new information, or tried to. With familiar inadequacies welling up, Cale again wondered if he possessed the maturity needed to handle this job. Monroe might well have carried his *cigarillos* in that tin. Or jerky. Or a deck of cards and poker chips. An experienced lawman would have looked in there to find out. That was obvious now.

Cale wished he had acted prudently. He had been convinced he knew where the tin had come from, so much so that he had never thought to look at the contents. Now he pulled the hinged lid open. The tin was filled with cash.

Taylor moved closer. He spoke a single word: "Caliente."

Sam Aikens whistled when he saw a young fortune in greenbacks in the tin. Several hundred dollars in various denominations were neatly packed in there.

"Caliente?" Sam repeated. "What about Caliente, Mister Taylor?"

"We figured Monroe got away with cash from the sale of stolen livestock down there," he answered. "Looks like he did . . . almost." He turned to Cale. "You said Monroe's at the Circle M?"

"I left him in irons there," Cale said. "I'll pick him up on my way back to town."

Taylor paused as he thought about that. "No, Parker, you stay here."

Cale had not expected to be overruled, and for a moment all he could do was stand mute.

"I'll take Monroe to Red Rock," Taylor went on, "and turn him over to Heck Jones. Then I'll raise a posse. While I'm doing that, Parker, you backtrack those thieving bastards. Track them from the Diamond Bar. Find out where they went, if you have to get down on your hands and knees to read sign." He added: "We'll meet at the Circle M headquarters, and go from there."

Taylor added for Aikens's benefit: "With a bunch of men armed with repeating rifles, we'll run the rustlers to ground and recover your livestock."

"Appreciate yer help, Mister Taylor. Sure do."

Cale shook his head.

Taylor eyed him. "Something on your mind, Parker?"

"I'll lock Monroe up," Cale said. "It's a job that comes with the badge."

"You take your duties as sheriff seriously," Taylor said,

"and I applaud your dedication. I knew you'd make a good lawman. I was right, wasn't I?"

Cale met his gaze, jaw clenched.

"But it only makes good sense," Taylor said, "for you to track rustlers while I raise a posse. Like I said, we'll meet at the abandoned Circle M, ready to ride. . . ."

Cale interrupted: "No, sir."

Taylor's expression hardened. He was accustomed to giving orders, a leader of men rarely if ever crossed, and now it was his turn to be silenced. He cast a measured look at Cale. Sam Aikens spoke up.

"Hold on, young' un, jest hold on. Sounds to me like Mister Taylor's got a good plan. You oughta do this thing jest like he's laid it out so's I can get my livestock back."

"Stay out of this, Sam," Cale said, and in a glance saw a look of surprise flare in the old rancher's eyes. "I took an oath. I'll do my duty."

"But you oughta listen to Mister Taylor. . . ."

"Sam, I told you to stay out of this," Cale repeated. He saw the look of surprise turn to anger. Aikens stared, silenced and clearly mystified by his friend's refusal to agree to take the best course of action.

Cale no longer worried whether he possessed the maturity for this job. He had made one error today, but now he saw through Taylor's scheme. He knew what he had to do. This was not the time or place to explain it to Sam. He turned to Taylor.

"Griff Monroe's my prisoner," Cale said. "I'll take him in, lock him up, and write down the charges just like Joe Gilmore showed me. The circuit judge is due in town in five days. That'll give Monroe time to think about a confession."

"Wish I could stop you from making another greenhorn mistake," Taylor said.

"I figure I'm right about this," Cale said.

Taylor studied him. "There's something else you'd better figure on."

"What's that?"

"Folks in Red Rock are taking a wait and see look at you," he replied. "Fall down on the job, or even stumble, and you'll lose public confidence. Then you'll lose that sheriff's star just like Baldwin lost it."

Cale knew the rancher meant county commissioners when he said public. He well remembered Taylor held sway over them.

"I'll take that chance," Cale said.

"Chance?" Sam repeated angrily. "I'm the one who's running a chance . . . a chance of losing my Diamond Bar. What the hell's wrong with you, young 'un?"

"Griff Monroe will be up against a long prison sentence or a short one," Cale explained.

"That don't do me no good," Sam said. "Not one bit."

"I think it might," Cale said.

"How?"

"If I drop the assault charge," Cale said, "he'll be handed a shorter sentence. How short depends on how much he tells us about rustlers in Red Rock County. I figure he'll break and tell us where we can locate your steers."

Cale stole a look at Taylor. The man was pensive. This plan had taken shape in Cale's mind moments ago, and he did not know if it would work. Sam Aikens clearly did not. The old rancher studied the ground at his feet and slowly shook his head in disgust and anger.

Taylor broke the silence. "You're determined to go through with this harebrained scheme, Parker?"

Cale nodded.

"Then I'll see you in Red Rock," Taylor said. He turned away and headed for the corral in long strides.

Red Rock Signal

Definition of a Pessimist: The man who wears a belt and suspenders.
Advice for the day: Be an Optimist and leave home either the belt or the braces.

Wisdom for the day: Greet every sunup.

Truth for the day:
The man who is optimistic one day at a time is no Optimist.

"Stop! Edna, stop! Stop right here!"

Eddie was on her way to the mercantile when her mother lifted a hand and barked out commands from her wheelchair.

Eddie halted. One city block ahead, a commotion erupted among three men on the boardwalk. She saw them grappling near the red and white striped barber pole marking the location of Dave's Tonsorial Parlor.

Eddie recognized Cale and Heck. The third man was unknown to her, clearly a man under arrest. Bare-footed and bound in wrist irons, he used his upper body to fight them. He head-butted and struggled mightily until he was brought under control. Ahead and across the street onlookers stopped. They gawked until Cale and Heck shoved their prisoner into the barbershop.

"Did you see that?" Marietta demanded of her daughter. "Fighting . . . right here in the middle of town in broad daylight. One of them . . . one of them was that saddle tramp, Carl Harper. He and the other one beat that poor man. Beat him until his face was bloody. Did you see? Did you?"

"Yes, Mother."

"That's the kind of lawman this burg got after Joe Gilmore left," Marietta said. "Take me home, Edna. Take me home right now. I don't know why you were so determined to bring me here in the first place."

Eddie had awakened early this morning, filled with purpose. "Mother, I wanted to show you something. I still do."

"Show me? Show me what?"

"Something important," Eddie replied.

Marietta blinked. "Well, what is it? Where is it?"

"It's in the Sears and Roebuck catalogue displayed in the mercantile. Here. Look. You can see it through the window."

"A catalogue? That's all?"

Eddie had wheeled her to the plate glass window of the false-fronted store, the largest in Red Rock. For once Marietta Pauls neither protested nor exclaimed. She was silenced the moment her daughter pointed to the wedding dress pictured in the Sears & Roebuck "wish book".

**TO
CALE PARKER
COUNTY SHERIFF
RED ROCK COLORADO**

**—ARRIVE RED ROCK FOURTEEN AUGUST—
PURPOSE: SERVE ARREST WARRANT—**

SUBJECT: FREDERICK ALLAN MONROE AKA
GRIFF MONROE—REQUEST ASSIST- ANCE—
**FROM
JOSEPH GILMORE
UNITED STATES MARSHAL
DENVER COLORADO**

"I know you're in with Taylor," Cale said to Griff
Monroe. "What I don't know is how deep."

He leaned against the barred door to the cell while
Monroe sat on the bunk, head down. Scrubbed and freshly
shaved, the prisoner wore a spare shirt and trousers from
his saddlebags. His belt, boots, and socks had been taken
from him.

"You don't know much," Monroe said.

Griff Monroe had resisted all the way from the Circle M
to the barber shop where Cale and Heck forced him to take
a hot bath. Earlier, even though bound in wrist irons,
Monroe had tried to escape on his white horse. If there was
another escape attempt, Cale figured bare feet and sagging
trousers might slow him down.

"What did Taylor promise you?"

Monroe offered no reply.

Cale recalled the night he had been pistol-whipped and
kicked. Before the beating, Monroe had claimed *my* range
and *my* livestock. "Land and cattle? Is that what he said
he'd give you?"

Monroe did not answer.

"You might as well tell me," Cale said. "You're not getting either one." He let Monroe think about that, and went
on: "You and Taylor figured out a way to sell stolen cattle
in Caliente. When that S and RG man came into the
cantina, telling you there had been a miscount, that was

your signal to ride out of there. While your Circle M cow-hands were getting shot up, you were on horseback, leaving with all of the money in your saddlebags. That's how this thing stacks up, doesn't it?"

Monroe raised his head, glowering. "You don't know what you're talking about." He added: "Nobody was supposed to get shot."

Cale eyed him. Griff Monroe was a big man, tough as a cedar stump, but mention of the shooting in Caliente seemed to stir him.

"No matter what Taylor promised," Cale said, "he'll throw you to the wolves." Trying to sound like he knew more than he did now, Cale added: "I'm telling you for your own good."

Monroe did not reply.

"You may not believe it," Cale said, "but I'm the best friend you've got in this town."

"You're right," he replied. "I don't believe it."

"Assaulting a lawman goes down hard enough," Cale said, "but you've got more trouble headed your way."

Monroe stared at him. "What do you mean?"

"Joe Gilmore's coming to town," Cale said. "He has an arrest warrant with your name on it."

"Gilmore," Monroe repeated.

Cale nodded.

"He's some kinda U.S. marshal now, ain't he?"

"Yeah," Cale replied.

"That means he can take prisoners across state lines," Monroe said.

Cale nodded again. "What's the charge against you?"

"Go to hell."

"Instead of sending me to Satan before my time," Cale said, "tell me what you know about rustling in this end of the county. Come clean, and I'll drop the assault charge against you."

Monroe fell silent for a long moment. Then he stiffened. He spoke without turning to face Cale. "Get outta here. Go on. Get the hell outta here."

Cale got out. Leaving Heck in the sheriff's office, he walked to Seventh and paid a visit to Eddie. He wanted to see her before returning to the sheriff's office to relieve Heck. Cale doubted Taylor would try to spring Griff Monroe in a nighttime jail break, but at the same time he did not want to make another clumsy mistake. He figured he'd better be ready for anything, and either he or Heck would be on duty day and night until Joe Gilmore's arrival.

To Cale's surprise, the doorbell was answered by Marietta. She opened the door and looked up at him, her expression turning to a scowl.

" 'Evening, Missus Pauls," Cale said.

Jaw jutting, she backed the wheelchair away and reached for the door handle. "I have nothing to say to you." She added: "Neither does Edna."

"Reckon I'd like to hear that from her," Cale said.

"You'll hear nothing from her," Marietta said. "Now or ever. Leave. Please leave."

Cale gazed down at her. Eddie's description of the accident that crippled her came to his mind, and he thought about the ordeal of pain this woman had faced every day since that awful moment. He recalled a phrase he had read in a book once, and now he repeated it, inserting the name of his beloved: "I will honor Eddie's wishes."

"Then leave!" Marietta said angrily. "Edna and I witnessed your brutality! You and your deputy beat that poor man today, beat him when his hands were tied behind his back. He was bleeding. Who's next? Will you sneak up behind Edna and me again, and beat us until we're bloody?"

"Mother!"

Pounding footfalls made Marietta turn to face her daughter. Her long calico dress lifted to her ankles, Eddie hurried down the hallway toward the door.

"Mother!" she exclaimed again.

Cale stepped back when Eddie grasped the handles of the wheelchair. She pulled her mother around, and leaned close to her.

"What are you doing?" Eddie demanded in a fierce whisper.

"I am informing this brutal man he is not welcome here," Marietta replied. "We both saw what he did today, didn't we . . . ?"

"Have you heard an explanation?" Eddie asked.

Marietta shook her head once.

Eddie turned to Cale. "Tell us what happened."

Cale looked into their eyes. He saw his future wife and his future mother-in-law—one questioning, the other glowering.

The next day Henry Taylor kept his word. He swept into the sheriff's office, stern of gaze, and, after a sidelong glance at Heck, he faced Cale.

"Well, Parker?"

Cale eyed him, seeing rage barely concealed beneath a polished surface of manners. "Well, what?"

"Did your prisoner crack?" Taylor asked in a mocking tone. "Did he reveal the location of Diamond Bar steers?"

"All he's revealed so far," Cale admitted, "are new ways to tell me where to go."

"So what's your plan now?" Taylor asked.

"Turn Gilmore loose on him," Cale replied.

"Joe Gilmore?" Taylor repeated in surprise.

Cale picked up the telegraphed message from his desk. He gave it to Taylor, and watched him read the hand-printed words.

"What's this all about?" Taylor asked, looking at Cale.

"I don't know any more than what you're reading there," he replied. "I questioned Monroe, but he won't talk about it."

Taylor thrust the message at him, and gestured to the outer door of the cell-block. It was closed, and locked.

"Let me have a crack at him."

Cale stood. "No, sir."

Taylor faced him. "Parker, open the cell-block door. Open it, so I can go in there and question the prisoner."

Cale repeated: "No, sir."

Anger flashed in Taylor's eyes. "You had your chance with him. Now I'll grill him, man to man. If I pry some answers out of him, we can locate Mister Aikens's livestock and herd them back to his range."

Cale heard a high-minded tone of noble purpose in his voice. There was a time when that resonant voice had impressed him, even stirred him to action. Not now.

Taylor's expression darkened. "As a duly-elected Red Rock commissioner, Parker, I am issuing you an order. Open that door."

"My sworn duty is to make arrests and guard prisoners," Cale countered. "When Joe Gilmore was sheriff, no one without a badge was allowed in the cell-block. That's my policy, too."

The rancher was flustered. "Your harebrained scheme won't work. You should have gone after those Diamond Bar steers when you had the chance. Monroe's a tough nut. You won't crack him. Neither will Gilmore."

"I'm not finished with him," Cale said.

Taylor asked: "Dreamed up one more harebrained scheme, did you?"

Cale decided to play another card, hoping this one was an ace. "I aim to question Monroe about you."

"Me?" Taylor said. "What are you talking about?"

"I have a witness," Cale said, "who saw you and Monroe in the Circle M horse barn."

"He's a liar," he said.

"Someone is," Cale said.

"Who is my accuser?"

Cale figured Taylor had surmised the witness was Rollie, but the rancher could not say so without revealing the truth.

Taylor seemed eager to challenge him, but the moment of conflict passed. Turning abruptly, he departed without a word to either Cale or Heck.

Cale moved to the window. He saw Taylor head for the Colorado House in long strides.

Heck whistled softly. "You faced him down, Sheriff," he said.

Second time in two days, Cale thought. He turned to Heck. "Buster Baldwin crossed Taylor," Cale said. "Look what happened to him."

"That was a whole different deal," Heck said. "Baldwin's dumb as an ox. Taylor respects you."

"No, he doesn't," Cale said.

Heck looked at him questioningly.

"You heard him say he didn't care about my age," Cale explained. "I've been thinking about that. I'm younger than the other riders in these parts. I figure he knew that just by looking at me."

"What're you driving at?"

"Taylor got me appointed sheriff so he could ride rough-shod over me."

"Well, if that's what he did," Heck said with a grin, "he figured wrong. You've got sand, and now he knows it. I'll tell you one thing for certain sure. If Taylor takes your star like he took Buster's, he'll get mine, too."

"I appreciate that," Cale said. "But you have to earn a living. If the time comes for me to turn in this piece of tin, do what you have to do."

Heck shrugged. "A man with a fair horse and a good rope can always earn his beans and bed."

In truth, Cale was proud of himself. He had stood up to one of the most powerful men in the county, twice, and on both occasions he had not backed up an inch. He felt a new sensation, an afterglow of some sort, as though he had crossed a threshold.

With Heck on duty, Cale tried to sleep after sundown. His room was hot, and he lay awake, his mind full, his eyes open. Finally he dozed, awakening in a sweat. He splashed water on his face from the basin on the dresser, pulled on his boots, and tromped down the outside staircase as he left the boarding house. He walked to Broad, relieving Heck several hours early.

"Monroe wants you," Heck announced the moment Cale cleared the door to the sheriff's office.

"What for?"

"Palaver," Heck said.

"Palaver," Cale repeated.

"He's been bellowing like a bull in a bog," Heck said. "Says he'll talk to you, nobody else."

Chapter Sixteen

"Get Pittock."

Cale eyed Griff Monroe behind bars. Still robust, the man sat down on the bunk, bowed by the weight of his troubles.

"Pittock," Cale repeated. "Why?"

"None of your business," Monroe said. "Just get him."

Cale eyed him. "This isn't the Circle M, Griff. You don't give orders here."

"The hell I don't," Monroe said, standing up. He came to the door and grabbed the bars. "I give you orders, Parker. You foller 'em. Hear?"

Cale met his gaze. Even in defeat, Monroe looked capable of bending iron bars and busting out of his cell, a strange, fearsome creature—half ox and two-thirds gorilla—no cage would ever hold.

Suddenly impatient, Monroe cursed him. "Kid, if you want something from me, you gotta give me something. I told you what it is. I want Pittock. Be a good boy, and go get him."

They stared at one another for a long moment before Cale left to do his bidding. He had to admit he had never met a man like Griff Monroe before.

Cale found Ben Pittock in his print shop, front door locked. He tapped on the window. Pittock appeared out of deep, dark shadows, as though emerging from a vat of ink.

"Locked up tight," Cale remarked when Pittock opened the door.

"Ever since those S and RG goons came to my alley

door," Pittock said, "I've been a tad careful with both doors."

"If that pair comes back to Red Rock," Cale reminded him, "let me know. Heck and I will even up the score."

Ben Pittock thanked him for the offer, and this time he did not decline aid from a "gendarme".

"What can I do for you, Sheriff? A print job?"

Cale shook his head. "I've got a man in jail asking for you. Name's Griff Monroe."

"I've heard of him," Pittock said. "Aaron Miller's ranch foreman." He thought a moment. "Hardcase, isn't he?"

Cale nodded. "He seems to like that reputation."

"What about him?"

"Says he wants to talk to you."

"Why me?"

"I don't know," Cale said. "He has information I need, and he says he'll answer my questions after he talks to you. That's why I'm asking this favor on short notice."

"I see," Pittock said. He untied his ink-stained apron and tossed it toward his desk. It missed, landing on the floor like a dismembered torso sprawled amid the clutter of torn and wadded proof sheets, lead pigs for type, and slats from packing crates.

Pittock shrugged, and headed for the front door of his print shop. "Let's go hear what this Mister Griff Monroe has to say for himself."

"You're looking at a dead man."

Cale stepped aside while Griff Monroe stood in his cell and faced the newspaperman on the other side of the bars.

"I want my story to be knowed, Mister Pittock, knowed by folks who think poorly of me."

"I'm listening," Pittock said.

251

"I always figured Robby Ray James would send for me one day, so I ain't surprised. Not a lick."

"Who?" Pittock asked.

"Robby Ray James," Monroe replied, "sheriff of Tilden County, Ohio. Gilmore will haul me in irons from this stinking jail in Red Rock County, Colorado to the gallows in Tilden County, Ohio. Sheriff Robby Ray James is gonna hang me when I get there. Reckon he's knotting the noose right now."

"Were you convicted of murder?" Pittock asked.

Monroe shook his head vigorously as though setting the record straight. "Waitin' for Robby Ray to line up a jury of folks who wanted to see me dead didn't strike me as a fine notion."

"You fled from an arraignment?"

Monroe nodded. "Made my way out West. Over the years I worked on farms and ranches from there to here, doing 'most any paying job. I've got a string of horses now, but time was, I didn't own nothing. Even the clothes on my back and the beat-up boots on my feet were hand-me-downs." He drew a breath. "But that ain't it. What I want folks to know comes before that. . . ."

In his youth Griff Monroe had struggled to earn enough money to support himself and his younger sister, Ellen. Their parents, an aunt and uncle, and one set of grandparents had perished in the boiler explosion of the *Midnight Star*, a steam-powered paddle wheeler plying the Mississippi River. Once the family's meager savings were depleted, Griff labored at numerous jobs in town, chores mostly, as he struggled to feed and clothe Ellen and himself. They lived in the poorhouse on the edge of town, and knew all the shame that went with it.

Sheriff Robby Ray James took an interest in the pair, and

aided Griff in his constant search for work. The sheriff's teen-aged son took an interest in Ellen. Convinced she needed to be protected, Griff was soon at odds with young Robby Ray. They fought. Griff sent him home with loosened front teeth and a broken nose. Ellen rebelled. She ran away. Returning after two days, she promised her brother never to run away again. She admitted seeing young Robby Ray. He had forced himself on her under a moonlit pier, raping her while the waters of the great river slapped against pilings. Four months later she was showing.

"Then she disappeared."

Pittock repeated that hollow word: "Disappeared."

"Oh, I hunted for her, hunted ever'where," Monroe went on. "All that time I knew, I just knew. Couldn't hardly eat. Couldn't hardly breathe. Then one day that kid smiled at me. No reason. Young Robby Ray James passed me on horseback, looked down his crooked nose at me, and smiled." Monroe drew a deep breath. He exhaled. "He done killed her. I knowed that sure as I knowed anything. He done killed her and buried her somewhere, some place where I'd never find her, and here he comes on his big damned horse, smirking at me. I'm the sheriff's son, and you're a low-life, and there's nothing you can do to me. Nothing." Monroe stared into space. "He was wrong about that. Young Robby Ray James, he sure was wrong about that."

Pittock broke the silence when he said: "You killed him."

"With my bare hands," Monroe said. "Choked him until the life went out of his eyes."

"Did he confess?" Pittock asked.

Monroe nodded. "Said he never meant to kill her."

"Anybody else hear his confession?" Pittock asked.

"No. I killed him quiet. Killed him under that pier down by the river."

Pittock asked: "Did you ever find out what he did with her body?"

"His scrawny neck snapped afore he could tell me," Monroe replied. "Not knowing where Ellen is . . . not knowing . . . damn . . . that's what put a knot in my gut."

Cale asked: "Did this kid look anything like me?"

The question drew a curious look from Pittock.

Monroe shook his head. "No, you don't look a thing like him, Parker. Hell, I know what you're getting at. I've thought about it. I had plenty of time to think when you left me chained to that pump out on the Circle M. You're a young pup wearing the badge, and I reckon seeing you ride high, wide, and handsome brought ever'thing back . . . ever'thing I've tried to forget. Trouble is, a man can't forget. The more time goes by, the more I can't forget. I still dream about little Ellen. She wasn't nothing but a skinny kid with freckles on her cheeks." He added: "Reckon a noose will put an end to them dreams."

Cale watched Monroe's expression, seeing a rugged face battered and bruised by his fists.

"Mister Pittock," Monroe said now, "that's the story I want published in your newspaper. Ever' word is true. I want folks to read it, folks who think poorly of me."

Pittock nodded thoughtfully.

"Will you put my story in your paper?"

"Yes," Pittock said. "Yes, I will." He looked at him and added: "I'll need a few more details, Mister Monroe. When I come back, I'll bring paper and pencil."

After the newspaperman left, Monroe faced Cale. "I'm sorry about the way I've treated you, Parker. I sure as hell am sorry about it. Turns out you made me pay, in spades. I had a whupping coming, I reckon. I just never figured you'd be the one to do it."

Cale did not know what to say, but he knew the question he had to ask. "I want to know about Taylor," he said.

Monroe grew pensive. Cale figured the man's thoughts were still in Tilden County, Ohio where vivid memories were laced with tragedy, poverty, rage, fear, revenge, regret. Too young to shoulder adult responsibilities, Monroe's was a tale of survival—splitting wood, hauling water, burning trash, shucking corn, weeding gardens, tending animals— any paying chore he could find within walking distance of the poorhouse. Then Ellen, pregnant well before the full flower of womanhood was upon her, was murdered by a young man who went free.

"I want to know about Taylor," Cale said again.

Monroe blinked. "What about him?"

"He promised you a ranch and your own brand," Cale said, "after you stole enough cattle to drive his neighbors out of business. That's the truth, isn't it?"

"I figured I had one chance to live a decent life. . . ." Monroe's voice trailed off as he moved away and slumped down on his bunk again.

"Will you testify before the circuit judge?" Cale asked.

"Don't worry, Parker," Monroe said. "I'll keep my end of the deal."

"Tell me about those Circle M cowhands who stole the cattle with you."

"Not much to it," Monroe said. "We skimmed profits from a rich rancher or two. That's all there was to it. Ranchers steal mavericks from each other all the time. Why do you think most of 'em pack a running iron?"

Cale was uncertain if Monroe was trying to convince him, or himself.

Monroe went on: "I never aimed to take the money, but when I heard shootin' from the Caliente sale barn, I got the hell outta there. Nobody was supposed to get killed. Taylor set it up that way. Buster Baldwin went wrong when he pulled the trigger."

"Taylor told you about that when you met in the Circle M horse barn?" Cale asked.

"Yeah."

"Did he tell you to rustle steers from the Diamond Bar?" Cale asked.

"Yeah."

"Sam Aikens isn't rich."

"It was Taylor's idea," Monroe said. "Said he'd let old Sam live on the place even after he bought him out. Me, I drove Diamond Bar critters to a seep ten, twelve miles east of the Circle M headquarters. Due east, good water and plenty of graze to hold 'em. You'll find 'em out there, kid, along with my string of saddle horses."

Cale thought a moment. "When you stand before the circuit judge, Taylor will call you a liar. Plenty of folks will believe him."

"I don't give one damn about that," Monroe said. "I got nothing to lose. Marshal Joe Gilmore's gonna haul me off in irons, and Sheriff Robby Ray James's gonna fit me for a noose. I've got nothing left but the truth."

Cale left the cell-block. In his office he stood at the window, looking past the painted star to Red Rock's main drag. Aware of Heck's gaze, he turned to his deputy. He knew what they had to do, and, as he spoke to him, the knowledge of what was to come filled him with a sense of dread that was almost overpowering.

"You're gonna do what?" Heck asked.

"Arrest Taylor," Cale replied.

"That's what I thought you said," Heck said. He studied him. "Just how do you aim to pull that off?"

"I've got an idea," Cale replied. "I'll need your help."

Mr. Henry Taylor
Colorado House

If you want to interview the prisoner, come to my office. Right away.

                                    Cale Parker, Sheriff

The truth was stretched to full measure, but Cale took some satisfaction in the fact that it was not a lie—not an outright lie. Taylor had requested permission for an interview with the prisoner. Cale aimed to give it to him. He left his penciled note at the desk of the Colorado House. Within the hour Henry Taylor hurried across Broad and entered the sheriff's office.

"Change your mind, Parker?" he asked, barely concealing a gloating note of triumph in his voice.

"Griff Monroe's tough," Cale said, "like you said."

"I'm a fair judge of horseflesh and men," Taylor allowed. He added: "After I grill Monroe, we'll set matters straight, once and for all. You'll see."

"Yes, sir," Cale said. He stood. "Leave your revolver out here, and I'll take you in."

Taylor paused. "I must question the prisoner alone, Parker. Man to man."

"Yes, sir," Cale said. He reached to his holster and took out the Whitney, placing it on the desktop. "No guns allowed in the cell-block, Mister Taylor. Not even mine."

Taylor hesitated. He opened his jacket. Pulling a pistol

257

out of his holster, he set the gun on the desk beside Cale's large revolver.

Key ring in hand, Cale moved past him. He unlocked the outer door to the cell-block, opened it, and entered. Taylor followed him in. If the rancher was aware Heck was close behind him, he gave no sign of it. The first cell was empty, the barred door standing open. Cale reached out as if to close it, momentarily blocking the rancher's way.

Heck closed in, angling to his right. The moment Cale grasped a bar to the door of the empty cell, Heck shoved Taylor. The rancher was knocked off balance, grunting in surprise. Heck pushed him again, harder, and Taylor lurched into the empty cell, arms flailing the air. The moment Heck stepped back, Cale swung the barred door shut. He locked it.

Regaining his balance, Taylor stood in the jail cell, amazed and dazed. He blinked. The fact that he had been tricked seemed to seep into his awareness like a desert spring where water came to the surface one droplet at a time. Then his mouth twisted in rage. As though awakening, he whirled to face Cale and Heck. He bellowed like a scalded hog, still too surprised to be coherent. That moment of confusion passed.

"What . . . what the hell . . . what the hell do you think you're doing?"

"You said you wanted to grill Monroe alone," Cale said, backing away.

In the next cell Griff Monroe chuckled. Taylor reacted to the taunt.

"Open this door! Open it! Let me out of here!"

Since pinning on the badge, Cale had weathered impassioned cussings from men like Buster Baldwin and Griff Monroe, but their verbal lashings were weak compared to hot invective issuing from Taylor's mouth like lava. Then, out of breath for a moment, his vituperation died out.

Cale emulated Joe Gilmore. Instead of reacting angrily to a cursing, he spoke calmly to the man. "You are under arrest, Mister Taylor," Cale said. "The charge against you is cattle rustling."

"It's a lie!" Taylor exclaimed. "Lie!" He cast a glance at Monroe in the next cell, and quickly turned to Cale. "I don't know what this man told you . . . but you can't prove anything."

"I have witnesses who will testify," Cale said.

"They're lying!"

"Everyone except you is lying?" Cale asked.

Taylor cursed him again.

"The circuit judge will hear your side of it," Cale said, and turned away.

Taylor grasped a bar with each hand. "Let me out of here!"

Another volley of shouted curses followed Cale and Heck out of the cell-block. The voice was silenced only when Cale closed the outer door and locked it.

The arrest of Henry Taylor was not known in Red Rock until Ben Pittock returned to interview Monroe. Cale had already decided to admit Pittock into the cell-block. He escorted him in without advising him of new developments. The newspaperman took four steps and abruptly halted, dumbstruck, staring in disbelief.

Pittock saw Henry Taylor lying on the bunk in the first cell. In the next cell, Griff Monroe lay on the narrow bunk, bare-footed. Taylor did not move. The rancher stared at the ceiling, looking like he had been slugged.

Pittock turned to Cale. "What's going on here?"

The sound of his voice seemed to revive Taylor. "Ben!

Ben!" Taylor left the bunk and rushed to the barred door. "Ben, get me out of here."

When Pittock only stared, Taylor raised his voice as though speaking to a man gone deaf.

"Go get Josh Everts!" Taylor shouted. "Bring him here! Now!"

Pittock backed away from this verbal fusillade, still absorbing the disparate elements of the strange scene before him.

"Mister Pittock came here to see me," Griff Monroe said, "not you."

Taylor turned to Cale and pointed at him. "You'll take my place in this cage, Parker. Just you wait. You exceeded your authority. Your turn is coming." As though shooing a slow-moving hound, Taylor called out to Pittock again. "Ben! Ben, go on! Get Josh!"

Pittock turned. On his way out, he said to Monroe: "I'll come back and talk to you later."

Monroe scowled. "Don't waste no time, Mister Pittock."

Cale escorted the newspaperman to the outer office, and locked the cell-block door behind them. Pittock stood in the middle of the office, collecting his thoughts. He dragged a hand through his mustache, his gaze moving from Cale to Heck, and back to Cale.

"What's this all about?" Pittock asked.

Cale described the charges against Taylor, enumerating witnesses and evidence. He talked about the expedition to Caliente and the later testimony from Rollie and from Griff Monroe.

"Taylor lied about meeting Monroe in the Circle M horse barn," Cale said. "That's when I knew he was guilty."

Pittock shook his head in a gesture of increased admiration. "You make a strong case . . . very thorough. For myself, I just can't believe it. Henry Taylor. . . ." Pittock fell silent, then added: "Nobody in this town's going to believe it, either."

Cale did not attempt to prevent the newspaperman from leaving the office. He was obviously within his rights to go to the bank. Cale figured Everts would find out sooner or later, anyway, and this step merely meant sooner. He was right. From the time Ben Pittock left the office and returned with Joshua Everts was a matter of minutes.

Pittock stood aside while the banker confronted Cale. Not a man to curse, Everts, nevertheless, was forceful in his demand for an explanation.

Cale again recited evidence proving Henry Taylor was involved in the theft of cattle as a means of acquiring range land and water rights in Red Rock County. Hatless, Everts's forehead sweated to a shine. The banker stroked a trimmed muttonchop on his jaw. Unlike Pittock, he was not persuaded.

"Cut him loose," Everts said, dismissing all that he had heard with a wave of his hand.

Cale made no move to comply.

"Parker, I said, cut him loose. Let Henry out of that cell. Right now."

"No, sir."

"If I must," Everts said in mounting anger, "I'll bring the county commissioners in here. We will strip you of that tin star. You saw what happened to Baldwin. You'll be sent packing, too, should you defy the county commissioners. I'm ordering you, Parker. Let Henry out."

"No, sir."

"Consider yourself fired, Parker," Everts said. "Take off that badge and get out of this office."

Everts turned his attention to Heck. "Mister Jones, it appears to me that you are next in line to assume the position of sheriff of Red Rock County. Will you accept the job?"

Cale turned. He saw Heck stand, and move to the gun rack. He unlocked the chain and pulled out a double-barreled shotgun. After checking the loads, he faced the banker, barrels up with the stock braced against one hip.

"Mister Everts," Heck said, "I work for Sheriff Cale Parker. I'll work for him until the day he tells me I don't. You won't take a badge off either one of us. Leastwise, not until we're ready to hand 'em over, polite like, on our way out the door for the last time."

"You're rogue lawmen," Joshua Everts said, "both of you. You'll end up in prison."

"Not if Mister Taylor's guilty," Cale said.

Everts studied him. "What's your game?"

"The circuit judge will come in on the train in two days," Cale said. "I figure he'll listen to the testimony and make a decision. That's what judges do, isn't it?"

Everts scowled, openly angry now.

Cale had not intended his question to be sarcastic. He was uncertain when a judge would turn the case over to a jury. He had never witnessed court proceedings, and simply posed the question. Now he watched Everts leave the office, neck bowed.

Pittock had watched and listened, a pencil poised over his pad of paper. "I don't know how this thing will play out, boys, but it's the biggest story to hit this town since I've been here."   •

They were interrupted by a mournful sound. In the distance a train whistle blew. Frowning, Pittock looked in the direction of the depot.

"Unscheduled."

Neither Cale nor Heck understood the significance of

Benjamin Pittock's remark until he answered their unspoken question.

"Last time an unscheduled S and RG train rolled into town," Pittock said, "two passengers arrived . . . goons sent by S and RG bigwigs to influence the content of my paper."

The steam whistle sounded again in three shrill blasts. Cale crossed the office. Opening a desk drawer, he pulled out two pair of wrist irons.

"Mister Pittock," he said, straightening, "let's go meet that train."

Eddie was caught by surprise. She heard thudding footfalls on the planks leading to the porch, and in the next moment Buster Baldwin kicked in the front door. She ran down the hall toward the lurching figure, as though somehow her tone of voice would turn him back.

"Get out of here! Get out!"

Baldwin lunged. Before Eddie could change direction, he grabbed her dress front. The fabric tore when he yanked her off her feet. Her kicks and pounding fists had no effect other than to bring a guttural laugh from him. The smell of alcohol on his breath and soured sweat rising from his body at once sickened her and sent fear surging through her.

"I know what you damned Paulses think of me," he said. "Don't think I don't. You all got your pinched noses turned up so you don't have to smell shit. You think I'm a pile of shit, some pile that gets stepped on . . . hell, you ain't steppin' on me no more. . . ."

Baldwin's words were slurred and made little sense, but he was a strong man and no matter what Eddie did—kick, flail, bite—she could not break his grasp or escape the stench.

He carried her to her bedroom off the rear hallway of the

house, and flung her onto the bed. Opening his trousers with one hand, he grasped her throat and held her down with the other. Then he shoved her dress up, exposing the loosely gathered fabric of her bloomers. She kicked. He swatted her, hard. Reaching up her thigh, he grabbed a handful of the cotton cloth and pulled, pausing only when a voice behind him called his name.

"Deputy Baldwin!"

Eddie saw him turn away. He looked back and released her. She raised up far enough to see the wheelchair in the doorway, and her mother's distraught face. Marietta lifted her hand.

Eddie saw blued steel. Her mother held the small revolver Roger had given to her.

"You get out of this house, Deputy Baldwin!" Marietta cocked the pistol, clumsily pulling the hammer back with both thumbs. She aimed at his crotch, one eye squinted shut. "You get out of this house. Get out, or I'll shoot that thing off. I will, Deputy. I will shoot if you don't get out."

To make her point, Marietta tilted the barrel toward the ceiling and pulled the trigger. Amid the resounding report of a .32-caliber round and a cloud of powder smoke, a shower of plaster drifted down to the floor.

"I will shoot you, shoot you right down there, Deputy Baldwin." Marietta gestured with the pistol.

"Deputy!" Baldwin exclaimed. "Deputy! I ain't a deputy no more! I was sheriff until the crooks stoled my badge!" He edged away, holding up his trousers with both hands. "Can't you get that through your head, you crippled-up old bitch?"

"Bitch," Marietta repeated.

Eddie saw her cock the hammer with two thumbs again, taking aim as she squinted both eyes this time. Yanking the trigger in a jerking motion, she fired the pistol. The bullet plowed into the wall behind Baldwin, missing him by inches.

Baldwin carried a revolver, but had no taste for exchanging bullets with Marietta Pauls. He staggered to his left, looking for a way out. The wheelchair blocked the doorway. Eddie rolled off the bed and came up on her feet. She rushed to the door. Pushing the wheelchair back, she gave Baldwin room to retreat.

"Better get out of here," Eddie said to him over her shoulder. "Neighbors heard those gunshots. Somebody will come to see what happened."

Baldwin staggered out of the bedroom. He headed down the hall where the broken door stood open. Stopping long enough to button his trousers and adjust his cartridge belt, the stout man lunged outside, stumbling down the slanted planks to the walk.

"Edna, he called me a bitch. Old bitch. Did you hear that?"

"Yes, Mother," Eddie said.

"Such a rude man," Marietta said. "How many times did Deputy Baldwin put his manured boots under our table on the ranch? Many's the time we fed him and poured his coffee. Now he calls me a bitch. An old bitch." She thought about that. "I only meant to scare him off. Now I wish my aim had been true."

Eddie reached down and gingerly lifted the revolver from her mother's grasp. "Good thing you had the gun," she said.

"I keep it close when I'm here alone," Marietta said. "I don't know what to expect in this town, and I just feel better with that gun in my lap."

Setting the pistol on her dresser, Eddie picked up an

ivory-handled hairbrush. She turned and faced the beveled mirror on the wall. Her auburn hair was speckled with white plaster dust. She brushed it vigorously.

"You're . . . you're going somewhere?" Marietta asked.

"Town."

"Town? Whatever for?"

Eddie glanced at her. "To do something I should have done a long time ago."

"What?"

"Report Buster Baldwin to the sheriff," Eddie replied.

"Take me with you."

Eddie shook her head. She brushed her hair straight back, and let it cascade into place. "I want you to stay here, Mother."

"I won't," Marietta said.

Eddie turned to her.

"Take me with you, Edna. Take me, or I'll wheel myself to Broad."

Chapter Seventeen

At the depot Cale met the S&RG with Ben Pittock at his side. A dozen children had sprinted from town, and they gathered on the platform to watch the arrival of the unscheduled train. Four girls jumped rope and the boys played chase as the earth-shaking locomotive eased past them, a hissing beast belching black smoke and cinders.

The locomotive pulled a coal car, a Pullman with curtained windows, and a red caboose. No flat cars, no boxcars, no cattle cars. When the engine vented steam and slowed at the water tower farther down the tracks, two burly men swung down from the passenger coach to the platform. Neither carried a grip nor any other luggage. They made their way through the cluster of excited children, and strode across the platform toward Broad.

Cale glanced at the newspaperman. "Those two?"

Pittock nodded, a doubtful look in his eyes.

"Something wrong?" Cale asked.

"I don't know what plan you have devised," Pittock said, "but, if you're counting on me, I must confess . . . well, I am a wordsmith, not a pugilist."

"Reckon that makes us a team," Cale said.

Pittock looked at him questioningly.

"Pugilist is one of those big words I can't spell," Cale explained. "You take care of the spelling, I'll handle the rest." He handed Pittock the wrist irons and added: "Wait here."

Intent on heading for Broad Street, the two men from the Pullman did not notice Cale until he intercepted them. Crossing their path, he forced them to halt when he stepped in front of them. One was stocky and red-bearded, wearing a black suit with a dark green vest over his white shirt. The other was dressed similarly in a brown suit, sporting a thin mustache and a clean shave over high, pointed cheek bones. Both men wore narrow-brimmed hats and polished shoes favored by city men of means.

"Howdy, gents," Cale said.

They studied him, surprised by his maneuver. Cale saw them take note of the star pinned to his vest. The man with a thin mustache spoke first.

"What can we do for you, Sheriff?"

"You can get back on that coach," Cale said.

"What?" he said.

"Get on it," Cale said, "and go back where you came from."

The pair exchanged a puzzled glance before turning their attention back to Cale.

"What the hell's going on here, Sheriff?" It was the man with the pencil-thin mustache who spoke. With a pointed nose, his face took on the appearance of a prairie rodent. In a whining tone of voice, he seemed distressed and offended by unjust treatment from a lawman.

"You're getting back on the coach," Cale replied, "that's what."

"You've got no call to horse us around like this," Rat Face said. "We haven't committed any crimes."

"Disobeying a lawful order," Cale said, "is a crime."

The stocky one spoke up. "We're here on a private business matter, Sheriff. After we complete our business, we'll leave directly."

"I'll tell you one more time," Cale said.

The two men eyed him with growing anger.

"The easiest way for you to get out of Red Rock," Cale

said, "is the way you came in. Take my advice, or you'll get a long look at the inside of my jail."

Rat Face asked with growing anger: "What the hell is this all about?"

Cale lifted a hand, gesturing toward a row of baggage carts at the far end of the platform. The pair turned. Pittock stood there, watching them.

"Recognize him?"

Neither man answered.

"Name's Pittock," Cale said. "Last time you gents came to town, you put him on the floor."

Rat Face started to deny the accusation, but Cale silenced him with a raised hand. "So Mister Pittock and I took a vote," Cale went on. "We voted you out of town."

The two men looked at one another again, clearly unprepared for Cale's aggressiveness. Both were angered, both unwilling to comply with his demand.

"We didn't come all this way to be run out of town," Rat Face said. "Not by some tinhorn lawman out here in the middle of the desert."

The stocky one added: "Sure as hell."

"If you have a complaint," Cale said, "take it to the railroad bigwigs who paid you to rough up a newspaperman."

Face reddened now, the stocky man swore.

Cale remembered a speech Joe Gilmore had used on a belligerent drunk outside a Red Rock saloon. "You don't want to see the inside of my jail. It's filthy. Stinks. Men have been peeing on the floor in there for years. Worst thing about it, I'll fine you after I lock you up. Every day you stay in that stinking hell hole costs you money. Gents, leave town now while you've got money in your wallets and the shirts on your backs."

The two men were unimpressed by the speech. Rat Face

269

spoke up, still whining. "Damn it, Sheriff, we have a legal right to be here. Like he said, we'll leave when our business is finished."

"I gave you a couple chances," Cale said. "Now you're under arrest. Both of you."

"Big talk," Rat Face said. He eyed Cale, clearly measuring him as an opponent. "You don't look big enough to back up your mouth."

The stocky one added: "You don't even look old enough to be sheriff."

Cale took off his hat and tossed it aside. "I'm old enough to know a couple of railroad goons when I see them."

The pair glanced at one another again, silently agreeing on a plan. Rat Face edged closer, fists balled while the stocky one slowly moved to his left.

Cale's fists went up. He became aware of movement behind the two men. He looked past them. Children clustered nearby, silent now, and watchful. The only show more entertaining than the arrival of a locomotive was a fight among grown men. This one came with an added feature— two against one. Wide-eyed, the children of Red Rock turned their backs on the train and stared.

Cale sensed Rat Face would throw the first punch, and he was right. The man lunged. He tried to deck Cale with a punch straight from the shoulder. Cale deflected the fist, aware of the second man closing in. Cale took a chance. Instead of retreating, he stood firm. The act of bravado cost him a blow on the side of his head from Rat Face. The punch was solid. Side-stepping, Cale quickly turned. He fought off dizziness and punched the stocky man. His fist landed squarely on his jaw. The big man wobbled, eyes slowly blinking.

Relying on agility and hand speed, Cale spun around to

confront Rat Face. Feinting once, he threw a series of jabs followed by a stiff right to the chin. That one connected. The man's head snapped back. Cale saw a glimmer of fear in Rat Face's eyes. Blood trickled from a mouth hanging open now. Closing the distance, Cale again feinted with his right. The man flinched. He threw a clumsy, looping blow that landed high on Cale's shoulder. Cale bent at the waist and came in low. He hit Rat Face down there, his left and right fists driving like pistons. The heavy punches, in Powell's words, "knocked the breakfast out him." Cale saw Rat Face's eyes squint shut as he doubled over. He popped him again, unloading a hard, slashing blow to the jaw. Rat Face fell to the timbered platform, rolling over on Cale's hat.

Cale frowned. He turned to the stocky one. Still unsteady, the man blinked like a mustang that had collided with a snubbing post. Cale drew his right arm back, set his feet, and hit the dazed man with a stiff right. The punch to his jaw buckled his knees and sent him sprawling to the platform.

Cale straightened. He caught his breath, and dug the pointed toe of his boot into the man's ribs. With a pained moan, he raised a hand and begged Cale to stop. Behind him, the cluster of children cheered.

"Two against one, the sheriff won!" they chanted. "Two against one, the sheriff won!"

Joined by Ben Pittock, Cale locked wrist irons on both men. Pittock helped him pull them to their feet, at once exclaiming over Cale's pugilistic skills.

"My word . . . I've never . . . never seen . . . anything . . . anything like that . . . a masterful display . . . manly arts . . . truly masterful."

Cale picked up his hat. The brim was bent back. He

straightened it, and tried to brush off the dirt while smoothing creases where the crown had caved in. He shook his head in dismay. No self-respecting man would be seen wearing the emblem of a saddle tramp—a crushed, dirty hat that probably had been discarded by a respectable gent. Or worse, by another tramp. Cale worked on the hat, a good one purchased to impress the prettiest lady in town. He suddenly looked at Pittock, just then aware that something had happened to silence a talkative man.

"Looks like there was one more passenger on that train," Pittock said.

Following Pittock's gaze toward the water tower beyond the depot, Cale saw a man standing there. Lanky and full-bearded, he stood at the far end of the loading platform, unmoving, a black valise at his feet.

"Joe Gilmore," Cale said.

"Did you arrest everybody in town?"

That was the question Gilmore posed as Cale and Heck locked the two S&RG men in separate cells. In the cell-block, Griff Monroe watched silently from his bunk.

Cale heard Henry Taylor confide his dilemma to Joe Gilmore. The rancher demanded freedom. The two men shook hands through the bars, and Gilmore nodded his assurance. Taylor stopped protesting. Cale left Pittock in the cell-block to complete his interview with Griff Monroe. He led Gilmore and Heck to the outer office, and closed the door.

Joe Gilmore listened to Cale cite the evidence against Taylor, clearly unsettled by the recitation. Cale finished the account with Heck's help, information including details of the Caliente fight and wide-ranging thefts of steers in Red Rock County.

"You claimed there wasn't much trouble in these parts," Cale said. "I've had nothing but trouble since you left."

"Guess I had all the troublemakers buffaloed, didn't I?" Gilmore said with half a grin. "Looks like you're up to the task. When you pinned on the badge, I don't believe anyone in this county had you pegged for a fighter. Monroe sure as hell didn't."

Heck added: "Baldwin, either."

Gilmore asked about Buster Baldwin. While Cale brought him up to date on the man's truncated career as sheriff of Red Rock, Gilmore looked around the office, his gaze drifting to the window where the out-size star was painted on the plate glass. Children had tagged along from the depot, and several still lingered outside, resuming their play in the street while keeping an eye on the sheriff's office in case another event was worth watching today.

"Like I told you," Gilmore said, "I have a warrant for the arrest of Griff Monroe. When I got your wire, I went through old Reward dodgers in the Denver office. Turns out Monroe's wanted in Ohio. For murder. Federal marshals have been hunting him for a long time. I'm obliged to you for bringing him in. You made my job easy." Gilmore paused. "As to the matter of Henry Taylor, turn him loose."

"Huh?" Heck exclaimed.

Cale stared at the lawman.

"You heard me," Gilmore said.

Cale heard. The request was tendered in a respectful tone of voice as though Gilmore had addressed an equal, one lawman to another. At once, though, he was aware of an overriding fact: United States marshals outranked county sheriffs.

"Monroe is locked up on a charge of rustling," Cale said.

273

"I have two witnesses saying Taylor's up to his neck in this thing. How can I cut him loose while Monroe's behind bars for the same crime?"

"Here's what you have to look at," Gilmore said. "Cut Griff Monroe loose, and what will happen?"

"He'll ride out," Cale said.

Heck added: "Straight for Mexico on his big white horse."

Gilmore nodded in agreement. "If you cut Henry Taylor loose, what will happen?"

Cale shook his head. "Reckon I don't know what he'll do."

Heck shrugged.

"Everything that man owns," Gilmore said, "is either out there on the T-Bar-H Ranch or locked up in Josh Everts's bank vault. I don't know if Henry's innocent or guilty. I know he is an ambitious man. A lot of ranchers are. The most ambitious man I ever met was Tom Pauls. That didn't make him a crook." Gilmore concluded: "Son, when the circuit judge arrives, Henry will be in town. He'll come before the judge and fight for his life. You can count on that. Now, go unlock that cell and turn him loose."

Eddie pushed the wheelchair along the boardwalk, passing Pittock's print shop and the mercantile. Ahead, her gaze was caught by children ranging in the street in front of the sheriff's office. A moment later the door to the office opened.

Eddie saw Cale step out, and hurried along, calling out to him. He turned and lifted his hand in greeting. She saw that he was followed by two men.

"Look," Marietta said. "That's Joe Gilmore."

Realizing Gilmore had arrived on the train, Eddie was

even more surprised to see him accompanied by Henry
Taylor. She watched as the rancher paused on the boardwalk and adjusted his hat. Shielding his eyes against the
bright sunlight, he was a man reveling in new-found
freedom. In the next moment Eddie heard pounding footfalls.

That hollow drumbeat of boots reminded her of the
sounds she had heard moments before Buster Baldwin
kicked in the door. She turned now and saw Baldwin. He
lunged out of a narrow passage between two false-fronted
shops. Drawing his revolver, he ran headlong toward the
men gathered in front of the sheriff's office.

Eddie shouted too late. Baldwin had raised his gun as he
lurched toward the three men. Nearby, children stood
frozen in fear. They stared at a wild-eyed gunman, each of
them rooted, breathless, silent.

Marietta was not breathless. She cried out, shrieking a
warning of her own. Her voice seemed to ignite Baldwin's
rage.

"Bastards! Bastards! You bastards . . . you're nothing
. . . nothing . . . nothing but crooks!"

Eddie saw Baldwin level his gun and snap off a quick
shot. The bullet struck Taylor at the base of his neck. He
went down. He lay on the boardwalk, gurgling as though
drowning in his own blood. Then she watched Gilmore
reach for his holstered revolver. Baldwin's second bullet
struck him in the leg. Spun around by the force of it, the
lawman limped away until he fell to the street, clutching his
thigh.

Cale had dropped to one knee. He cocked his long-
barreled revolver and drew aim at Baldwin. He hesitated.
Panicked children broke and ran in front of him, as quiet
and swift as a flock of sparrows taking wing.

Baldwin fired, missing Cale and the children. He swore and charged.

Unable to get a clean shot, Cale became a still target. Eddie saw Baldwin halt, aim, and fire again, point-blank. The bullet creased Cale's head and sent his hat sailing through the air.

In the next instant, Heck burst out of the office on the run, bent low, revolver in hand. Baldwin swung around, and fired at him, too high. Heck dove into the street, rolled, and came up shooting. Three bullets struck Baldwin in the center of his chest, driving the man back on his heels.

Eddie watched Baldwin totter, a look of disbelief etched into his face. He sank to his knees on the boardwalk, toppled over, and rolled off the planks to the street. He lay on his back, lifeless eyes staring skyward.

The aftermath brought silence. Eddie heard her mother sob. She saw Cale slowly stand, holstering his revolver. Bareheaded, blood trickled from the wound in his scalp. Heck got to his feet.

Eddie knelt at her mother's side and took her hand. Perspiration drenched Marietta. Both women were transfixed by the sight of such carnage. Before them lay three men, one dead, one dying, one wounded. The wounded man, Joe Gilmore, clutched his thigh. His woolen trouser leg seeped blood, but he managed to stand.

Gunfire still rang in Eddie's ears, and acrid powder smoke stung her nostrils. For the moment she was too shocked to speak or even to comprehend all that had happened before her eyes. The fight that had erupted with terrifying suddenness and a roar of gunfire had ended just as quickly. She saw Cale move to the prone figure of Henry Taylor. He knelt. Gilmore limped toward them. Heck reached out, steadying the lawman.

From this distance Eddie heard that gurgling sound again. The muted voice of Taylor carried to her, but she could not sort out his words. Then silence settled over them. Gilmore's shoulders quaked.

She saw Cale stand. He untied his bandanna, wadded it, and pressed it to the side of his head. Eddie left her mother and hurried to him. She helped him blot the wound, relieved to see that it was superficial.

"Cale?" Eddie whispered.

He pulled his gaze away from the body of Henry Taylor and looked at her.

"What did Mister Taylor say?" she whispered.

"He admitted to it."

"Admitted what?" she asked.

"Stealing cattle," Cale said. "He said he got on the wrong trail after Tom Pauls died. He figured he could get more range land, more water. He never meant for those cowhands to be killed in Caliente. He said Monroe knows the truth."

Eddie wrapped her arms around him. He kissed her cheek. While they held one another, townspeople ventured out of the shops. They gathered on the boardwalks, bunching in small groups, Ben Pittock among them. Adults were silent. So were the children of Red Rock. Then, as if heeding a signal known only to them, the children scattered, all of them running for home, all of them with stories to tell.

As a result of circumstances no one in Red Rock could have foreseen, the former sheriff returned to the sheriff's house. It seemed fitting for Gilmore to be in familiar surroundings for a few days while he was on the mend. Bandaged, well fed, and fussed over by Marietta and Eddie,

Gilmore readily confessed to visitors that he had never had it so good.

Cale and Heck met the county commissioners in the sheriff's office. Cale had sent word of his resignation to Mister Everts at the bank. He turned in his star, the Whitney revolver, horse and saddle, and a tobacco tin filled with cash. Led by Everts, the commissioners trooped into the office for the purpose of talking him out of it.

There would be no talking. Cale had made up his mind. He was not cut out for the job. He had only to reflect on his experiences while wearing the badge to know it. All too vividly, he recalled the evening he had nearly gunned down Rollie, an innocent man, unarmed. Worse, in fragmented dreams now, he saw children crossing in front of his gun sight, and awoke in a night-sweat, believing he had pulled the trigger.

Cale did not know what he would do, but he knew he would never pin on the star again. Just as he knew he was not cut out for the job, he knew Heck was. On Cale's advice, the commissioners elevated the deputy to the position of sheriff of Red Rock County.

In time for the funeral of his long-time friend, Taylor, Joe Gilmore was up and limping around, restless and well enough to leave town with his prisoner. Cale accompanied the lawman and the shackled Griff Monroe to the loading platform. Heck had ordered the engineer to stay in Red Rock until all passengers were ready to board, and now the locomotive was ready to depart.

"I shouldn't have set Henry free," Gilmore confided to Cale. "If he'd been locked up in that cell like you wanted, he'd be alive today."

"Baldwin aimed to kill him," Cale said. "On that day, or any other."

Gilmore nodded slowly. "That's what I keep telling myself. Damn. Henry was no outlaw. Not in the days when we fished mountain creeks and told tales over campfires, he wasn't." Gilmore paused. "Once a man gets on a wrong trail, it's hard to get off it. Damned hard. I've seen other men caught up in greed with one crime leading to the next. It cuts deep to see it happen to a friend, though."

With a last handshake, Cale said good bye to the man still referred to locally as "the sheriff". He watched him board the coach with his prisoner. Griff Monroe cast a glance back at Cale, then the big man turned, and entered the coach.

Two passengers were already aboard. The pair of S&RG men had jumped at a new offer from a new sheriff—leave town on that Pullman, and don't come back.

Cale settled up with Wade Powell. He packed his belongings in a beat-up canvas war bag the liveryman gave him. Months ago Powell had taken it in exchange for services from a cowhand who was broke. Now Cale thanked him for that as well as for the medical treatment and boxing lessons.

"You helped me stand when I could have buckled," Cale said with a last handshake.

"Where do think you're going?" Powell asked.

"Don't know yet," Cale replied.

"This damned desert gets under a man's hide," he said. "Hotter than hell, and colder than hell. After you've cooked in summer and froze in winter, and lived to tell about it, it's hard to leave. Plumb hard."

"Maybe I'll come back before too long."

"Oh, you'll come back," Powell said. "Sooner than you think."

Cale studied him. "You must know something I don't."

"There's plenty I know," Powell said with a grin. "Go on, now."

Cale moved out of Bess Loukin's boarding house, and expressed his gratitude to her before leaving. In a quick movement, she hugged him. On Broad, Cale walked past Ben Pittock's print shop. The front door stood open. A shadowy figure moved about inside—the newspaperman working on his next issue, Cale figured.

He had passed the recessed doorway of the print shop when he was hailed. He stopped, and turned. Pittock came out, waving a folded sheet of paper as he caught up with him.

"I've been watching for you," Pittock said. "Monroe wanted you to have this . . . his words, my writing."

Cale took the piece of paper from Pittock's hand. Unfolding it, he read the words carefully printed on it:

Take my gear, Parker. Guns and everything in my saddlebags. My string of horses, take them, too. Hell, I got no use for them no more. I told you where you will find my saddle stock. If you cannot find where I said, then you do not deserve them.

G. Monroe

"Did he say anything else?" Cale asked.

Pittock shook his head. "Not only is this document Monroe's last will and testament, those were his last words, period." He added: "Griff's a man ready to die, Cale. He wants to get it over with."

Cale thrust the paper into his pocket, and bid Pittock good bye.

In truth, he did not know what he would do. He knew he

had to leave this town. The thought crossed his mind that he could sell Monroe's horses and gear and buy a ticket, departing in an upholstered coach seat, instead of riding the rods underneath. Somewhere up north he would find work, he figured, and considered returning to North Platte, Nebraska. Heck had spoken favorably of Cheyenne, Wyoming, too.

Cale rehearsed an imaginary conversation with Eddie, silently telling her he would be gone for a time. He planned to return when he had made a place for himself, somewhere, and hoped she would wait. He went over this in his mind, looking for the right words. He had not found them by the time he reached the end of the boardwalk and turned off Broad on Seventh. He walked to the sheriff's house, and mounted the planks to the door. He dropped his war bag on the porch, and turned the bell handle.

The second ring of the doorbell was answered by Marietta. He had expected Eddie, and was surprised to see her mother. Marietta gazed up at him from her wheelchair.

In that moment Cale realized he had fulfilled this woman's prediction. With his battered and bloodied hat clutched in his hands, a fresh wound on his head, and an old war bag, her worst fears came true. He was a saddle tramp, a drifter on the move again, and he had come for her daughter.

Marietta wheeled her chair around. Lifting her hand in a terse gesture, she led him into the drawing room, empty now. Cale cast a puzzled look at her. She insisted that he sit down, and turned to face him. They were silent, unblinking and stilled for a moment that seemed to stretch into eternity.

"I have been wrong about you, Cale Parker," she said at last. "Grievously wrong. I offer my apology, and seek your forgiveness."

Too surprised to speak, Cale did not immediately realize she interpreted his silence to be intransigence. Marietta went on to describe her tumultuous emotions upon seeing Cale risk his life during the gunfight. He had avoided harming the children scattered on Broad Street. That was the moment, Marietta said, when she knew she had misjudged him. She raised a hand and pinched two fingers together.

"That bullet came this close to killing you," she said. "This close, and you held your ground. I have never seen such bravery." She went on: "I was surprised, but Joe Gilmore wasn't. He speaks highly of you. He told me, if he'd ever had a son, he wished for him to be like you."

Cale eyed Marietta Pauls. Already the longest conversation he'd ever had with her, he sensed it was not over yet. He was right. She changed the subject.

"As you know, Edna's father is not here to look out for her. It is up to me to pose the time-honored question . . . young man, just what are your intentions regarding my daughter?"

Cale smiled. "If she'll have me, Missus Pauls, I aim to marry her someday."

"You have my blessing."

"Thank you, ma'am," he said.

"You did not say so," she said, troubled. "Do I have your forgiveness for my rude behavior toward you?"

"Yes, ma'am," Cale replied. Marietta Pauls was a formidable women, and he chose his words before continuing. "I figured you had me spotted for a hardcase. I figured you aimed to protect your daughter from making a mistake, a bad one."

"Yes, that is true, quite true," she said. "I am glad to hear you say it in plain English, just as Tom would have.

Edna tells me you are a lot like him. Well, I assure you, Tom was one of a kind. I've got a feeling you are, too." She went on: "Now, on to another matter. In the words of my children, I have regained my senses."

"Ma'am?"

"I have decided to move back to the ranch," she said. "The coffin will be moved, as Roger wished. I shall live out my days on the Rainbow, and someday my gravestone will be on the crest of that rise overlooking the home ranch. I shall be at final rest there alongside my husband and our old friend, Spud Jenks." She paused. "Hilda Bulla has agreed to work for me. She will move her herd to the ranch and live there. With our reservoir, her dairy cattle will flourish, as perhaps her business will, too. With both of us being widows, we have much in common. We have already discussed traveling to Denver two or three times a year where we may enjoy cultural events. Hilda is strong and can see to my needs." She smiled. "Perhaps Mister and Missus Cale Parker will care to join us."

"Yes, ma'am."

"Did you happen to notice two of our saddle horses in Powell's livery?"

"No, ma'am."

She smiled. "My sons wanted to surprise you."

Cale realized Wade had known something he did not, after all.

Marietta turned her wheelchair toward the hallway and called out. Footfalls sounded. Presently Eddie, Roger, and Alex filed in, all of them smiling as though bearing the secret of the century.

Cale stood, and Eddie came to him.

Marietta said: "This man intends to marry you, Edna."

Eddie smiled. "I've been waiting for him to ask."

She pressed against Cale and kissed him on the cheek. Brief as it was, that kiss in front of her family spoke volumes.

"Well?"

"Eddie," Cale said, "I can't ask you to marry me. Not right here in front of everybody."

"Why not?" she asked.

"It just . . . it just isn't done that way."

"How have you done it before?" she asked.

"Well, I haven't, but. . . ." He felt his face grow hot, and saw Roger and Alex grinning as they enjoyed his misery.

"But, what?" she asked.

Cale thought about it, and took her hand. He swallowed. "Eddie Pauls, will you marry me?"

"Yes!" she said, and hugged him.

He held her for a long moment, and heard her joyous shout.

"Yes, Cale Parker! Yes!"

He kissed her again, and then he spoke to her. "I aim to leave Red Rock County and get established somewhere. Maybe Cheyenne. I figured . . . well, I figured I'd send for you."

"Cale," she said.

He looked at her.

"How can I say this?" she went on, casting a glance at Roger and Alex. "Cale, you had a proposal for me. Now my brothers have one for you."

Roger said: "You know we need a rider. If you agree to take on that job, we have a long range plan that involves you and Eddie."

Cale looked at the brothers. "What is it?"

Alex spoke up. "We plan to buy the Circle M from Aaron Miller. Taylor never finalized the deal, so we'll move in and take it."

"If you're willing," Roger added, "you and Eddie can manage the ranch."

"Tell him the rest of your plan," Eddie said. "Tell him."

"Well, if we can swing it," Roger said, "we'll buy the T-Bar-H when Taylor's estate is settled. Rollie's working on an offer. If it all comes out, we'll put both ranches under our brand. We'll all be equal partners."

Alex said: "What do you say, Cale?"

"I'd say," he answered, smiling at his fiancée, "that I have changed my plans."

Eddie turned in the saddle as her gelding splashed across Ute Creek. She waved at her mother. Hilda Bulla stood behind the wheelchair on the verandah of the home ranch. Marietta vigorously waved back. No one but Eddie would ever know, but that energetic wave signaled a new message. Unlike the past when Eddie had left the home ranch for a horseback ride alone, her mother did not give voice to her worries. Now she waved good bye, smiling at her daughter.

Crossing the creek, Cale rode at her side. She admired his new stockman's hat. For their last picnic, she remembered, he had bought a new hat, too.

Now with a picnic basket tied behind her saddle, Eddie was taking the man she loved to a favorite place on the ranch. Rainbow Arch reminded her of the brilliant rainbow they had observed from the abandoned homestead, and she wanted to show it to him. She recalled his remark that day—*fire in the rainbow.*

Eddie knew her brothers trusted and respected Cale, and welcomed him into an ambitious partnership. Roger and Alex knew the plan suggested by Rollie was sound. She was proud of her brothers and recognized their growing maturity. They had become more serious since the death of their father, revealing, now, only brief glimpses of the rough-housing and rowdy behavior she had enjoyed when he was alive. She missed their rambunctiousness, sensing the shouted insults and horseplay were behavior consigned to the past.

Eddie reflected on the passing of generations. She thought about others who had come this way, the countless families known only by hand prints and scratched images on a red cliff, by pottery shards, by chips of milky flint. She looked ahead. Far in the distance the first sandstone spire came into view. Thoughts of past generations loomed large in her mind as her own marriage drew near. The date had been set, and Ben Pittock had agreed to walk her down the aisle on "her day".

The thought of it thrilled her. With marriage came a new promise, a promise of life. One day her children would pass this way, too.

Red Rock Signal

We witnessed an act of savagery, an assassination committed by a man gone mad or crazed by demon rum. We seek justice, methinx. We demand it. We are all in agreement. The assassin must pay with his life. The self-confessed murderer must hang. That is justice. So we believe. Or do we?

Read on, if you dare to examine facile judgments. You will discover a simple matter of justice can take on complications.

For nothing in this life is simple or ordinary, methinx. In this case, for example, the end of the story comes first.

As your faithful editor must report, word arrived in Red Rock by wire. A terse message bore the signature of United States Marshal Joseph Gilmore, the text informing us a murderer was brought to justice in Tilden County, Ohio. Admitting guilt, the murderer was hanged.

Justice was served. A simple matter?

Read on, dear readers. For this is the story of Griff Monroe. . . .